DEVIL

SAVAGE BROTHERS MC— TN CHAPTER

JORDAN MARIE

Cover Art by Robin with Wicked By Design

Model: Gabe LaDuke

Photographer: Wander Aguiar with Wander Aguiar Book Club

WARNING: This book contains sexual situations and other adult themes.
Recommended for 18 and above.

❀ Created with Vellum

Savage Brothers MC
Tennessee Chapter
Book 1

Logan is a complication I didn't count on.
I need to stay away—too many lives depend on it.
One wrong move and everything around me will crumble.

But his graveled voice calls to me.
His wicked smile takes my breath.
His blue eyes intoxicate me.
His heated touch seduces me.
And his hard body promises hot nights beyond my dirtiest
fantasies.
Saying yes would be wrong.
But being wrong feels so good.

DEDICATION

To my husband, I love you beyond words. Our story may be ordinary, but our love makes me feel extraordinary.
Jordan

PROLOGUE

Devil

I'VE HEARD most of my life that a man shouldn't let his dick lead him. I don't know who the fuck came up with that, but it sounds like a boring life. Leading with my dick has led me to some of the sweetest pussy a man could hope to touch and quite simply, I'm a man who likes to fuck. I'm also a man, not a boy. I'm almost thirty-six years old and I live my life exactly like I want. I don't have bullshit that holds me back.

I take what I want.

Sanctimonious assholes can look down on me and how I choose to live my life. They won't be the first and they probably won't be the last. While they're doing that I'm usually swimming with pussy in my bed. That's my life and I make no apologies. The woman—or women—know the score before they climb in and join the party. They get what they want and I get what I want. It's a beautiful bargain. The only loyalty I have is to my club.

Until her.

I used to look at bastards like my Vice President Crusher and just stop and wonder how one pussy could wind his dick so much that he'd be willing to give up other women. That kind of bullshit confused the hell out of me. The thought of just having one woman for the rest of my life terrified me *and* my dick.

Until her.

One look at her and it was like I was struck by lightning. Sounds like a fucking cliché, but it's true all the same.

I'm standing in the pharmacy aisle at the local K-Mart stocking up on condoms. I might like sticking my cock in a lot of different holes, but I do that shit smart. One, I'm partial to my dick and I'm not sticking it in any snatch where it's going to come out looking like it's been stuck into a beehive. Women can look smoking hot on the outside, their pussy can smell like fucking lilacs in the spring—but inside it can be deadly. I will never be caught without a condom and that's the fucking truth.

I usually order the damn things in bulk, but there's been hurricanes everywhere and I'm not risking my dick because of a delayed shipment.

I wheel my cart around—only having a cart because I'm a lazy ass motherfucker who wants to lean on it, but also because the boss told me to pick up some beer and shit for the club. Other chapters have open bars and crap. Our group is smaller. There's a room, there's a fucking wall of refrigerators and a bar where the alcohol goes. There's no bartender and we stock that shit ourselves. We're trying to convince our Prez, Diesel, to get the prospects to do that shit. But the bastard has been dealing with people trying to steal his kid since day one almost, and he's very picky about who he trusts. Prospects for the club have guarded access at best until they prove themselves, and there's very few of those. I can't say as I blame him.

My usual brand of condom is the "Legend." I don't mean to brag, but fuck, the name fits my cock. It's made for big and wide, both of which—thank God—is me. If I was one of these poor bastards born with a pencil dick I probably would have swallowed a bullet by now. Some men can deal with that blow from Mother Nature—hell, maybe they even compensate by learning to use their tongues to bag their women, fuck if I know. I just know I'm *not* one of those men. I love my dick and it works out well the women do too.

They don't sell Legends at K-Mart, and that sucks. I find the extra-large, ribbed for her pleasure and extra strength latex and grab those. I throw about ten boxes in the buggy and they slide down until they're leaning against the three cartons of beer.

"Planning a party?" a soft voice asks me and that's when it happens. The moment my dick gets so tangled up in a woman the bastard will never get free—which sucks, because my dick and I are attached.

She's beautiful. A long, silky-haired brunette with eyes the shade of whiskey. Her skin is a golden tan and so smooth I ache to touch it just looking at her. She's dressed in a white skirt that hugs her curves—and she's got a lot of them—and falls just at the edge of the prettiest knees I've ever seen. Her legs don't have stockings on, it's just them, and they're as golden as the rest of her. A woman who lays out in the sun and lets the rays worship her body. That's the image that comes to mind and I fight down the urge to adjust myself—evidence my dick has the same image.

"I was, until I saw you. Do you like parties, Angel?"

Her eyes blink at my pet name. Her body stiffens, but that could be because my eyes are still glued to her ass and the way it stretches the material of her skirt. I finally drag my gaze back to her top, which is just as good. She's wearing a soft pink top with a high collar that doesn't give me a chance to see her cleavage—and that makes me damn sad. Still, it hugs her tits and those are nice and big. A man could bury his face in them if he felt the urge to go motor boating and he could bury his dick in them if he wanted to go face surfing.

The best of both worlds.

3

"I have a feeling I'm not really into your type of parties," she says, her voice a mixture of laughter and sweetness. It's a damn good voice, perfect, and goes with the rest of her.

Damn.

"What's your name?"

"Does it matter?"

"My heart will wither up and die without it," I answer, making her laugh, those beautiful pink-glossed lips of hers spreading into a smile.

I can't stop myself from letting my eyes travel up and down her body one more time. She's got these white shoes on with a wide heel, her toes peeking out of them.

I'll fuck her while she's wearing nothing but those shoes.

"I think you might be lying to me," she murmurs.

"You ready to roll, man? Diesel will have our asses if we don't get back," Fury says, rounding the aisle that me and my dream woman are standing in.

"In a bit," I tell him, not taking my eyes away from her.

She looks at Fury and I don't like it. I frown because that's the moment I know I'm in *real* trouble.

For the first time in my life I feel jealousy.

Fury has no trouble getting women. He doesn't get as much pussy as I do, but only because he doesn't try. Women tend to flock to him, digging the bad boy vibe mixed with the blond hair and blue eyes look that could have him mistaken for the boy next door.

She turns back to look at me, her eyes finding mine, and the look on her face is thoughtful.

"Enjoy your party, boys," she says softly, and then starts to move around the corner. I reach out and grab her arm. I instantly love it, and curse myself for it.

Electricity and heat shoot through me like a bolt of lightning. That hasn't happened before. I've never felt anything like it, but it's there. I think she feels it too, because she jerks in my hold. Or fuck, maybe she's just unnerved because a man she doesn't know is putting hands on her. Couldn't blame her for that. I've never done something like this in my life—but I don't let her go.

"How about I let Fury take the shit back and I take you out for a drink instead?"

She swallows; I know because I'm watching her that closely. She rubs her lips together, spreading the gloss on them even more, and I feel the exact moment a shiver runs through her body. She's not immune to me, or I'm freaking her out. That seems fair, since my reaction to her is doing the same to me.

"What about your party?"

"You and I can have our own party," I tell her easily and I hear Fury mumble in the background, but I tune him out.

"I don't think I'm the kind of girl who goes to your parties," she laughs.

"Devil, come on. We got to get a move on," Fury growls and swear to God I'm going to junk-punch his whiney ass for sounding like a harping girlfriend.

"Devil?" she asks, and I grin.

"That's my road name, Angel."

"Angel? Devil? That's kind of lame, isn't it?"

"I think it's more like fate," I answer, loving the way she's relaxed into my hold.

"I'm not your angel. Trust me on that one," she laughs.

"Are you ready, Sister?" Another woman comes around the corner, looking at my Angel.

"In a minute," she says.

"Is there a problem, gentlemen?" the other girl says. I give her a glance. She's passably pretty. She's wearing a longer skirt, and a shirt that is buttoned up to the neck. Her hair is in a bun and she's showing no skin except her face and hands. On some women you'd get the urge to undo the hair and see what's she's hiding under those clothes. This woman doesn't give you that urge. This woman makes me feel like one look and she could cause my balls to go into permanent hiding. It's unsettling, to say the least.

"No problem, I was just asking… your sister's name."

"And I wasn't giving it," she laughs, taking her arm out of my hold. I let her go, but I sure as hell don't want to.

"I'm going to make it my mission to find out your name," I warn her.

"My life is more complete, then," she jokes.

"Mother Lisa will be waiting for us," the other woman says.

Something is nudging into my brain—which is mostly fogged by the beautiful woman in front of me.

"Mother Lisa? Kind of a strange way to refer to your mom, isn't it?" I question.

"It's not when she's the Superior."

"The Superior?" I ask. Not quite getting it.

"As in Mother Superior," she smiles, and that smile is a little too sweet.

"I—"

"Oh shit. You two are nuns?" Fury asks. My body stiffens and I jerk as if I've been punched in the gut—because I have.

"Told you I wasn't the girl for your parties," she says, and then turns back to her friend. "I'm ready. You gentlemen have a good evening. Nice meeting you… *Devil*," she adds and then just like that, she leaves me standing with a cart full of condoms and without the first urge to use them tonight.

Damn it.

TORRENT

"*I* can't believe he's out here again," Elise mutters under her breath. I fight the urge to roll my eyes. Elise is hard to take on most days.

I've not minded my exile into self-denial of all things wonderful—I mean not really. I've missed things. I've missed my home. I've missed a good cold Sangria, I've missed talking with my girls, and I've definitely missed sex. Then again, I'm a normal twenty-six-year-old woman who really, *really* liked sex—not that I got to have it that much. When your father threatens to kill a man for touching his only daughter, it tends to slow the flow of willing partners. There's not that many men willing to take on a man who looks like like my dad, especially if he has a reputation to back it all up.

All that said, if I had to pinpoint the one thing that annoys me most about this situation, it would be putting up with Elise. That's saying a lot, especially since there are days that I crave going out for hot nachos and Cherry Coke or, better yet, a strawberry daiquiri, or heck, even the option to walk around naked in my bedroom and paint my nails. There's also days I'd kill to just dye my hair. I did that regularly in my old life. The life I was forced to leave three *very* long months ago. I've done it because Dad and Wolf asked me to. I did it because my father might be a cold-hearted bastard to most people, but he loves me. He'd die for me in a heartbeat—and I don't want him to die. I also did it because my father will kill for me in heartbeat—and has. If I think about the men he's killed while I've been in exile, I'd probably have to go for penance a lot more often than I do.

Still, when I agreed to go somewhere safe, I didn't realize what my father meant. I pictured a luxurious apartment with a pool and a gym. I pictured a cabin in Alaska with a roaring fire and a sexy wilderness guide. Hell, I even began daydreaming about an island with a sexy cabana boy, wearing loose, white pants that swayed in the breeze and showed off his rather large attributes as he stood over my lounger, fanning me with a large palm leaf.

Nowhere—and I do mean nowhere—did I picture myself pledging myself to the Lord and not being able to wear what I want, speak how I want, or even freaking eat like I want. I realize I probably sound like a petulant child, but at this point I don't give a damn. I sigh as I look around the picnic area, wondering if somehow anyone can read my thoughts and I'll need to say penance for those too. Elise keeps droning on and on and I'm resisting the urge to shut her up—by throat punching her and fixing it so she can't talk. I think I'd probably be doing everyone in here a favor at this point.

I might be tuning her out, but the subject of her whining hasn't left my mind at all. I pretend to be uninterested, but I do look over Elise's shoulder to see Devil in the background.

He's leaning on his bike, his arms crossed at his chest. He looks like he doesn't have a care in the world, but I know that's not true. He's been staring in my direction for the last ten minutes. I can feel the intensity of it, even at a distance. He's been doing this at least twice a week for the last month and a half... *ever since I met him buying condoms at K-Mart.* The thought makes me want to smile, but Elise is watching me too closely so I push a spoonful of cereal in my mouth to hide it.

It sounds like I'm full of myself, but I'm pretty sure he's here to see me each day. It's taken effort not to go over to him and ask. Being quiet and naïve is not who I am. Not asking someone outright what I want to know goes against my personality. At first I worried he was one of Dad's enemies, but the more I see him, I'm thinking it's not true. The fact he's a biker is just a coincidence...

Which is more than a little scary.

"I'm going to report him to Mother Lisa," Elise announces and those words I hear—those I don't blot out.

"You will not," I respond and my voice is as cold as steel. I've played under the radar and I've never drawn attention to myself, so the change in my voice and demeanor is something that can't be missed. Perhaps that's the reason everyone around us goes silent.

"Tori—"

"You will mind your own damn business," I order and I ignore the gasps from the other girls. "And if you so much as breathe about him to any of the others I will make you regret the day you drew your first breath."

"You can't do—"

"You don't know anything about my life before I came here, Elise. Trust me when I tell you that I can and I will."

Elise goes visibly pale. I am my father's child, and I think she can see that in my face—or at least sense it. Maybe she's not as stupid as I gave her credit for. I'm mad. I'm so seriously pissed off right now that I don't have words to describe it. Only I'm not mad at Elise. I'm mad at myself. I have no idea why I reacted that way. Sure, I hate Elise, but I'm here for a reason and showing my ass over a man I don't even know does nothing to help my situation. I push my food away in irritation.

I look up to see everyone staring at me. I cross my arms at my chest and put on my favorite fuck-you face and wait. They all nervously look away and begin eating. Eventually they begin talking again about the charity bake sale the convent is hosting later in the week. In the background I can hear the roaring of a bike, the pipes raking. I look up, even after telling myself not to. Devil is straddling his bike, revving up the motor and he's looking over his shoulder...

Directly at me.

Our eyes lock and then I watch as he puts on his shades, turns and takes off.

Damn... I think I'm in trouble.

DEVIL

"*A*bout time you got here. The party started without you," Fury laughs, slapping me on the back.

I look around, taking a deep breath. The scene tonight is exactly what I like. Half-naked to completely naked women everywhere, booze and assorted joys to explore if you want, and people having a good time. It's the life I embraced when I set out to become a member of the Savage Brothers. It's a life I've enjoyed for fucking years.

Who in the hell knew talking to a woman—*one look at a woman* —could change everything. Instead of being here and enjoying the party I've been stalking a woman I can't touch. I feel like a fucking creeper. I'm keyed up and pissed—even when I don't have a right to be.

"I don't give a fuck about the party," I grumble, grabbing a bottle of Jack and ignoring the glass. I look around the room one last time and this is not where I want to be.

"Hey! Where ya' going?" Fury asks, but I ignore him and keep walking toward the back.

I push through the doors and take in a deep breath when I hit outside. These doors lead to our courtyard out back. It's not much more than gravel. None of the men here enjoy mowing grass and since Diesel keeps a tight rein on our prospect numbers, gravel is easier. There's a few fifty gallon drums on concrete blocks that we throw a fire in when we have a party, a few picnic tables scattered here and there and a couple homemade brick and steel grills. Nothing fancy, but it works. That seems to be our motto. It's actually suited me better than most clubs we visit.

Tonight it annoys the fuck out of me.

I feel like I'm caged inside my own skin. When I get like this—and that's not often—I want to ride or fuck. Tonight, for whatever reason, fucking is the furthest thing from my mind. I'm ignoring the fact it has anything to do with the brunette who is torturing me lately. She's not available and whatever this voodoo is that has my dick twisted up over her will pass. All I need to do is wait it out.

"What's wrong with you, man?" Fury asks after following me outside. I sit on one of the tables, my feet on the bench, open the bottle and take a big swig from it while looking up at the stars in the Tennessee sky.

"Got my mind on shit," I growl, which isn't a lie. It definitely is —even if it shouldn't be.

"You're starting to get as broody as Diesel, dude, or that fucker you talk with every once in a while—Beast."

The irony in that makes my mouth twist in self-derision, because I'm forever nagging Beast, trying to get him back into the land of the living.

"You ever miss Ellie?" I ask Fury. Ellie was his old lady. The two of them were inseparable for over a year. Something happened between them—I don't know what and I don't think anyone does. Fury closed up over it. All I know is that one day Ellie was here and the next she was packing her shit and heading out of Tennessee. We could all see it was tearing Fury up inside, but he stood and watched her leave. He didn't try to stop her... *Not once.* The men and I have never brought her up, because we see the pain in Fury every damn time something happens to remind him of Ellie. Last Christmas, a few weeks after Ellie left, a Christmas card came for her and Fury stayed drunk for a fucking week. He broke windows out of the club and threw chairs—breaking them and fuck, anything else he could get his hands on. The man was torn the fuck up… *Which means* it's fucked up I'm asking about her now, but I can't seem to stop myself.

"She made her choice," he answers, his face changing to the point it's almost painful to look at. He looks like he's been carved in damn stone.

"Still, man—"

"I don't know what the fuck has got you like this, Devil, but I'm not talking about this shit."

"A woman," I mutter, taking another drink. "A motherfucking woman," I answer, feeling like the sad fuck I am.

Fury watches me for a minute and then the bastard takes my bottle, using his shirt to wipe off the rim of it.

"I'm not going to give you fucking cooties," I growl, barely feeling the buzz of the Jack, even if I've managed to drink a fourth of the bottle in two gulps.

"I've seen the bitches you play with. I'm not taking any chances," he laughs, though his voice still sounds angry. He takes a drink, letting out an "Ahhh…" as the burn moves down his throat. Then he takes another drink.

I jerk the bottle back before he can drink it all and ruin my chance to get shit-faced.

"Haven't played with any bitch in so long I think my dick is dead," I admit sadly.

"You're really that sprung over that nun chick?" he asks, as if he can't believe it. And I can't say as I blame him. I can hardly believe it myself.

I've been stalking her. There's not another fucking word for it; that's what it is—and I've been doing it for over a month. I can't explain why. There's something about her that captured my attention from the very beginning and it's not letting me go...

She's not letting me go.

"There's something about her," I mumble.

"Yeah, her pussy belongs to God," Fury smirks and I want to hit him. I want to smash my fist into his face and keep hitting until the frustration inside of me is gone.

"Didn't know you were religious," I respond instead.

"Didn't say I was. I only know you're shit out of luck," he says with a shrug. "You'd do better to get back to the party and find you a bitch in there and fuck her out of your system."

"And that works for you?" I ask, knowing that it doesn't. It's the reason we aren't allowed to talk about Ellie.

"Trust me, Dev. Women aren't worth the pain, man. They never are."

I listen to him, and I do it taking another drink.

What I don't do is go back to the party and find another woman, knowing I'll be outside that damn convent tomorrow looking for a certain brunette.

TORRENT

He's not there.

As I look out across the street, disappointment sinks in. I really thought he would be there. I've started looking forward to seeing him and this is the first time he's failed to show.

He's given up.

That's good. He needed to give up. I need him to stay far away from me. Logically I know all of this, but it doesn't mean I have to like it. I feel letdown by Devil, even if I shouldn't, and the weight of that emotion is almost crushing. A smart girl would go back to her room and pretend to be a good little girl. I'm not smart. If I was, I wouldn't be in the mess I'm in right now.

I catch the other girls working in the garden and I sneak away. I look over my shoulder repeatedly, afraid someone will see me. I can cover if they do, but I need a break—even if it's a small one.

I turn the corner of the building and lean against it, breathing deeply. This place is historic and so old I swear it was probably standing before Tennessee even became a state. The block is covered in green ivy halfway up and it sticks into my back, but I ignore it. I'm wearing a white uniform, including the damn veil and coif on top of my head. I thought nuns wore black. I could handle black a little more. At least I'd feel more at home in it. I rip the top off my head; it's fucking hot and I'm not sure how much longer I can handle being here. I know I promised my dad, but damn, nothing seems to be changing and I miss my old life.

"That looks better."

My head jerks up when I hear his voice.

"What are you doing here?" I ask, my head tilted to the side so I can watch him closely. I was kind of hoping I had embellished how good he looks. I didn't. He's tall and wide, his skin a golden tan and his hair is copper brown and when the sun hits it I see those highlights even more. He's wearing jeans that look lived-in and hug him in all the right places—so much so that my mouth waters. I force myself to look at his face—and not the bulge pushing against the zipper in his jeans. His eyes are blue. They're not a normal blue. Jesus, they're a dark, sparkling blue and they send goosebumps over my body and it's so intense my nipples freaking tingle. To disguise my reaction to him, I take out a few of the pins that didn't come out of my hair and then sift my fingers through it.

"Wanted to see you, Angel," he says, but he's different. He's not smiling or cocky like he was the first time we met. He's staring at me and he's completely serious... so serious that it's unnerving.

"What for?"

"Been asking myself that for a while now."

"You got a smoke?" I ask him, figuring it's best not to comment on his reply.

"Do nuns smoke?"

"This one does." I shrug.

He takes out a pack of cigarettes from the pocket on his cut and reaches it over to me. I take one out, silently congratulating myself that my hand doesn't shake. When I bring it to my lips, he digs in his pocket again and brings out a lighter. He lights it, his gaze holding mine. It's the simple act of lighting a cigarette, but it feels more intense.

Probably because I'm playing with fire, literally and figuratively.

"Thanks," I tell him, ignoring the fact that my voice is hoarse.

"Is smoking a sin?"

"Depends on what you're smoking, I guess. Is that why you're here? Church is usually on Sundays."

"I don't think they let the Devil in church. Pretty sure that's against the rules."

"The purpose for church is to save lost souls, *Devil.*"

"Mine's a little more than lost."

"What makes you say that?"

"How about the fact I want to rip that get-up off of you and fuck you against the building right now?" he asks and for a minute my heart stops. My body feels flushed and heat invades my system, inching up my spine.

I take a big drag off my cigarette, hoping the nicotine soothes me. *It doesn't.* Instead I'm having visions of Devil fucking me, my body pressed into the brick as he slams inside, filling me...

"Did I leave you speechless, Angel?"

"Just enjoying my cigarette," I tell him, doing my best to keep my voice even and unaffected.

"You should give those up," he responds.

"Why's that?" I ask, shaking off the ashes of the cigarette and taking another drag. I'm going to have to get back to the others, and I wish like hell I didn't have to. I can't stay with Devil though. It's not safe...or sane.

"Because I want to kiss you."

"And my smoking would stop that?"

"No, but I'd rather taste you than a cigarette."

"You smoke though. Isn't that kind of a double standard?"

"What do you mean?"

"Are you going to stop smoking so I'll kiss you?"

"If you want to kiss me, Angel, fuck yeah, I'll give them up."

"Just like that?" I ask before I can stop myself. I ground my cigarette under my shoe, but I never look away from him.

I'm not sure I can.

In answer, Devil takes his cigarettes out of his pocket and throws them on the ground. I watch as they hit the green grass and then his foot comes down and smashes them under his boot.

"Exactly like that."

"I better get going," I tell him, feeling unnerved and very tempted to kiss him.

"Don't leave," he orders—and it's definitely said like an order.

"I need to get back before they miss me," I explain, but we both know I'm running and we know why, because I've not been entirely successful in hiding my reaction to him.

"Give me something," he says as I start to turn away.

"I'm not kissing you," I tell him, because I know if I do there will be no coming back from it.

"I could make you like it," he says. I see a ghost of a smile on his face. His lips are mostly hidden by his well-groomed beard, but when he smiles his forehead crinkles.

"That's what I'm afraid of," I tell him with complete honesty.

"Then give me your name."

I start to lie to him. It would be safer to lie, but for some reason I find I don't want to.

"Torrent," I tell him, and start backing away, unable to turn away from him.

"Torrent…" he repeats and he says my name like it's candy on the tip of his tongue and he's savoring it, enjoying the flavor so much he's memorizing it.

Damn.

"What's your name?" I ask him, and when I do I fully expect him not to tell me. I know that a road name is special and most men only go by it.

"Logan," he answers, surprising me.

"Logan," I whisper, nodding my head in a yes motion, because the name fits him. It's strong, rough and yet smooth. I like it and I like that he has it. It would have made it so much easier if his real name had been George or Martin—heck, Herman would have been great. "Goodbye, Logan," I whisper, the act of saying goodbye somewhat painful.

"I'll be seeing you again, Torrent."

"I don't think that's wise," I tell him, shaking my head negatively.

"Probably not, but it's going to happen," he warns.

"Then maybe we both better start praying, Logan," I warn him and that makes him smile again.

Too bad I'm not kidding.

DEVIL

"*Y*ou're looking good today, Angel."

"Give it up, will you?" She laughs, but she keeps walking toward me. "You really like stalking me, don't you, Logan?"

"I really like it when you use my name," I answer her instead. It's useless to deny anything. We both know I'm stalking her. Hell, if I could get away with it, I'd throw her over my shoulder and drag her back to my... I really need a place of my own. I don't want to spend all my time with Torrent at the club. If I convince her to give us a shot, I need to work her slowly into my life. I don't want to make her afraid.

"You're such a dweeb. What could you possibly get out of talking with me? There's no future in it and I doubt you're looking for much more than an easy lay. In case you were wondering, Logan, I'm not easy."

"I never thought you were," I laugh, scratching the side of my face as I add another note in the mountain of them my brain has made when it comes to Torrent. "You sure as hell don't talk like any nun I've ever been around," I mutter.

"Have you been around many nuns?" she asks with a smile.

"Well, no, but you aren't what I imagined. You don't even dress like one," I tell her and my eyes rake up and down her body. She's wearing pants. They're wide in the legs and don't cling to her, but you see her hips and her shirt does hug her large breasts. Fuck, she's beautiful.

"I've not taken all of my vows yet," she says, avoiding my eyes.

"So you're saying I still have a shot," I press, and the freedom I feel inside at her announcement is indescribable.

Shock moves over her face, I see it clearly, and her eyes widen with surprise.

"A shot? Are you for real, Logan? Or are you wanting to see if you can get in the nun's pants? Do you have a bet with your buddies or something?"

"I've been called a bastard before, sweetheart, but never because I've bet on a woman. That's not my style. I like women but I always—*always*—respect them."

"Always?" she asks, clearly not believing me.

"Unless they do something to lose it." I shrug.

She stares at me intently for a few minutes and neither one of us talks. I don't know what she sees, but she seems to instantly relax.

"Why should I give *you* a shot, Logan?" she asks when she sits down beside me.

I try to concentrate on her words, but when she gets close, I have to fight the urge to take her into my arms. Doing that will fuck up everything.

"Because you want to," I respond with a smirk.

She shakes her head and I get the feeling my answer disappointed her.

"You're just like every other man I've met."

"What does that mean?" I ask, but I ask because I want her to talk more about herself.

"My family, the men are always cocky—so sure that they are the answer to every problem a girl could have."

"That's a bad thing?"

"It's no longer 1950, Logan. Women can find the answers to their own problems," she murmurs. "Maybe all they need from a man is support."

"Support?"

"Someone to talk to, a hand to hold…"

I pick up her hand. She stiffens immediately, but she doesn't pull away.

"I think I could handle that," I tell her and for once I'm entirely serious.

I thread my fingers through hers and entwine them.

"There's no way this can work, Logan," she argues.

I turn into her, letting my fingers brush against the side of her face.

"I think it can," I tell her, my gaze locked with hers. A man could drown in her eyes.

Drown and die happy.

"You're a dreamer," she scoffs.

"That's not the first time I've heard that, but Angel, tell me something."

"What?" she asks softly, her tongue coming out to caress her bottom lip. I want to moan as I watch its slow movement, but I manage to keep from it…

Barely.

"What would the world be without dreams?" I ask.

Torrent doesn't answer, but she sits beside me for another ten minutes. Not speaking, but holding my hand. For now, that's more than enough. I'll hope for tomorrow.

TORRENT

hree days.
 That's how long since I lost my mind.

I can't say what made the final break. It could be the tall, built, sexy biker with beautiful lips, blue eyes, brown and copper tinted hair. It could be the fact I've been living in a nunnery for way too freaking long. Maybe it's hereditary; Lord knows my mother was always a few French fries short of a Happy Meal.

I couldn't tell you why I'm being so stupid. Maybe it's a mixture of all those reasons and more. All I know is that this is day three I'm meeting Logan. Day three of risking my cover, and it's definitely the third day I'm falling deeper in lust for the biker named Devil.

I haven't kissed him—though I've wanted to. I've not told him a lot about my life—though the temptation to do that was there too. I've held hands, listened to his stories about his brothers. I've laughed at his jokes, and shared a few cold sandwiches he brought.

I'm in trouble and when I say that, I mean that there is this giant sign above my head in flashing neon that says *"Stupid!"* and there's an arrow under that word pointing directly at my head. I know all of this logically, but when I make it to the park, this time wearing jeans and a shirt—that I hid under the long black uniform dress I normally wear for confession—I find I don't give a damn. I want more time with Logan and I want to do it as me... *Torrent Bishop*. Not the make-believe Torrent I've been forced to become.

"Damn, Angel."

"What?" I respond, wondering if something is wrong.

"You're trying to kill me, showing up here like that. You can't tell me this is what nuns normally wear," he grumbles, his voice doing like it always does and sending sparks of awareness instantly through my body. Sometimes when he says my name, I swear it feels like a physical caress.

I start to tell him what I originally wore and stored behind a tree when I got away from the others. The girls are working at a local farm today with some children. I pretended to be sick, and stayed back as everyone else boarded on the bus. It was a little dangerous, but like I said, I'm insane and spending time with Logan has become as essential to me as air and water.

"Whatever," I mutter, walking closer to him. "If you don't like it, you don't have to look."

"Oh, I like it, Torrent. I like it too damn much," he says, scratching his beard. I almost giggle at the look on his face. It's clear he's struggling—but not that much, since his gaze is zeroed in on my ass. Devil is an ass man, that much is clear.

"Horn-dog."

"Arf, arf, baby," he jokes and I giggle. "How long do we have today?"

It's a simple question, but it causes my body to heat and my heart-rate to kick into overdrive. I can't stop myself from looking over my shoulder in the direction I came. I half expect to see the other girls, including the Mother Superior, standing there ready to...

Crap. I don't know what they would do, I only know whatever happened next wouldn't be good.

"An hour or so," I tell him, knowing that's pushing it. Most everyone might be gone, but there are still people at the convent and if one of them decided to check on me and discover the pillows under my cover...

"How do you feel about riding a bike?" he asks, surprising me.

I can't stop the smile that stretches on my face. I miss so much about my former life, but one of the biggest things—outside of father and my friends—has been riding. I was on a bike practically before I could walk. My dad bought my first bike when I was a teen and the bike I have now was built exclusively for me, by him. I cherish it and I miss it every day.

"Umm..."

"Never mind. I can tell from that grin plastered on your face you want to. You're a different kind of woman, Torrent."

"You don't know the half of it," I mutter under my breath.

"But I want to know more," he says, proving he listens to everything I say—even when I'd rather he didn't.

He takes my hand and I almost close my eyes at the feel of his fingers linking through mine. My heart squeezes in my chest and I feel flushed through my whole body—especially between my legs.

Logan struts, there's no other way to describe it, as he walks back through the park. Immediately I know that he's proud to be seen with me. I don't have any illusions about my appearance. I look decent, but because of my family and the way I was raised, most boys I've been around are intimidated by me. They've definitely been afraid to make a move. Which means most of my boyfriends and the men I've let into my life have been part of the club, and have been a closely guarded secret. Shit, if Wolf knew I was trying out the other brothers he'd flip his shit. Wolf intimidates the hell out of me, and the only thing I do know is I am not cut out to be his old lady—even if I thought of him like that... *Which I don't.* Wolf is practically the same age as my father, a habitual cheater on his women and hard partier. No way is that the kind of man I want.

Logan...

The truth is, I don't know what kind of man Logan is, but the man I'm getting to know could win my heart as well as my body— that much I know and I should be scared instead of being happy. But I'm not. I'm happy. Logan's hand in mine fills me with so much happiness, it's kind of scary. I'm on the back of his bike without really remembering how I got there. I was too caught up in spending time with Logan, of having him close to me and smelling that masculine scent and that sexy as fuck aftershave he wears.

"You get on a bike like you've done it for years, Angel," he says and he's looking over his shoulder at me. His dark eyes are trying to see inside my brain. I know a flash of panic, but I shrug it off.

"Not the first bike I've been on, Logan."

He nods in agreement, but doesn't comment. Instead he hands me a helmet. I curl my nose in distaste.

"Put it on, babe. Not risking you getting hurt," he orders. That's sweet and all, although I'm not really sure how I feel about it. Most of the men in my dad's club wouldn't be caught dead with a helmet on them or their old ladies. Still, I shrug it off and put the thing on.

We drive ten minutes down the road, and cut off on an old dirt road that I had never noticed before. I'm not real familiar with this area in Tennessee. I'm from the opposite end of the state essentially, but it's clear that Logan knows this place like the back of his hand.

My hands are wrapped tight around his stomach, my legs pressing into his thighs. The vibrations of the bike are working through me and I'm aroused.

Painfully so.

It's more than just doing without sex for a long time too. It's the fact that I'm more sexually attracted to Logan than I've been to any other man in my life. Hell, I'm lusting after him and it's not purely about the sex either. For the first time in my life, I actually really and truly like everything about Logan. The more time I spend with him, the deeper that goes—which has never happened before.

After going down the dirt road he cuts off again, this time in front of a sign that reads: *Lake Conte Public Boat Ramp.*

He drives down the small incline and then parks his bike under a huge willow tree. The tree might be the biggest one I've seen, the branches spanning out so far it encompasses the entire ramp, shading it.

I slide off the bike, my legs shaky—not from riding, but from the need to be touched. Even through my pants, I can feel the muscles of my pussy clenching in hunger, the wetness painted on the inside of my thighs, and I know without looking that my nipples are so hard they're probably visible even through my shirt and bra.

Logan steadies me and then reaches under my chin and takes the helmet off of me. He lays it on the seat of his bike and I rifle my fingers through my hair, trying to tame it—although I'm sure I'm not successful at all.

Logan reaches into his saddle bags, taking out a paper sack from one and a blanket from the other. Then he grabs my hand and leads me to the other side of the old tree. I watch as he spreads the blanket with quiet efficiency.

"Time for a picnic," he says as he sits down on the blanket and pulls me down to join him.

"We couldn't picnic at the park?" I ask, thinking that might have been safer. It might be hard to resist Logan out here... alone with him... his eyes sparkling in the mid-day sun... with him smelling like a freaking god of sex and leather.

"This is prettier," he says, and I can't deny that at all. He reaches behind him and picks up the paper sack he placed on the ground earlier, as he spread the blanket. He takes out a peach Nehi soda for me with a grin. During one of our conversations I let it slip that it was my favorite drink ever and he laughed at me, but it's clear he took notes and that thought makes my heart feel... full. Then he takes out a can of beer—which he proclaimed was his favorite drink ever during the same conversation. I curl up my nose and he laughs.

"That crap still tastes like warm piss," I tell him—exactly like I did before.

"Angel, have you ever drank a bottle of piss?" he asks, still laughing at me.

"No, but if I did, it would taste *exactly* like that. You can just tell."

"You can?"

"It's the smell. It smells like piss that's been sitting in a toilet for hours without being flushed."

"Maybe we should change the subject. It's going to make it hard to get romantic with you if we don't," he says, taking out a couple of sandwiches.

"You shouldn't be trying to get romantic with me, Logan."

"You can't deny there's something between us, Angel."

"There's a pull between us, I'll admit that."

"It's something we should investigate," he says plainly, his dark gaze boring into mine.

"It's something I'm not free to investigate," I tell him, and it's the truth—even if it's not for the reasons he believes.

"Not yet," he responds and in a way he could be right, so I don't say anything further.

Maybe because I'm hoping he's right.

DEVIL

She's gotten quiet and I've probably pushed too far, too soon. I'm not used to reining myself in around a woman. Time to try and lighten the mood. The last thing I need is for her to take off running.

"I slaved over this lunch all morning, I hope you like it," I joke, taking the sandwiches out of the plastic zipped bags.

"You made these yourself?" she asks, an eyebrow cocked, showing her disbelief.

"I sure did, with my own little hands," I tell her with a wink.

"There's nothing little about you, Logan."

"Glad you noticed. Now dig in."

She looks at the sandwich and then back at me. She picks it up and brings it to her nose, smelling it.

"Peanut butter and jelly?" Her voice is a mixture of laughter and disbelief. Her eyes almost sparkle when she looks up at me. "You spent all morning making peanut butter and jelly?"

"Hey, it's a lot of work putting enough peanut butter on one side and getting the ratio to jelly correct on the other side," I defend.

"You do realize they sell it already combined in a jar, right?"

"No shit?"

She studies my face and must realize that I'm completely serious because she cackles with laughter so hard she snorts— which only makes her laugh harder.

"I take it you don't really grocery shop? Unless of course it's for condoms and beer," she adds, still sounding like she wants to laugh again. I watch as she meticulously tears the crust off of her sandwich. For some reason that simple act is appealing to watch.

"That's pretty much it, yeah," I answer, not bothering to deny it. "Though it's starting to look like all I'm going to need is the beer." That declaration stops her mid-bite. "Haven't used one since I laid eyes on you."

"Am I supposed to be flattered?" she asks while licking peanut butter off of her lips.

"Unless you like the fact that you are helping my balls to turn blue, then no. I'm only stating a fact."

"If you're waiting for me to put out, your balls are going to be in sad shape, Logan."

"Some things are worth the pain."

"You're insane," she responds, not looking at me.

"I think that's already established, babe. I'm sitting here across from a woman I can't quit thinking about and I haven't tried to get between her legs once."

"You haven't?"

"Trust me: when I try, Torrent, you will know."

"That sound ominous." She sighs. "Maybe it would be better if we stopped meeting each other," she says, not looking at me.

I take a bite of my sandwich as I mull over her words. What she says has merit and she might even be right—but that doesn't mean I like it, or that I'm going to do it. I have a bad feeling that I couldn't stop seeing her even if I wanted to.

"Is that what you want, Angel?" She doesn't respond and still doesn't look at me. "Is that what you want, Torrent?" I ask her again, putting my fingers under her chin to bring her gaze up so she looks at me. I apply enough pressure that I don't allow her to look away. Her answer is important. I need to know where her head is.

"It should be," she answers.

"But it's not?" I press.

"No… it's not," she answers.

"Then you'll meet me tomorrow?"

"Will I be treated to peanut butter and jelly sandwiches?"

"Nah. I have something better planned for tomorrow."

"Better than peanut butter and jelly?"

"Definitely."

"Then how can I say no?" She laughs and I make a vow to myself to make her laugh like that again tomorrow.

TORRENT

"*I* really shouldn't do this. If I get discovered..." I'm muttering this to myself, knowing that I'm playing with fire. Sneaking away to picnic with Logan yesterday was crazy. Doing it again today is worse. Most of the sisters are gone again, this time to work on a project with Habitat for Humanity. They left me behind, thinking I'm sick again. I spent the morning wrapped in a million blankets and a heating pad, all so that when Sister Marie came in I'd have a small temperature.

Realistically I was going to hell before I came to the convent. Now, I'm pretty sure I have a table reserved with my name on it.

"You'll be all right either way," Logan says, tugging on my hand because I'm falling behind.

I look at our joined hands before I move. That's another problem. I keep finding myself holding onto Logan's hand. I am not a touchy-feely type of person. Hell, I've never wanted to hold someone's hand before. Yet, I find myself doing it all the time with Logan. *And when did he become Logan in my mind, rather than Devil?* I'm losing it completely and if my father finds out, there will be more than hell to pay.

"Easy for you to say, Logan. You have no idea how much is

invested in this," I grumble, letting my annoyance bleed through. The one thing I don't do is let go of his damn hand.

"Invested in this..." he says, as if he's puzzling over the words. "You mean in becoming a nun? How do you decide to do that, by the way? Do you just wake up one day and say, hey, today is the day I'm going to give up sex for the rest of my life?"

"Does everything revert back to sex for you, Logan?"

"I'm a man, so most things do," he answers. "But I'm not going to lie, Torrent, I'm finding that with you I seem to think about sex even more than normal."

"I suppose I should be flattered."

"Is flattery going to make you strip and jump my bones?"

"Jump your bones?" I giggle.

"Well, jump just one in particular," he answers, and he somehow wiggles his eyebrows and that makes me laugh harder. "My very *big* boner."

"You're crazy. You know that, don't you?"

"Crazy for you," he jokes and it hits me right then.

I might be twenty-six years old, and I might have lived a good life, but until right now while holding Logan's hand, I'm not sure I've been particularly happy. I'm happy now. Happier than I can ever remember, and the reason makes my heart quake in fear.

It's Logan.

"Where are we going, anyway?" I ask him, doing my best to *not* think about what that revelation means. I can't have Logan...

"We're hiking."

"Yeah, but where to? I thought this was lunch. I am on a time limit here, you know."

"You said you had more time today," he reminds me.

"Well, yeah, but I was thinking a couple of hours, not all day," I grumble, trying to keep my panic at bay.

"I'll get you back in time, Angel. I promise."

"Logan—"

He turns to face me and, using our joined hands, pulls me in closer to him.

"I need you to trust me, Torrent. You don't know me that well yet, but you need to know that I would never do anything to hurt you. I joke, babe, but I do care about you."

I look into his eyes, his face, and I memorize it. From the slight curl in his reddish brown hair, the slight scar on his forehead and the groove under his eye that shows he smiles often. I take it all in and if I were to ask myself later, this would probably be the exact moment that I fell in love with Logan.

"Okay," I whisper, feeling like my heart is in my throat.

It's a feeling that stays with me, even when we reach the top of the mountain and a waterfall comes into view.

"How do you feel about skinny dipping, Angel?"

That groove under his eye deepens and his eyes twinkle.

Maybe this is when I fall in love with Logan.

DEVIL

"*I* am not skinny dipping with you, Logan," she says, shaking her head, but for a minute I catch a look in her eyes. She may say no, but I think she *wants* to say yes. It's not much to hang my hat on, but it's there.

"I could make you like it," I tell her with a wink.

"Probably," she agrees.

We stand there looking at each other and I know she has to feel the pull between us. Hell, I can even tell her body is reacting to it, but she doesn't reach out.

"Ready for lunch?" I ask when it becomes clear that she's not going to give in. I feel more than a little stupid, but I'm not giving up. I want Torrent, and I want her in ways I've never wanted another woman.

"You did promise something better than peanut butter and jelly," she says, smiling at me. There's a sadness in her eyes that I don't like.

"That I did," I respond, leading her over to a clearing by Grotto Falls. Grotto is a hike that I like to take often. It's not that far from the main road and though I hate the busy nature of the Smokey Mountains, I do love the scenic areas. It's also why Diesel decided to relocate our crew here. He wanted the privacy the mountains offered him and thought it would be a good place to raise Ryan.

Once we make it to the clearing I spread out a blanket. There's no one here today, which is good. During the peak season for hiking there's usually quite a few here. I'm thankful I seem to have it and Torrent to myself. I sit down first and look up at her, reaching my hand out. She takes it almost reluctantly and sits down across from me.

"What's for lunch?" she asks.

"First, a little something to wet your whistle," I tell her, handing her a cold soda from the small cooler tote I've been packing.

"Oh... Dr. Pepper...*fancy.*"

"Only the best for you, Angel. Next the appetizer."

She looks at the candy bar I handed her and laughs.

"*Snickers?*"

"In case you get... *Hangry.*"

"You really are insane, Logan."

"Eat up before it's time for our main course."

"I can hardly wait to see what it is," she says, shaking her head.

"Tell me more about you," I urge her as we unwrap the candy bars.

"Like what?"

"I don't know. Anything. What made you decide to become a nun?" I ask. I should have waited to spring that question on her because I asked it mid-bite and she chokes and starts coughing. I lean over to maybe slap her on the back or something, but she motions me away and gets the cough contained. I open up her soda and hand it to her to drink.

"Did you seriously just ask me that?"

"It's a legitimate question. I mean, there had to be something to trigger your decision. Maybe you watched too many Whoopi Goldberg movies."

"What?"

"Sister Act?"

"I have no idea what you're talking about, Logan."

"You've never seen that movie?"

"I don't really watch a lot of movies."

"Oh... Okay. So tell me something else. Anything. What was your childhood like?"

"Good."

"You're going to have to give me a few more words than that, Angel."

"How about you tell me about your childhood first?" she says instead.

I study her for a minute and decide to give in. I want to know more about her, but maybe if she finds out more about who I am she will finally realize she's safe with me.

"What do you want to know?"

"Where did you grow up?"

"New Orleans."

"Why doesn't that surprise me?" she laughs. "Was your mother a voodoo priestess?"

"Fuck no," I laugh. "But those women scare the fuck out of me."

"It's not very manly to admit a woman scares you," she points out.

"*Christ.* Have you seen some of those women? I swear it's enough to make your balls shrivel up."

"I don't really know about that, since I don't have that particular part on my anatomy."

"Thank God for that, woman."

"You're horrible," she laughs. "Okay, so what was your mom like?"

"She's truly one of the best people I've ever known in my life."

"That surprises me," she responds, pulling her legs up against her chest. Her gaze studies me and I leave myself open. I want her to be able to see everything. I don't want secrets between us, and I know that keeping them is not the way to make her feel safe with me.

"Why is that?"

"Well, you're a biker. Every biker I've ever met has childhood issues."

"Have you met many bikers, Angel?"

"I've known my fair share." She shrugs, and something about the way she says that piques my interest, but I decide to let it slide for now.

"Hate to break it to you, but my old man is a pistol who retired from the army and still gives everyone around him hell, and I had the sweetest mother ever to take a breath."

"Had?" she asks, quick to pick up on my words. I like that. It shows she's really paying attention.

"She passed away two years ago. Breast cancer."

"Oh, Logan, I'm so sorry."

"Life is hard, Angel. She was a good woman, she got a shitty draw that she didn't deserve, but she fought like a warrior. Cancer is a fucker that doesn't give up sometimes."

"I know," she whispers, her face sad.

"What's your story, Torrent?" I ask, knowing she has one.

"My brother. He had a brain tumor."

"*Motherfucker.*"

"Yeah, it was bad," she answers. Her voice catches and I see the cost of those memories on her face. I reach out and take her hand, needing to touch her. When she doesn't pull away, I press my luck and gather her up and pull her into my lap. I hold her close. "It broke my father. He became someone I didn't recognize for a while. Luke—my brother, got so bad there at the end. He couldn't talk to say anything to us. He didn't have control over his body. Even touching him brought him pain. The night before he died he would get so scared if we weren't right beside him. He couldn't talk, but his eyes followed Dad everywhere," she whispers, tears rolling down her face.

"I'm sorry, Angel. I'm so sorry."

"I never saw my dad cry until then, Logan. And he didn't just cry... He emptied his soul out with tears as we said goodbye to my brother."

I don't know what to say to that, so I continue to hold her, stroking my hand up and down her back, trying to bring her comfort. Inside I can't help but think this is another sign that Torrent is meant to be mine.

TORRENT

TWO WEEKS LATER

"*I* want out of here," I growl to my old man. I don't get to see him often and the fact that I'm in a confessional at midnight talking to my father through a screen is a bad sign.

"There's been a complication, Torrent."

"No. There can't be complications. When I agreed to this you said it would be a couple months at the most. You *promised* you would get this shit handled. I am not spending my life in a convent, Dad."

"I need to keep you safe, Tor," Dad says and his voice is laced with worry. A month ago I would have listened to that and backed off. But that was before Logan. Everything has changed now.

I need out of here.

"Then lock me down at the club. You've done that before. Just get me the hell out of here," I hiss, so frustrated I want to scream.

"I can't do that yet, Tor. I have to find out who the mole in my club is, and I can't do that if you're there."

"Dad—"

"No, Tor. You know I always try to let you have your way, but not on this. You can hate me if you want, but I need to make sure you're safe."

40

"I don't hate you. I'm just not really fucking happy."

"Don't say fuck, Tor," he grumbles and it makes me snort with laughter. "You're in a holy place."

"You're a freak, Dad."

"Never claimed to be anything different."

"If I stay you have to push to get this crap figured out. I need out of here."

"You can't see it, Tor. But I am pushing. I also need you to stop playing with fire."

"What?" I ask, my heart beating harder in my chest. I don't know how he knows, but intuitively, I'm sure he does.

"That fucking biker that's been sniffing around you. End it, Tor."

"Dad—"

"I want better for you, but even if you end up with a club member that's fine. The Savage crew are—"

"Don't. Most people talk about us like that."

"That damn bunch deserves it. They're a bunch of nomads, junkyard dogs that have set up shop and got adopted by a crew out of Kentucky. They're worthless. I don't want my baby girl mixing with them. Besides, you know Wolf would kill a mother-fucker stupid enough to lay a hand on you."

"I'm not Wolf's property. I've never seen Wolf like that," I sigh. I'm tired of this argument. It never seems to go away.

"Maybe not, but that doesn't mean he didn't claim you years ago. The only thing that's stopped him is the fact you want a life outside of the club."

"The only thing that's stopped him is *me*, Dad."

"We'll talk about this later, but you need to cut loose the fucker sniffing at you. Do it today, Tor."

"Dad—"

"If you don't I will, and you won't like how I do it. There are people looking for you, people in my own fucking circle. You have to keep your head down."

41

He's right. I know he is. But the past two weeks have been the best in my life. I haven't been able to go away with him again, but we've been meeting at the park across from the convent. I do it while I'm supposed to be saying my devotionals and it's been the only thing that has kept me sane.

Logan is a little cocky, but I like it. He's kind of cute, if that can be said about a man who oozes testosterone out of every pore in his body. He's dirty—deliciously so and I always leave him wanting more. Dad's right. I am playing with fire. We almost kissed the other day. I can't keep doing this. And Dad's not lying. If he is the one to put a stop to it, I won't like how he does it.

"I don't—"

"Do it, Tor."

"Fine, I'll do it," I say, my stomach instantly tightening and leaving me feeling sick.

"Good girl. I'm not sure when I will get back here, but I'll get word to you next week and let you know if I've had any luck."

"You need to hurry this up, Dad. Because if you don't, I'll pull myself out of here."

"You always were a pain in my ass."

"Like father, like daughter," I laugh. I put my hand up against the screen and he does too.

"Love you, baby girl," he mumbles and I smile.

"Love you too, Dad."

He leaves and I stay where I'm at. I don't want to risk going out and hugging him, even if he is wearing a priest's robe. All I need is for Elise to come in and ask me why I'm bear hugging a priest. The bitch would tell everyone and then I'd have to kill her and I have enough on my plate.

Like how to say goodbye to Logan, when it's the last thing I want to do.

DEVIL

"*You're* late, Angel," I tell her as she walks toward the bench I'm sitting on.

Our bench.

I've been meeting Torrent here for the last couple of weeks, and we've not even kissed. I've not touched her since that day I held her in my lap, except for holding her hand a couple of times. Still, I've enjoyed my time with her more than with any other woman I can remember. She's got a wry sense of humor that keeps me on my toes. She's sarcastic and witty and when she laughs I swear I feel it hit me deep inside. She feels like pure sunlight when it shines on you after a week of rainstorms.

I've been a lover of women my whole life, but I'm not stupid. Eventually, I knew I'd find the one that I wanted to keep. I didn't want a club girl. There's nothing wrong with them; I never wanted to claim an old lady who had been hardened by the life we live. I never wanted a woman in my bed who also warmed my brother's bed. That makes me a bastard, I freely admit it. It doesn't alter the truth. I wanted something special when I decided to settle down and Torrent is definitely something special.

There's only one major problem with her and that's the vows

she's made for her life. She refuses to talk about it, and so far I haven't pressed her. But the other day we almost kissed and I saw the want in her eyes. She wanted my lips on hers. It's time I start pushing her, because I don't have a choice. I want her and I'm getting damned tired of holding back.

"I started not to show at all," she says and right away I can tell she's different today. Colder. There's no welcome in her eyes, no smile on those cherry lips, and not one hint that she's happy to see me. The abrupt change from this to the way she treated me yesterday is jarring.

"What's wrong?" I ask, knowing something is.

"What could be wrong?"

"Because you're coming off like an ice queen ready to freeze my damn balls," I tell her bluntly. Torrent might be wearing the garb that says she's innocent, but she hasn't been acting that way with me and I've never pulled punches when talking to her. I'm not built that way. I am who I am. She seemed to have accepted me like that, but today I can see her visibly blanch at my words, as if they shock her...or she finds them distasteful... finds *me* distasteful.

What in the fuck has changed?

"Do you have to talk like that?" she whispers, looking around as if she's embarrassed by me. I don't know why Torrent is acting like this now, but I know I don't like it.

"You didn't have a problem with the way I talked yesterday," I remind her. "Or the day before, or the day before that—"

"I did, but that's part of the problem, Logan."

I resist the urge to close my eyes when she says my name. Hardly anyone calls me Logan, and I'd be lying if I said that I don't enjoy it when Torrent does. I like my name on her lips—probably too much.

"I didn't realize there was a problem," I mutter, because apparently there is. She's not even sitting down this time. She's standing

in front of me wearing that damn nun garb—this time in black—
and wringing her hands.

"What are you doing here?" she asks and her face looks almost
panicked. I don't like it at all. Torrent should only be smiling.

"Having lunch with my girl," I tell her, hoping to joke enough
so that she relaxes. Immediately I know that strategy isn't going
to work.

"That's just it, Logan. I'm not your girl. I'll *never* be your girl.
My life is planned out and there's no room for you in it."

"You can always change your life, Torrent. Just because you
made plans in one direction, it doesn't have to stay on that path."

"What path would it take? You expect me to give up all of my
plans so I can warm your bed?"

"Would that be so bad?"

"Do you *really* expect me to give everything up to crawl under
your sheets a couple of times?"

"I was thinking more than a couple," I joke, and again it's clear
now is not the time to joke.

"And then what? What happens to me once you got to corrupt
the innocent little girl and move on?"

"Maybe we need to take a step back and breathe here, Torrent.
We can start by you telling me what's going on inside that pretty
little head of yours."

"I'm not taking a step back. What's wrong, Logan? A woman
starts talking about the future and you get nervous?"

"I didn't say that," I growl, getting tired of trying to be patient
and logical here. If she wants a fight, then I can fucking give her one.

"That's what I heard," she yells back. "I'm out of here."

I grab her wrist when she goes to turn away from me. She will
not dismiss me. I don't know what's going on here, but I'm damn
well going to get to the bottom of it.

"We're going to have this out."

"We're done talking..." she argues back. "*Forever.*"

"No, we're not. First you're going to tell me how yesterday you were sweet as pie and today you're acting like a raging bitch."

I barely get the words out and she slaps me across the face. I let her, her anger feeding mine, but then I pull her to me and slam my lips onto hers. I kiss her hard and fast. I kiss her like the punishment it's meant to be. My tongue pushes to get in her mouth and when she doesn't immediately open for me, I wrap my hands in her hair and yank hard. When she gasps out in pain, I press my advantage, plundering her mouth, conquering it and not letting her say no to me.

Her fingernails bite into my arms, scoring the skin. She tries to pull away, but I tighten my hold. She doesn't give in to the kiss, but I get the strangest feeling that she's allowing it—that she's not fighting it as hard as she could. That's the last thought I have before hunger takes over and I get drunk on the taste of her. My hand moves up to her breast, squeezing it and playing with her hardened nipple. I break away from her mouth and she moans as I pull up that damn garb she has on, hating it—but happy it gives me such easy access. My hand finally touches the flesh of her thighs and I focus between her legs. She's wearing silk panties. I didn't expect that. The heat and wetness of her pussy is against the pads of my fingers, and I press in, immediately feeling the pulsing of her clit.

To hell with this shit. I'll finger-fuck her into submission and I won't stop until she's begging me for more.

"Oh my God!"

Torrent and I break apart at exactly the same time. When I look around I see that damn woman that was with Torrent at K-Mart the day I first met her. Now she's standing there watching us and my fingers are clearly pressed between Torrent's legs and I'm sure that's not lost on her. Hell, even if it is, she can't miss the way my other hand is possessively owning Torrent's tit.

I pull away from Torrent, not wanting to cause her problems, but it's best this shit happened. It's time Torrent comes to terms with the fact that she wants me—as much as I want her. She's on fire for me. She can't deny herself, she can't deny us—not anymore.

Torrent takes a couple of steps away from me. Her dress falls down, covering her, and when she looks at me, there's a war going on in her head. I can see it clearly. Her eyes aren't hiding anything from me.

"I never want to see you again. I don't have any room for you in my life, Logan. Don't come back."

"Tor—"

"I mean it. Stay away from me. If you don't you will live to regret it," she says and then she takes off running.

Away from me.

Her friend gives me a strange look and then goes after Torrent.

I'm left standing here wondering what in the fuck just happened.

TORRENT

"*D*addy?"

"It's Wolf."

My hand tightens on the phone. It's one in the morning and Sister Victoria came and got me out of bed to tell me my father was on the phone. Dad's taken great pains not to contact me directly where others were involved, so a phone call—especially at this time of the day—scares me.

"What's going on?"

"There's been some new developments at the club. Your father…"

"Is something wrong with my dad?" I ask, and I don't keep the terror out of my voice—*I can't.*

"He's fine, Torrent. I promise you, but we had to take him underground."

"Underground? What does that even mean? I want to see him, Wolf."

"Torrent—"

"I mean it. Either you come and get me or I'll come to you. I don't give a damn."

"I'll arrange it. It will take a me a couple of days to arrange it and make it safe for you."

"But…"

"Your dad is fine, Torrent. I promise you. But you have to help him right now and you have to do that by keeping yourself safe."

"You promise me that he's okay?"

"I promise. Give me two days."

"One."

"Damn it, Torrent—"

"One day, Wolf. Then I'm out of here, either with your help or without it," I warn him and I hang up before he can respond.

I walk out of the office and find Sister Victoria in the hall, waiting for me, her sullen face searching mine.

"Is everything okay?"

"My father has taken ill. I may need to go to him immediately."

"I—"

"I already know the rules, Sister Victoria, but my father is all I have left in this world and if he needs me, I'm going to be by his side and no one will stop me—not even God."

Shock moves across her face and I see it right before I turn away.

I march straight to my room and start packing. I'm not giving Wolf time either. I'm leaving this damn place tonight. I need to know what's going on with my father and I can't trust any of his men to get to the bottom of this. The club my father loved, the club I grew up surrounded and adored by, has turned into a nest of vipers. I can't help my father by hiding away, that much is clear. I've given up too much to sit on my hands and lose my father too.

It's time I remember I have my old man's blood running in my veins. If we can't trust his men to put an end to this, then by God I will. I'm not helpless. I can find things out and maybe Logan would be willing to help if he knew the truth. He might be pissed that I was lying to him at first, but he's no stranger to our world. He'd understand. I sigh because my heart aches even thinking

49

about Logan. I hated walking away from him. He's come to mean a lot to me in such a short time. Maybe it will never go anywhere, but I wanted the chance to find out.

I zip up my duffle bag after tossing in the few items I have left that are mine. Then, I throw on my jeans and T-shirt that I showed up here in. I always feel better in my own clothes. I sit down on the bed and lace up my boots and head out.

Luckily Sister Victoria didn't follow me, or alert anyone else. The place is deserted. Still, I walk as quietly as I can and only breathe when I get to the entrance. I undo the deadbolts on the double doors and open one just enough to slide out. I keep my front facing the inside of the convent, my back out to the sidewalk as I do my best to make sure no one inside sees me. Turns out that is my biggest mistake. Because before I can so much as scream a large gloved hand is clapped over my mouth and I'm pulled away.

I fight.

I truly do.

I kick, I hit, and I try to slam my head backwards into my abductor. Nothing works. I twist, trying to get to my side so I can aim my kicks better, but the man holding me—and I'm sure he's a man; his grip is too solid and hard, and squeezes even tighter. I'm afraid he's going to crush my bones. I reach behind me and my hand hits skin and I dig my nails into the meaty flesh. I hear the man scream and I know a moment of victory before blinding pain thrums through me as I'm hit hard on the side of my head.

Pain explodes, my vision goes white, gray and then bleeds into a dull blur before I sink to my knees and the world goes completely black.

DEVIL

"*C*an I help you?"

I look around the inside of the chapel and shift uneasily. It's been a long fucking time since I've been inside any church—much less a convent. The walls are stark white, the floors wood that's so old it's almost black in color and the trim has been painted the same coal black. This room looks so barren, so devoid of anything warm and inviting that I don't know how Torrent could survive here. I look up to the front of the chapel and it's different from the rest of the room. There's a statue of the Virgin Mary, rows of candles and a sacrament table. The bright reds used to add color shine vividly, drawing my attention. I force myself to look away.

"I'm looking for Torrent," I answer her, clearing my voice and shifting back and forth on my feet. I feel way out of my depth here for sure.

"Torrent?" she parrots, studying me. "Are you her natural father?"

I blink. Fuck, I'm not that old. Torrent is younger than me, sure—but she's not that damn young.

"Hell no," I answer before I can stop myself and I instantly see the distaste on her face. "I'm... I'm a friend."

"A friend?" she asks, her eyes narrowing.

"This is the guy that Sister Torrent was sneaking off to see, Mother Superior," a girl answers from the corner of the room.

I look over at her and it doesn't surprise me that it's the chick that followed Torrent to the park three days ago.

Three days.

I haven't seen Torrent in three days. I kept going to the park, hoping she'd change her mind or at least come back to scream at me—*something.* But she's been silent. I haven't so much as caught a glimpse of her and that's bullshit. She owes me at least a little more of an explanation.

"I see," the woman referred to as Mother Superior responds and I swear the temperature in the room drops another ten degrees.

"I want to see Torrent," I state again, refusing to back down. If this gets her in hot water, then she has no one to blame but herself.

"I'm afraid that's impossible," she responds.

"*I'm afraid* that's not good enough. I came here to see Torrent and I'm not leaving until I do. So you need to get her... *Now.*" I counter.

"I can't do that."

"Yes, you can—"

"She means she can't because Torrent's not here," the other girl answers snidely. I don't like the bitch. Sometimes you can look at someone and see the hate in them. This girl is chock full of hate. How they ever let her in this place I don't have any idea. I thought nuns had to be loving and giving? The only thing this chick could give you would be a fucking headache.

"Where is she?"

"She left," the girls answers, speaking over top of the other one.

"Where did she go?"

"I—"

"That's enough. Go back to your room, Elise. This is not your concern."

"But—"

"*Now.*"

"Yes, Mother Superior," Elise says. She casts me another look full of hate and bitterness and walks away.

"Where is she?"

"I'm afraid I do not know. One of the sisters reported that Torrent got an urgent call in the middle of the night from her family. She was missing when we reported for breakfast the next morning. She left in the middle of the night and took all of her belongings."

"Did you contact her family?"

"We did, not that I can see that it is your business. How well do you know Sister Torrent?"

"I know enough to know that she doesn't belong here," I growl. I want answers and I'm not getting a damn one.

"Where does she belong? With you?"

"She'd be happier with me than here," I defend, suddenly feeling like an idiot.

"Just because one gives their life over to God, it doesn't mean they are unhappy," she says and immediately I feel out of my depth.

"I didn't mean that… *Not exactly.*"

"If something is not your choice that doesn't necessarily make it a wrong one."

"I'm sorry, Sister…" I'm getting the feeling that I've had my ass handed to me.

"In any event, Torrent isn't here and I don't know where she is."

"You don't know how to contact her?"

"I'm afraid not. She had family, but we don't have their information and—"

"But—"

"And even if I did, Mr....?"

"Dupree," I answer, feeling the last hope I've harbored fade away.

"Even if I did, Mr. Dupree, I couldn't give it to you."

"I want—"

"I don't have any information, but maybe you should consider something, Mr. Dupree."

"What's that?"

"Maybe Torrent left because she made her choice and you weren't it," she says and then she walks away.

She leaves me standing there and with her she takes away the last hope of talking to Torrent.

It's over.

No... That's wrong... It never really began.

Torrent was never in my reach.

DEVIL

"*W*hat in the hell is wrong with you lately?" Diesel asks. I look up at the son of a bitch and frown.

"Not a thing, why?"

"Ever since I sent you on that errand for Skull you've been sullen as a damn mule."

"Sometimes that country boy in you comes through, Diesel," Fury cracks, thinking he's funny. Diesel flips him off and ignores him. He's not wrong but Diesel doesn't laugh much these days. Hell, considering they've tried to kidnap his boy over and over, I can't say as I blame him. Diesel is a walking poster child for why you should be careful where you stick your dick without protection. Of course no one realized Vicky was a complete whack-a-doo—until it was too late.

"Well?" Diesel asks and I run my hand through my hair and look at the almost empty bottle of beer I'm holding. He's right. I'm a fucking mess. I've been grieving the loss of Torrent for a fucking month. Grieving a woman who was playing games and was never mine.

Grieving a woman who didn't bother to say goodbye.

Okay, she did say goodbye, I just didn't realize it at the time. I sure as hell didn't think she would walk away that easily.

"He's fucked up over a woman," Fury smirks, taking a pull on his beer.

"When in the hell did I miss that? I don't remember you bringing a woman around here."

"I—" I start but stop when Fury answers for me—*again*.

"He didn't. Hah, that's the best part of the story. He wouldn't dare bring this woman to the club, man."

"Why in the fuck not?" Diesel growls. "The club is part of who you are, Devil. Shit, you've been in this life as long as I have. We were born into it."

"He—"

"Will you fucking shut up, Fury?" I growl, draining my bottle. I aim it toward the trash can which is probably twenty feet away. It goes too far to the left and crashes on the floor. Seems to be a symbol of my life right now. "Last time I checked I could talk for myself," I mutter, rubbing my hand over my face.

"I liked you better when you were a cocky motherfucker," Fury grumbles, walking off.

"Join the crowd," I say with a sigh, liking myself better back then too.

"Speak," Diesel commands, sitting down on the sofa beside me and taking the spot Fury left. I manage to hold in a curse. The last thing I want to do is talk to Diesel about women. I think he's pretty much sour on women in general and who in the hell could blame him?

"I let my dick lead me where I didn't belong," I answer, my voice hoarse as images of Torrent smiling and laughing come to mind.

"Women. The downfall of every fucking man since the beginning of time," Diesel answers, his voice sounding way too tired.

"This wasn't her fault really," I respond, feeling the perverse need to take up for Torrent—to defend her to one of the men who mean the most to me.

"Why's that?"

"She was off limits. I knew that. I still had to try."

"Fuck, dude. I never figured you for the type to do that."

"Do what?"

"To mess around with another man's old woman."

"She's not. Not really. Fuck, it's one of those gray areas."

"Gray areas?" The asshole laughs at me, and I can't say as I blame him.

"She wasn't really married."

"That's what they all say."

"Damn it. I'm serious. She wasn't married, or hell even claimed —*not really*." I rub my hand over my face, scratching my jaw. "At least not to a real person," I mutter.

"Say what?"

"I said, she wasn't married to a real person. Torrent... she's not what you're thinking."

"What is she? Christ, is she one of those people who marry Barbie dolls?"

"What the fuck are you talking about?" I ask Diesel, wondering if he's drunk. I didn't smell it on him that bad, but I'm kind of hammered myself, so who knows.

"She is... well she was... pledged, kind of..."

"Pledged? Did we go back in time to poodle skirts and fucking promise rings? What in the hell does pledged mean?"

"She's a nun."

"Get out of town," he says, his voice full of disbelief.

"Let it go," I growl.

"Shit man, you aim high, don't you?"

"Fuck you," I mumble.

"You got to get her out of your head."

"That's what I'm doing," I answer, holding up my liquor bottle and shaking it at him.

"What if I send you on an errand?"

"Why?"

"Skull is calling in another marker. Wants us to check on his boy."

"What did Sunshine do now?"

"You willing to go see him?" Diesel asks and I frown. If I leave, there's no chance of seeing Torrent again, but hell, there's no sign of her and even if I did… she's not mine.

She's never going to be mine.

If the last month has made anything clear, it's that.

"Yeah. Screw it. I'll head out in the morning."

TORRENT

$\mathcal{I}$ look around the small room, for the one hundredth millionth time. Nothing has changed. It's still nothing but a 4' x 6' box—*if that*. The floor I'm sitting on is rough lumber. I try not to move a lot, because if I do so I've learned I get splinters and in places I truly don't want them. There's a little light filtering in from the top of the box. It's coming in through the hole between the jagged wooden planks.

I moan as I move, my body sore from staying in basically the same position for a month and other things. When I first came to, after being unconscious, I panicked. Anyone would have, but it was worse for me because I'm afraid of small enclosed places. So when I say I panicked, I mean I freaked-the-fuck-out. So much so that they opened the top of my *"crate"* and when I lunged at them, they beat me back down—first with fists and then with a crowbar. I'm pretty sure I have a broken arm. I know my eye is swollen shut and infected—if the burning sensation I feel is anything to go by. It hurts to breathe so I'm not entirely sure what shape my ribs are in.

I've also lost track of how long I've been here. Everything is a blur from the moment I stepped outside the convent. I tried to keep count at first. Trying to judge the shift from day into night by the actions of people outside and how many meals they brought me. I think they bring one meal a day and it's usually toward the evening. I know it's evening when they feed me because there's a skylight above me and when they take the top off, it's the first thing I see.

The light hurts my eyes when they take the top off—a product of staying here in the dark for so long. I smell. There's no way to get around it. There's been no bathing, no personal hygiene concerns at all. There's only me... my wooden prison and small bucket across from me that I've been forced to use as a toilet. It stinks—though thankfully it is emptied once a day.

I'm living like a dog in a pound... probably worse.

I think I have a fever. I can't be sure. I'm always cold, but today I'm dizzy—even disoriented. I can hear voices around me, but I'm having trouble concentrating on them. I shake my head hoping to focus, but I end up moaning as the room spins harder.

"Sounds like the drugs are working."

"About time. Jesus, I almost dread pulling her out of there. She smells like shit."

I swallow down the bile that rises as I hear them talk about me. I *instinctively* know they're talking about me, but I can't...

"You would too if you've been in a box for a month. Stop your bitching and help me pull her out. The boss will be here today and he wants to see the merchandise."

"Dude, what's the endgame here? Do we even know? What the hell does he have planned?"

"Don't know, don't care."

"But—"

"You're getting a shit load of money for doing very little. Stop asking fucking questions. In our line of work that's a sure way to end up dead."

"Fine. Whatever. It seems a little screwed up if you ask me."

"Nobody's asking you shit. Let's pull her out of the pen and clean her up. Boss wants her in those clothes he sent over."

"Now that part I won't mind."

"What's that?" I hear one of them ask as the top of my crate begins to move.

"Strippin' the bitch. You see those Double Ds she's packing? Won't mind playing with those babies at all—not after we get rid of the smell."

"Do whatever makes you happy. Just remember your dick don't get in her, that's our only rule."

"Not like he'd know. Maybe that mouth…"

His words make the bile rush back and I vomit as the bright light from above pours inside my hell.

DEVIL

"*Y*ou back for good, man?"

"Yeah," I answer. "Got back in town last night."

"Was beginning to think you were going to move down there with Beast," Fury cracks.

"Aww. Did you miss me?" I crack.

"Like a case of the fucking shits," he responds.

"How is Beast?"

"Finally happy."

"Damn, really? Did he go back to his club?" Fury asks.

"Nah. Not yet. I think he and Hayden are going down that way in a couple of months. It will be hard for him, but I think with Hayden by his side he'll be okay. She's encouraging him to reconnect with his old life and his friends."

"That's good. Diesel said she was a good woman."

"One of the best," I agree and for the briefest second a picture of Torrent floats through my brain. I've done a good job of putting her behind me the last couple of months. I've had to. It's stupid to miss a woman who was never yours. I do, but I'm learning to live my life. I'm not going to grieve over a woman who didn't choose me—who walked away from me without a thought.

It'd be stupid. Besides Diesel, Fury and the rest of them are right. Torrent already had her life planned out and her choices made. There was no room for me.

There never was.

That's a hard pill to swallow, but it's the truth.

"Good. Now all we need to do is to get you back in the saddle with women—"

"Already done, compadre," I answer, cutting him off. I recline back and take a long pull off my drink. I think back to my little rendezvous with DD and Jenn. It wasn't bad for what it was, even if DD was too damn clingy.

"No shit? Who is it?"

"No one important. Just a couple of ladies that are friends with Hayden."

"Damn. Good for you. Sure as hell nice to have you back, old man."

"Good to be back."

"I'm headed out to Sal's tonight. You want to go?"

Sal's is a local strip club the boys hang out at a lot. I don't really have the urge to go, but I shrug it off. I don't really want to stay here either.

"Sure. Why not?" I ask.

I walk out with Fury toward our bikes.

I'm not going to lie. I think I did better away from Tennessee. Being back here makes me think of Torrent again, which fucks with my head. I ignore it though. Torrent is in the past. The one thing life has shown me lately is I want someone in my life that feeds my soul. I've seen what a difference it makes with Beast and that's what I want. I doubt I'm going to find it at Sal's, but I figure that's better than waiting for her to fall in my lap here at the club.

"Where you guys headed?" Diesel asks as we make it to the garage.

"We're going to head down to Sal's and check out the new talent he has. Want to join us?" Fury asks. Diesel's looking at me strangely. He's been doing that since I rode back in today. I see questions in his eyes, but I ignore them.

"Why not? Ryan's out for the night. Let me get Dani to check in on him," he says.

We watch as he walks away and there's something different about him. He's been that way since the last kidnapping attempt. His constant worry over his son is slowly getting to him. Crusher mentioned he's even talking about leaving the club and disappearing with Ryan. I'm hoping that doesn't happen—but, it's not like I could blame him if he does. Ryan needs to be his first priority.

"Diesel seem different to you lately?" Fury asks and I scratch my neck, wondering exactly how to answer that.

"He's got a lot on his plate," I finally say with a shrug and leave it at that.

"Yeah a night out at Sal's might be what the doctor ordered for all of us," Fury says.

Personally I think he's expecting too much from a night at a strip club. I'm tempted to grab a bottle of Jack and go back to my room, but I don't. I've made a decision to move on with my life and I'm damn well going to do it. I'm not getting any younger and I'm starting to feel way too old.

TORRENT

"What the fuck are you doing?" a dark voice growls. My eyes are swollen shut. The world is black and I couldn't see him if I wanted to. The voice sounds familiar though. I'm woozy, drifting in and out of consciousness, so I can't concentrate enough on it.

"Nothing—only having a little fun," the guy above me says. I hate him. I've vowed to myself over and over that if I ever get free I'm going to kill him first and I'll make it painful. The only problem with that plan is that I'm beginning to think I won't get free. Hell, even if I do I don't know what this guy looks like. I'll work around that, though, if I ever get the chance.

"You had strict orders not to hurt the merchandise, you fuck-head."

"Haven't touched her, just had to make sure she fell into line," he says.

I feel a hand tightening in my hair and yanking my head up. I moan from the pain that radiates so intensely through my head that I have to struggle not to black out.

"Fuck, look at her, asshole. How do you know you haven't given her brain damage?"

"What does it matter if I did? You just said you wanted her alive. I didn't think you meant I—"

"You aren't paid to think," the man growls and I hear the sound of someone being slapped. "You're paid to carry out *my* orders."

"I thought you were working for—"

"It's not who I'm working for. It's the fact you're working for me and I warned you. I don't want the package harmed. I have her sold, you fuck-wad. He's not going to want to pay for merchandise that looks like that!"

"What's so special about this bitch anyway?"

"She's wanted by a man willing to pay a fuck of a lot of money to get his revenge. She's the card he's going to play to get that revenge and because she's that important you don't fucking beat her until she's unrecognizable. That's all you need to know."

"Fine, fine. I'll lighten up. What's the next step?"

"Nothing right now. Thanks to you being so damned stupid, we will have to wait until she looks better to play out the revenge. At least until the swelling goes down enough you can tell who she is."

"How long?"

"A week. Keep your hands to your fucking self for a week. You need to bring her to heel, you do it without making a mark on her. You got it?"

"Got it."

"Good. I'll be in touch," the man growls and then I hear his footsteps walking away. My mind replays everything I've heard, but I'm too tired. I'm fading fast. I let myself go under. I'll try and replay everything later. Maybe I can find a clue as to who is pulling the strings then.

Right now it's taking too much effort.

DODGER

"I still say you shouldn't do this, Dodger man," Wolf growls. Frustration is thick on his face.

Wolf is my right arm. I trust him like he was blood. Fuck, he's the only man I can trust right now. I had to tell him about the note I found on my bike today. I rode into town to see if I could call some markers in and get some help. I've been going crazy trying to find a sign of Torrent. Getting the note saying they were willing to make an exchange—me for Torrent—was like an answer to a prayer. I'm not coming out of this alive. I've already accepted that. It doesn't matter. As long as I can save my daughter that's all I need. Wolf is going to help me do that. He's all I have. At least I know he loves Torrent. He's been in love with her for years. He'll protect her with his life. That's all I can concentrate on now. I can't be here to watch her spread her wings and find her way in life. I can only trust my best friend to make sure she's happy and I know he will.

"I don't have a choice, Wolf. They got my girl."

"So we go in there and get her—*together*."

"They know what I'm doing before I fucking do it. I can't trust my own club."

"We need another day or two, damn it. We'll find the mole and get it taken care of."

"What happens to Torrent while we're here playing with our dicks and—"

"They're not going to do anything with Torrent. They want to use her to get you, Dodger. We—"

"And they're getting me. I can't risk not falling to their demands. They want me to meet them out at the Watershed."

"The Watershed?"

"The old closed marina out on Route 38."

"Shit, that place has been closed for twenty years. At least let us—"

"Exactly. I go in defenseless as fuck and give them exactly what they want—"

"You can't..."

"And while I'm doing that, you come in with the three men of our club that we can trust and you get my girl."

"Damn it, Dodger. You're asking me to help you die."

"I've lived a good life. I don't give a fuck about dying—not if it means my girl will live."

"How do you think Torrent will like the fact that you're trading your life for hers?"

"She will understand in time."

"Bullshit."

"You'll make her understand," I tell him finally, looking up into his face and stopping just short of pleading for him to understand. I've never begged a motherfucker for one thing in my life, but I need Wolf to not fight me on this. I need him to make sure that Torrent not only survives this, but that she comes through it stronger and happier. Wolf is the key to that. My daughter is headstrong. She's like me in that respect and she will blame herself for my death. She's tried to fight having a life in the club, but in time she will see that the club is her family and that Wolf is strong enough to let her spread her wings, but make her happy too. They will be a good match.

"You're putting a lot of faith in me. Torrent hasn't ever listened to one thing I've said, Dodger. There's no guarantee she will in this either."

"When I'm gone, she'll look to you. She has trust in you, Wolf. My daughter might be stubborn, but she's smart."

"Hey, Dodger. You asked me to let you know if I saw anything funny during our lockdown," Big Tom says, opening the door, his face somber.

"Yeah?"

"Oh sorry. Didn't know you were in here, Wolf, but this can't wait."

"What is it?" I ask Big Tom. Tom stands about 6'4" and he weighs about three hundred fifty pounds. He's bald on the top of his head and his salt and pepper hair on the sides is cut short. I trust him almost as much as I trust Wolf. He and Wolf alone have been with me from the beginning. They're the only two left that I'm comfortable telling my plans to. There's two other men I feel are relatively safe, but the truth is when it comes to Torrent, I can't truly trust anyone but Wolf.

"Crash snuck out of the club a couple of hours ago. I did as Wolf ordered and I didn't stop anyone from leaving, so when Crash snuck out of the bunker, I laid back and followed him."

"Where did he go?"

"He drove out to the old marina. The one that—"

"Fuck! Crash is the mole?"

"It makes sense," Wolf says. "He's a transplant from another club. His loyalty wouldn't go as deep."

"I gave him a fucking home here. I let him into our lives," I growl, betrayal sitting deep in my gut, burning like a damn knife stabbing into me with a death blow.

"Is he still there?"

"Yeah. I left Dub watching the place."

69

"They better not see him," I mutter, still wrapping my mind around the fact that I finally know who in my club has been trying to get me.

"They won't, Dodger. You know how Dub is. If he doesn't want you to see him, you won't."

"Now we need to plan our next move."

"We already know it," I tell Wolf and our eyes lock.

"Dodger, now that we know who the mole is—"

"It changes only one thing."

"What's that?"

"I'm killing that motherfucker before I die," I vow. My options are limited, but if I have to wrestle the Grim Reaper himself to stay alive long enough to end Crash, I will.

"Damn it, Dodger—"

"Torrent is all that matters, Wolf. You know that. That's why I brought you into this. I can't do it alone."

"Damn it," he mutters again.

"You love her. I couldn't trust her life in anyone else's hands," I tell him. I see the exact second he accepts what I've already figured out is inevitable. I don't have a death wish. I hope a miracle happens and I survive.

I'm just pretty sure it's not going to.

TORRENT

"**W**hy are you doing this?" I ask again.

I don't expect an answer. I *never* get an answer. The response isn't verbal this time either. Instead, I'm blasted with the cold spray of the water hose. Water surges against my face. It's ice cold and a combination of the temperature and the way it's sprayed directly at my face work together to take my breath away.

I sputter and gasp, turning my head to the side and holding my hands up—all in some weak attempt to protect myself. That's a joke. There's no protecting myself. I couldn't even manage to beat them away from me so I could keep my clothes on.

I'm not sure which is actually worse. Being hosed down, or standing naked in front of a man I don't know and unable to see anything but the outline of him. I feel so powerless, like I have no control and I have to wonder if I will ever have control again. Over the last few days, I've been thinking and I'm pretty sure I'm not going to come out of this alive. I've thought about the people in my life, and wished I could at least say goodbye to a few of them.

This is going to hurt my father so much. Losing my brother

destroyed pieces of him, but if he loses me too... I swallow down the misery that threatens to drown me.

I feel the water slow and then—thankfully—it is taken away. I take in a deep breath. That is just as painful. My body is so sore from the beatings. I know my ribs are cracked—if not broken. He hasn't beaten me today and I'm thankful at least for that small mercy.

I hear steps walking toward me and try not to be scared, but I can't stop that emotion. I've been scared since I stepped outside of the convent. I've felt it for so long, it suffocates me now. I feel his hand wrapping around my hair, gathering it, holding it tight at the scalp.

"You're a hot little piece even looking like you do. I ought to break you in a little more for my boss, don't you think?"

I don't respond, but inside I'm shaking like crazy. I hope he thinks it is from the cold. I don't want to show that I'm scared —*not to these monsters.*

"What do you think? I bet you know how to suck a man dry, don't you? How about you show me what you can do with that mouth of yours?" he growls and then he uses his hold to force me to my knees.

I start screaming, I can't stop myself. I already feel lost and completely at my kidnapper's mercy. The thought of being forced... of them forcing themselves on me terrifies me beyond anything I've ever experienced. I know that if something like this happens, if this man is allowed to do that to me there will be pieces of me that I will never get back—parts of me that will not survive.

"What the fuck is going on here?"

I recognize the voice. He's the man from yesterday—the one whose voice sounds vaguely familiar. It does today... *even more so,* but I still can't place it. It's on the tip of my tongue but, I can't fight my fear enough to concentrate.

"Having a little fun," the man laughs, yanking my head harder and pulling me to him.

"I told you to not fucking—"

"I'm going to let her show me what she can do with her mouth. Hell, I'm only warming her up for—"

He doesn't finish his sentence. A gunshot rings out through the room and it causes my ears to ring. I scream, sure I'll feel blinding pain at any time. That never comes. Instead, the man lets go of my hair. I feel his body jerking against me and then I hear a large crash as he falls back and his body hits the floor.

"Fuck, Crash. Why did you do that?"

"Because you don't take orders. I gave you one fucking job you, asshole. You couldn't manage to do that and now you've used my fucking name!"

Crash!

The name rings in my head as loud as a damn siren.

Crash is a member of my dad's club. My father knew someone was trying to kill him, to bring him to his knees. That's why he put me in the convent to begin with. He wanted to keep me safe and out of harm's way while he found the source of the threat. I don't know Crash that well; I've talked to him a few times. I do know he was a respected member.

"What does that matter? There's nothing she can do about it. Not now!" the other guy yells, but another gunshot rings out. This one is so loud it is almost like I can feel the bullet whizzing past me. "Crash," the man adds, but this time his voice is filled with more pain and fear... I hear it, I recognize it at once, because it's choking on me. "Why are you..."

"You've fucked things up for the last time, motherfucker," Crash answers and then three more shots go off, one right after the other. I can feel a spray of liquid hit my face and I know right away it's blood.

Then Crash grabs me and hauls me back up on my feet.

"Don't... Don't do this," I stutter, knowing in my heart that I'm going to be next.

"Shut up, you stupid cunt. It's all ruined now. This wasn't the way it was supposed to play out. Your death isn't my fault. It's that stupid fuck's. You were supposed to survive this," he growls and bile begins to rise in my throat. I'm going to throw up. I don't want to die. There's so much more in life that I wanted to experience. I really wanted to see my dad again. I even wanted the chance to see Devil again—as hopeless as that whole situation is... I really liked him... I wanted....

He pulls me from the room. I keep waiting for the death blow, but that doesn't happen. Instead he shoves me back into the box. I may not be able to see but I definitely know when the lid closes, because any light I see through the shadows fades and I'm left with nothing.

Nothing but darkness.

DODGER

"*I* still say we need to go in together. We can let the gunfire rain down on them. We're stronger together," Wolf mutters.

We're parked on top of a hill, off the main road. Through the brush and the trees, I can see the outline of the old marina. Our club's not from here. This is not our territory but we made a temporary spot in this region the minute I lost contact with Torrent. I researched the area fairly good and I know the only real club presence is that damn Savage crew—which is really just made up of a bunch of nomads and under the protection of two clubs, whose strongholds are in Kentucky. They fly the Savage banner, but I don't think they have the full charter's protection. Dragon, the club president for the Savage crew in Kentucky, backs them though, and I know that fucker's firepower is impressive. I didn't seek them out for help and that might have been a mistake.

I can't trust my club now. Crash might have been identified, but does he have people within my club? Are there others I need to worry about? When you can't trust your own men, the last thing you want to do is trust others. So I purposely didn't announce our presence here. I left everyone in the dark. Now, I'm wondering if that was smart. If I had met with them, maybe I would have been able to trust them. It would have been good to have more firepower at my back. I get Crash was my weak spot and he went against me. It hurts that any man under my command would do that, but it feels better knowing who it was—instead of being left wondering. I can't even truly pinpoint when this shit started. I suspect it has something to do with the contract I turned down funneling women into Mexico. My men didn't like it. It meant a fuck of a lot of money for all of us. I'm a bastard and my hands are about as dirty as they come. I had to draw the line at that though. The women these men were paying for are my daughter's age. Turns out that even after all these years, I have a conscience.

"We can't go in shooting. I only have one goal here, Wolf. I want my girl safe."

"Damn it, Dodger. Are you listening to yourself? We don't even know if Torrent is in there."

"That's why Skeeter and Red are up ahead scouting it out. Hopefully they don't fuck up and get caught."

"They won't. They're the best, you know that. We both trained them."

"I can't fucking be sure of anything anymore."

"Crash might have been a motherfucking traitor, but it doesn't mean all of your men are, Dodger."

"Not my problem anymore. That will fall to you."

"Will you fucking quit talking like that? Are you really so damn eager to die?"

"Fuck no. But I've told you before—"

"Yeah, I've heard that shit. You'll excuse me if I try to keep your sorry ass alive."

"As long as Torrent is your number one priority." I shrug.

"She always has been," Wolf says and I don't respond.

I have a lot of shit on my mind, but I do know Wolf will take care of my little girl. I'm not worried about that. I just wish I could be here for her too. My skin feels like it's burning. I look down at my watch. The time I was told to be here is close. I'm going to have to get moving. They'll be looking for my guns and weapons. I'm going to be brought to them like a lamb to the slaughter. I have a couple of surprises though, and maybe if luck is on my side it will be enough to survive this—or at least for my baby girl to survive.

"She's in there, Dodger," Skeeter says and I look up to see him and Red coming my way. "They have her in a fucking crate in the back of the building."

"She's alive?" I ask, the thing that matters the most causing my heart to turn over in my chest.

"She is. We couldn't see her that good, but she's moving, Dodger."

I close my eyes as relief sweeps through me.

"Then I guess it's show time. You guys get in position."

"Dodger—"

"Save it, Red. Wolf already tried to talk me out of it and it's not happening. I'm going in front and I'll be the distraction. You guys have only one job and that's to go in the back and save my girl."

"Damn it—"

"*Enough!*" I growl, my frustrations boiling over. "I'm done discussing this shit. You know your job. Do it and I'll do mine."

I take off walking, leaving my club behind me. They don't matter anymore—nothing does.

Nothing but Torrent.

TORRENT

"*W*akey-wakey," I hear him yell before the top comes off of my crate. God, I hate him. I can see better this morning—not exactly clear, but I can make out faces. For instance, the guy grabbing me and pulling me from the crate is as ugly as I imagined he was. Most of his features are blurry, but I can make out his beard, which is bushy and unkempt. His eyebrows are much the same and his eyes are small and even though I can't focus on them I know that they are as cold as the rest of him.

"Ow!" I cry when he grabs me by the hair, pulling it.

"You got a date with your daddy," he growls and fear grips my heart so tightly I can't breathe.

"Please, don't bring my dad into this. You don't have to—"

"Good thing you're pretty because you sure are stupid as fuck. This has always been about your daddy, you bitch."

I let him drag me, I don't bother fighting—not now. I try my best to keep my head clear because I know I'm going to need it soon. He drags me to the wall that faces the front entrance and thankfully pushes an old tattered T-shirt over my naked body. It's not much—but I'm thankful for it.

My eyes are watering, but I can clearly make out a bright red double door. The man brings his knee up and plants it into my stomach. I go down instantly, gasping as the wind leaves my body. Once I hit the floor, he grabs one of my wrists, pulling it to a chair. Then he slaps a shackle on my wrist. I yank it, trying to get away, but I can't. It's attached to the leg of the chair. It's not like the chair is lightweight either. It's heavy and big enough that two people could probably fit into it. I pull again and again, hoping something is off and I can get free. The man punches me in the face and I instantly feel blood begin to seep from my lip. I go down, the world moving too swiftly and the pain colliding with nausea.

"Dodger's walking up the dock," another voice says.

"Please," I start, wanting to beg for my dad's life. I'd be willing to promise anything. I don't want my dad to die because of me.

"I really like it when you beg," the man laughs. He tightens his hand on my chin, lifting my head up, pulling me to him. My face is inches from him and he's leering—even through my bad vision and panic I can see that. "Give me a kiss. If you're good enough I might make you my pet," he says and his breath washes over me. With all the other odors around me I shouldn't be able to smell it as much as I do, but it's so strong it makes me sick. His teeth are black, as if he spends his time doing Meth. His bad skin would indicate that too. I can't even pretend to go along with him. Instead, I spit at him. He slaps me hard, my face jerking to the side with the force of the hit.

"Torrent!" my father yells from the door and he tries to make it to me, but two men grab him almost instantly. They're big men, but even then my father nearly drags them to get to me—that is, until one of the men hits him over the head with something and my father goes down, instantly knocked out.

I scream; I can't do anything else.

I'm powerless to help him... or myself.

DODGER

"Fuck," I growl.

My head feels like there's a damn Greyhound bus running through it. I look around, my eyes slowly and painfully adjusting to the light.

"Well, look at that. You rebound pretty good, Dodger—for an old man. You were only out a couple of minutes. Here I thought you'd sleep through all of the fun."

I look up and see a face I never thought I'd look at again.

"I should have known you'd be behind this."

"You should have known not to back out of the deal I brokered."

"I didn't ask you to broker it."

"But you've been around. You know the game. You wanted to roll the dice in your neighborhood, you got to play the whole game—not just parts of it."

"I will not run women in my city. I told you that. Fuck, most of those women are younger than my daughter," I tell Carter.

Carter is low-level slime. The Korean Mafia use him to broker their deals. He came to my club wanting to work out a deal with some petty shit. I'd use some of my pledges and younger members to act as enforcers for their illegal gambling and extortion rackets. It tried out my boys before I made them full-fledged members and kept our coffers filled with easy cash. Eventually Carter approached us about some drug smuggling. That turned into a more lucrative business and I didn't have a problem with it. When sex trafficking was on the table I said no. Most of my men were for it, but I didn't put it to a vote. I vetoed that shit immediately. That wasn't something I ever wanted to get into. I'm not a fucking saint and I'm about as dirty as they come, but I draw the line at kidnapping women off the street and shipping them out of the States. There's plenty of bitches that choose to spread their legs for money; I'm not about to force innocent girls into it. If someone did that to my daughter I'd cut their body into little squares and feed it to my fucking fish.

"And that's your downfall, Dodger."

"What's that?" I ask him, sitting up. A wave of dizziness falls over me, but I fight back. I can't be sure how long I've been out. I know Wolf and the boys are probably already working their way through the back of the building. I need to keep Carter distracted. I suspected it was an enemy. I had no idea it was the Koreans that called for my head. I actually feel better knowing it's this fucking punk. I'm even feeling better about my chances of survival knowing Carter here is calling the shots.

I move my hand to my back, feeling for my gun under my cut. I didn't really expect for it to be there. I know disappointment when I confirm that it's gone.

"Looking for this, Dodger?" Carter asks. I jerk my gaze up to him and see him waving my Glock. "You really are slipping, old man. Walking in here to try and save the day and instead you're at my mercy."

"I don't have much of a choice seeing as you have my daughter," I tell him and that's when I know I might have a concussion because until now, I haven't been looking for Torrent. "Where is she?" I growl. "I want to see her!"

Carter laughs as he takes a hit off of a blunt.

"You're in no position to demand anything, old man. The bitch wouldn't stop screaming when I knocked you out. I had to contain her."

Carter's smile is so fucking creepy that fear seeps into my bones.

"What did you do with my daughter?" I demand, doing my best to stand up. A man goes to grab me but I push him away. I sway on my feet, but I remain standing—even while Carter is laughing.

"Jin, bring Torrent in. I think dear old Dad should be able to see his daughter," he says with another grin. "At least one *last* time."

I try to still the chaotic beating of my heart and calm down. I can't lose my head here and I can't let fear rule me. I still have one weapon that Carter won't be expecting. Plus, my men should already be riding in to save Torrent. I have to stall for a little longer.

That's all... *just a little longer.*

TORRENT

I'm dragged back into the room. My dad's rough, unshaven face is the first thing I see. He's worried; there's even fear in his eyes and that looks wrong on him. His dark hair is marred with the dark stain of his blood from where he was hit earlier. I breathe deep, choking on my fear, but trying not to show it.

I'm holding onto one thing.

If my dad is here, that means his club is close by.

If I can keep my head and help him, we can survive this. It's a matter of holding on and not losing control.

"My girl," Dad all but moans.

His voice is filled with pain and I can see tears in his eyes. I can only guess how bad I look and I know that's what is causing his pain right now. I try to keep my own tears at bay. I don't really succeed. I stumble as I make it beside him. Dad wraps his arms around me and I go to him willingly and I hate that I cry, but I couldn't stop it now if I wanted to. I never thought I would feel his arms around me again.

"I'm okay, Dad," I lie. "I'm okay."

He pulls me in tight, tucking my head under his chin.

"I'm so sorry, Tor. I'm so sorry, my little angel," he says brokenly. "I'm so sorry I got you involved in this."

My dad sounds tortured and his body is shaking. My knees are weak and I know I'm leaning on him too much—*but I can't stop myself.*

"Isn't this touching? Too bad I don't have all day to watch it."

"Carter, you bastard. Let my daughter go. This shit doesn't have a damn thing to do with her," my dad yells. I close my eyes tightly, knowing the worst is coming quickly and not ready for this small reprieve to be over. I always thought I was brave, but right now I don't feel brave at all.

"It has everything to do with her," the man my father calls Carter responds. I process his name, commit it to memory, because somehow I want to be the one who takes his life… to take everything from him, like he's trying to do to me. Before I can do anything else, or even urge my father to quieten and wait for his men, I'm yanked away.

I scream because the hold on my hair is even more painful than before. My dad tries to pull me back, which causes more pain, but I do my best to hold onto him. For a split second I think we'll win the tug of war. Then fear blooms over Dad's face. I can see it take over his features, leeching into the characteristics on his face centimeter by centimeter—as if in slow motion—and draining the color from him. Then I feel the barrel of a gun pressed against my temple.

My dad lets me go. His hands go up to show he's not resisting as I'm pulled away. I try to beat the panic down, but a sob escapes because I know the farther I get from my Dad—the more these monsters gain control over the situation—the more likely neither of us will survive.

Where are his men?

My dad would never wade into this situation without backup, especially with my life on the line.

"Carter, stop this. Let Torrent go. This is between the two of us, not her. Let her walk out of here. You have what you want. You have me, let her go."

"You always were so damn short-sighted, Dodger. That's what has really caused all of this," Carter responds.

"Torrent doesn't have a damn thing to do with this!" Dad literally spits out.

"She has *everything* to do with this. You thought you could back out on the Koreans. You've built your life by showing people you're strong. Did you expect them to let you get away with making them look weak? You can't step in this world with one foot, Dodger. You know that shit. Now you have to pay the price."

"I said I'd pay it, but let Torrent go!" my dad pleads. The panic and fear in his voice is so potent I can feel it.

"Where would be the fun in that? Let me ask you, Dodger. When someone betrayed your club, what did you do to them? Did you show them any mercy? Their *family* any mercy?"

"I told you, you can do what you want with me! But—"

"But *nothing*! You aren't calling the shots here. *I am.* Now get down on your knees."

"I—"

"Get down on your fucking knees or lovely little Torrent here will have a bullet in her brain. Your decision, Dodger, but you might want to make it soon," Carter says. I bite my lip to keep from crying out when I hear the gun at my temple cock in preparation. I close my eyes and when I open them back up they're locked on my father's. Regret is shining in his eyes and that's almost too painful to see. My body trembles as he slowly drops down to his knees, his gaze never leaving mine.

Where is his club?!?!?

DODGER

I drop to my knees. I don't have a choice. I was hoping all along for a miracle and it's clear that's not going to happen now. I wish I knew what was happening with my men. I'd have thought they would have been here by now. Nothing about this is adding up. They didn't even have great security or else Red and Skeeter would have never found where Torrent was in this old building—not as easy as they did.

So what's holding them up now?

"I thought you'd see things my way, Dodger," Carter boasts.

"I'm sorry, Tor, baby," I murmur, giving up the last hopes I had.

"Daddy..." she whispers brokenly.

My beautiful daughter is so much like me. She always has been. She's headstrong and independent, impatient as hell sometimes but underneath it all she has a loyalty inside of her that shines bright. It's a loyalty that blinded me. I should have seen Crash for what he was sooner—should have investigated that harder... but I was too impatient to get to Torrent.

Too damn impatient...

"Chain her," Carter orders and hate and misery burn in my

gut. I still have a pistol hid down in my boot. I'm going to die, but I'm going to drag Carter into hell with me.

"Baby girl, do you remember when you were fourteen and Wolf and I took you to Hadden Park?" I ask her, hoping she gets it and quickly, before they lock her in the chains. She looks confused, but I see when the fog lifts and determination moves over her expression.

"Stop with the trip down memory lane," Carter says. The fucker is clueless and begging for his death—even if he doesn't know it yet.

"You've got me where you want me, Carter. At least let me say goodbye to my little girl. Please," I respond, the word making me nearly choke. I have to act as if I'm begging for crumbs from the son of a bitch, but it's not fucking easy.

He looks surprised, but his smile of victory is proof I'm only feeding his ego. I crumble down on the floor as if I'm completely defeated—as if I have no hope and that only makes the asshole smile that much more.

"Fine. Say your goodbyes, but don't worry, Dodger. I'll be sure to show your daughter a good time after your death. I'll make her scream in delight," he says and my hand shakes with the need to kill him now.

"Do you remember, Torrent? What fun we had that day?"

"I remember…" she murmurs.

"I was so proud of you. Wolf still talks about it," I tell her, trying to make sure she remembers what I need from her, without giving it away.

When Torrent was fourteen, there was a boy harassing her at school and making her life misery. Wolf and I decided to teach her how to take up for herself. We trained her that day in some ways to get the upper hand. She took to it like a natural. Hell, she even managed to bring Wolf down to his knees once. There's fifteen years between them because Wolf is five years younger than me, but sometimes I think that was when he began to see Torrent as something special.

And she is.

Torrent has always been special. There's a fire in her eyes that shines so damn bright you can't look away.

"He underestimated me," she says, and even now some of her cockiness fails to come through.

"Doesn't pay to do that to us, does it, Torrent? You were always your daddy's little girl."

"And proud of it," she murmurs and I can see her getting her body into position.

I move my hand slowly to my boot. I don't look at it while I do it, but I can watch as Torrent's gaze drifts down--watching. I slide my hand in and immediately grab the handle of my pistol.

"Okay, that's enough. Besides, your conversation reminds me of something I should tell you. You're really going to enjoy this one, Dodger. It's time—" Carter starts talking, and I worry I'm not going to have enough time to pull out the pistol, let alone aim it. Knowing what I'm thinking and proving that Torrent and I have always been connected, she lets out a loud moan, distracting everyone.

"Ohh! I think I'm going to be sick," she sobs interrupting Carter, which is good. The bastard is trying to torture me and I'm tired of listening to his damn voice.

Torrent sidetracks the room for a few seconds, but in those seconds everyone's eyes are on her and not me. I pull out the gun, bring it up and aim it at that son of a bitch, Carter.

"Now, Torrent!" I scream, unable to watch her as I level my gun at Carter and aim to shoot the bastard right between the eyes.

TORRENT

On Dad's command I bring my elbow backwards as hard as I can into the stomach of the man holding me. I wince at the pain. I'm weak, and I'm definitely not the woman who managed to get the best of Wolf all those years ago. I do have the element of surprise on my side and that is enough to make the man behind me stumble. A shot rings out and I glance up long enough to see my father shooting his gun. I grab the shackle that is near me on the floor. I didn't stay in them long earlier, but I hated them. They're heavy and that's all I need right now. I swing it upwards and back and slam it into the face of the man who mere moments ago held a gun at my temple. It connects and the man stumbles again. The corner of his eye is bleeding because the jagged end of the lock caught him there. The room begins to spin and I try to fight back the dizziness. My dad needs me right now. I have to help him. I can hear the sound of wood crashing and glass breaking, but I'm so disoriented I can't be sure where it's coming from. I look up to see the guy I hit aiming a gun at me. He's going to shoot me and there's nothing I can do. Before I can even process that, a body from behind me tackles me to the ground. I go down hard on the floor as the sound of the gun going off echoes so loud my ears hurt. The body on me jerks and I push against it enough to see that it's my dad. Another shot rings out and this time it's clear to me that my dad's body jerks and I know he's been shot. He's shielding me with his body, protecting me and killing himself.

I scream out, pushing hard, not wanting this. I don't want my father to die because of me. I wrap my arms around him, trying to move his body. My fingers instantly hit hot liquid and when I draw them back to look at them my hands are covered in blood.

"Daddy! No!" I scream and now I can see his face. His eyes are filled with pain. He looks at me, his face white.

"Love you, Torrent. You've always been my angel..."

His voice is broken and a trickle of blood drops from the corner of his mouth and lands on me.

"Daddy," I cry.

I know he's slipping away and the misery that's clawing inside of me makes it hard to breathe. All at once his body is lifted from me, an arm going around his neck. The man who had been holding me—Jin—has my father and he takes a knife to his throat. It happens quickly, but as I watch it feels like slow motion. The knife slices into my father's neck, and I watch every horrific second with a sense of disbelief...

This can't be happening.

All at once another gunshot rings out. The man who cut my father's throat lurches forward. He falls down, but I lose sight of him because my father falls down on me, his blood pouring over me.

"Why did you—" I hear a voice, but I lose track of it when my father is lifted off me. I look up to see one of my dad's men—Red. He lays my father gently on the floor. I scramble up, crawling to get to him. My dad's men have arrived, but in my heart I know it's too late. Another gunshot goes off and I look up to see Wolf standing and he's shooting the man who used his knife on my father. I clap my hands against my father's throat, but the blood keeps oozing against my hands, between my fingers and down Dad's body. There's so much blood there's no way he can survive. I have to stop it.

"Give me your shirt!" I scream to Red, to Wolf, to anyone who might listen.

"Torrent, baby—" I look over to see Wolf kneeling down beside me and Dad now and the pity on his face destroys me.

"Give me your shirt!" I scream again and he shakes his head.

"He's gone, Tor. He's gone, baby," he says and I know he's right, but I don't want to hear it. Instead I claw at my own shirt, tearing it from my body and taking the shredded pieces and pressing them against my father's throat.

I look at my father's eyes and they're wide open... open and lifeless...

"It's too late, Tor," Wolf says again and he pulls my body back into him. When I try to pull away, he wraps his arms tight around me, refusing to let me go. "It's too late, baby," he repeats. I try to resist him; I *need* to get to my dad. "For God's sake! Someone cover Dodger the fuck up!" he growls and I watch as they get some kind of coat or jacket and cover my dad's face.

"No!" I cry out, so much pain inside of me, I feel like I will never be able to survive.

"He's gone baby, he's gone," Wolf says in my ear.

"Nooo..." I whimper, the word torn from my very soul. I gasp, trying to catch my breath, but it feels like my chest is raw. I look down at my hands... hands covered in my father's blood...

And then the world goes black.

DEVIL

"*Hey*, Devil, you got a minute?" Diesel asks as I walk through the doors of the garage. I've been back home now for well over a month and I'm slowly starting to feel like my old self again. Whatever spell Torrent had on me during our brief time together is finally lifting.

"What's up, man?" I ask, walking over to him.

"It's about the shootout at the old marina around three weeks ago. You remember it?"

"Fury updated me on it. We going to deliver a message to the club that was in our territory?" I ask.

When news first filtered in through our contacts in the local police department about what happened, I know Diesel had Crusher checking it out. Nothing more had really been said about it, so I figured he'd decided to let it go. It's not like him, but his head has been elsewhere lately.

"I met with the leader last week while you and Crusher were in Kentucky at Dragon's. The way I figure it, they've lost enough and they're already back in Nashville. Wolf seems like a good enough guy. Can't hurt to keep friendly with them for now."

"Then what's up?"

"As a show of good faith, I'm going to go down for the ceremony of the man they lost."

"It was one of their men that died? Our contact said four died," I remind him.

"Yeah. Three were from a low level gang. They don't have real ties here. According to Wolf, their former president's daughter was in the area and this gang tracked her down and kidnapped her. The club came up quickly to retaliate and that's why they didn't bother with protocol."

"Fuck. I'm never having kids."

"I wouldn't give anything for Ryan, Ese, but kids make you damn vulnerable. You have too much to lose when it comes to them. It's one of the reasons I'm thinking of turning the reins over to Crusher."

"You love the club, man."

"I do. You guys are my family, but I need to do what I can to protect Ryan and being the leader of this club puts a mark on me."

I rub the back of my neck as I think over Diesel's words. I'd like to argue with him, but honestly, I'm not sure I can. I've never had kids; I've never had anyone that made me that vulnerable. If I did? I can't say I wouldn't be considering the same exact thing. I'm not about to speak out of my ass and offer him advice either. I haven't lived Diesel's life and I sure as hell haven't walked in his shoes. His decisions need to be his own.

"So we're headed to Nashville?" I ask instead.

"Well, more to the point, Murfreesboro."

"You okay to leave Ryan?"

"Yeah, Dani will keep him. He's comfortable with them and he and Dakota get along really well. Besides, if I don't take a break from being a dad for a bit, I'm going to go insane. We'll just be gone one night—two tops."

"When are you wanting to leave?"

"They're going to have a send-off for him tomorrow. It won't be a long trip, so we can leave early in the morning. That work for you?"

"Yeah man. I'll be ready to go. Maybe you'll do yourself a favor and get laid while we're away. I'm starting to think the Pope has more sex than you do."

"He probably does," Diesel mutters. "Shit, I doubt I even know how to pick up a woman anymore."

"Aww fuck, that's easy. It's like riding a bike."

"You mean once you do it, you don't forget?"

"Nah. I mean you tell a woman some bullshit about how they're special, then hop on them and ride them like a bike."

"Jesus, you're such an asshole."

"That's me. But I ain't lying. Maybe while I'm there, if the old man's daughter isn't a total barker I'll let her pour her heart out to me about everything she's been through and let her comfort herself by sucking my dick," I say with a wink.

Diesel shakes his head and starts to walk away.

"Try keeping it in your pants. I got the feeling the new President is sweet on the girl. Last thing I need is for your dick to cause a club war."

"Shit man, my dick is easy going. If I can't play with her, I'll find another chick. He's not particular and he only gets mean if he doesn't get petted."

"You're a fucking loon, Devil," Diesel yells over his shoulder as he exits the garage. I smile because at least I made the bastard laugh and that's better than the misery I see on his face most of the time.

TORRENT

"*How* are you doing, Tor?"

I tense when I hear Wolf. I fight to hide my irritation from him. It's not fair. It's just that he seems to check on me every hour on the hour. I get it. He's worried about me. It's not even that he's wrong to feel like that, because I do feel like I'm falling apart. I don't like being reminded that I'm as fragile as glass.

Cracked glass...waiting to shatter.

"I'm fine," I lie. The words feel so heavy it's hard to force them out.

I avoid Wolf's eyes and instead keep staring out my bedroom window, giving him my back. He comes up behind me and it takes everything in me not to jerk away when his hands drop down on my shoulders. I can see his face reflecting in the glass.

Wolf's a good-looking man. He's fifteen years older than me, but a blind woman would know his appeal. He's got warm brown hair the color of chocolate that's cut short and choppy and kind of lays around his head and looks easy and permanently windblown. He's got a scruffy beard that shows more gray in spots, which to be honest, gives him even more sex appeal. Plus, the beard is shorn close enough that it doesn't take away from any of his features. His face shows age, but even that can be seen as sexy. From the laugh lines around his eyes to the creases around his nose and dimples, he's got everything in him to make a woman weak in the knees. His lips are full and round and seem to stay in a permanent smirk…

Except for now.

Since my father died, Wolf is somber, concerned and protective—which is nice, but somehow adds to my misery.

"Torrent…" he whispers and I close my eyes as a wave of misery assails me.

"I'm okay, Wolf."

"Baby, you're not sleeping…"

"Sleep is overrated. Do I need to do anything for tonight?"

"Of course not. It's club business. It's been handled."

"I am the club now. I'm all that's left of…" I stop to take a breath and let it shudder through my body while I get control of my emotions. "I'm all that's left of my dad."

"He would be proud of you."

His words are hollow—then again, everything is now.

"I'll be ready," I assure him, dreading what's to come—*hating it.*

"You don't have to do this, Torrent. No one would think less of you."

"Except me," I respond with a tired shrug. "I will be at the part…party tonight," I tell him, choking on the word.

I know it's the club's way, but having a party to celebrate my dad seems wrong. There's nothing to celebrate about what happened to him—especially since Crash is the reason he's dead. I want to scream that from the top of the roof. I want to scream it at Wolf, but I don't. I just need to get through this. I need to be what Dad would expect—to make him proud. That's all I can do for him now and I owe him so much more.

"If you're sure?"

"I'm sure."

"Okay, baby," he says kissing my temple and squeezing my shoulders. I close my eyes at his tenderness. I don't deserve it.

I'm the reason my father is dead.

I wrap my arms around my waist wishing I could sleep through everything.

"We're going to do the ride to the cemetery today. We'll leave around five. You'll be on the back of my bike, Torrent."

"Wolf... I'm not... I mean I'm not..."

"And you don't have to be, baby. Not now."

He gives me one last squeeze and then leaves. I listen to his footsteps and once they fade away I sink to the floor. The view outside slowly blurs as the tears begin to fall.

DEVIL

"*How* ow is it fucking possible there's not one woman at this damn thing?" I mutter to Diesel.

We're all standing around a plot at the cemetery, waiting for the other bikers to file in. Diesel and I were at the back of the pack and we're already here. The dude's own men were in the front but they rode farther up the cemetery and are now piling in.

"Maybe they are back at the club waiting for the party?" Diesel answers, sounding like he could care less. Truth is he probably does. He hasn't looked at a woman since the last chick he trusted fucked him over. Violet was a sweet enough chick, until it turned out that she was Diesel's crazy ex's sister. Too bad the fucker doesn't like dick, because his taste in pussy sucks ass.

"If not, I'm ditching this damn thing early."

"You can't need laid that bad, asshole."

"Sometimes a sweet piece can cure an ailing soul," I tell him, grinning.

"I don't think it's your soul ailing. You might want to get your dick checked out if you're feeling bad. It has a bigger chance of coming into contact with... *germs.*"

I flip him off and he laughs. It sounds rusty on him; Diesel definitely doesn't spend his time laughing.

"Well hello there..." I say, ending in a long whistle as a customized Road King purrs by us. It's a beautiful electric blue girl, a real classic with ape hangers that add to the beauty. Her pipes rack so beautifully my dick throbs, but that's not what has my eye. No, what has it is the beauty on the back of the bike. She's got a helmet on with a face guard so I can't tell much about that. What I can see is the worn black leather riding outfit she's wearing that's clinging to her body so fucking perfectly I want to groan. She's leaning back and you can tell she's a natural on a bike.

She's wearing a leather cut and it hugs those luscious tits so much I want to cry mama and latch onto them. As they pass there's a patch on the back of her cut I read plainly and I hate it.

Property of Wolf.

"That's the guy I had the meeting with. Wolf... he's one lucky motherfucker," Diesel murmurs.

"Can't argue with that," I answer, mostly to myself. I have no idea if Diesel hears me. I'm too busy hating the bastard on the bike.

I start walking, falling in step behind Diesel as we head toward the cemetery plot. I try to keep my gaze on his back, but instead I watch the bike park up and the girl slide off. Her ass is as fucking amazing as the rest of her. Wolf gets off and his arm goes gently around the girl's back. Jealousy fires through me, which is a fucking alien emotion and I'm not sure I like it at all. The girl takes her helmet off and I curse the fact that she has her back to me. I want to see her face. She may never be mine, but I'd really like to know if it measures up to her body.

Wolf pulls the girl in closer, kissing her forehead gently and he leans down to whisper something in her ear. His movements show he values her, which is bad news for me, but proves the bastard knows what he's got. Long brown hair tumbles down the girls back once she's free of the helmet. It's beautiful. There's hints of dark blond and even copper shining through as the sun reflects on it. I've only see hair that beautiful one other time...

Torrent.

Fuck, now I am dreaming. That's just proof I need to get laid. I thought I was getting better about leaving Torrent in my past. The very last place I'd ever see Torrent again is on the back of some man's bike, encased in leather and attending a wake for a fallen member. I don't know what it is about that girl that got her hooks into me so deeply—but it's clear she still has a hold on me.

"Diesel. Good to see you here. I appreciate you coming out, man," Wolf says clasping Diesel's hand in welcome.

"We wanted to pay our respects. This is my Sergeant of Arms, Devil."

"Devil, good of you to come," Wolf says. I shake his hand, but my eyes go to the woman. Her back is still to me, but I heard a gasp when my name was mentioned. I'm even more fucked up than I thought, *or...*

"Do I know you?" I ask the woman's back, ignoring Wolf, which is probably not the wisest move on my part. I can feel his tension as if it was a physical force.

"Devil," Diesel says, and I know he's warning me. Shit. I shouldn't have addressed the woman—*I know that*—I just can't help myself.

"Come here, baby," Wolf says, taking the girl in his arms again and turning her around to face us. The placement of his arm and the look on his face give a signal of ownership. They're meant to warn me away. But I don't pay attention to that. *Fuck*, I barely glance at him. I'm too busy locking eyes with the woman who has haunted me. The woman with beautiful brown hair whose highlights sparkle in the sun. The woman whose whiskey eyes have haunted my dreams.

"Torrent," I manage to say, confusion laced in every syllable of the word.

"Torrent?" Diesel repeats. *"Your Torrent?"*

Wolf's growl is quiet, but definitely heard. He doesn't like Diesel's reference. I don't bother saying anything. I couldn't if I tried. I'm too busy trying to recover.

"Hi, Logan," Torrent says and until I hear her sweet voice saying my name I honestly thought I was suffering some kind of psychotic break where my mind made all this shit up.

But I'm not.

This is her.

This is Torrent.

My Torrent.

And she's wearing another man's colors and another man's cut.

"Ain't this a kick in the balls," I mutter, stepping back and feeling like I can't catch my breath.

Fuck.

TORRENT

ord? Don't you think I've received enough sucker punches?

I mutter that prayer in my head. I suppose instead of a prayer it's more of a what-the-fuck moment. There's a part of me that wonders if there is a God above, if he's punishing me for pretending to be a nun. Or maybe he hates me in general—that's completely possible.

As if today wasn't going to be hard enough, I had to run into the one man I've wanted to see for way too long and the one man that I never want to see again.

"Hi, Logan," I respond, wishing I could disappear. His blue eyes —the same ones that I used to dream about—feel like they are boring into me. Most of the bruises from my injuries have faded in the three weeks since my father's death. What you can still see I've managed to cover with makeup. The worst of the bruises are under my nose and the side of my mouth. There was a cut that got infected and even now it's still a bit puffy. It's hardly noticeable, but because I know it's there I act like I'm scratching the side of my nose and then turn a little to the side so Devil doesn't get a direct view. Wolf thinks I'm turning into him for comfort and as horrible as it is to let him continue to think it—I do. It works to my advantage right now.

"You know these men, Tor?"

"I met Devil during my time in... hiding at the convent," I answer Wolf, but I look at Devil from under my lashes. I see exactly when he understands, because his body visibly jerks.

"Convent? Is this *the* nun, man?" the man with Devil asks. I look at his cut and read his name. Diesel. I remember Devil talking about him during our lunches. My heart quickens at the thought he might have mentioned me to his president.

Devil looks at me. His blue eyes bore into me and I feel them as if they were a literal touch.

"I don't know who she is," his deep voice rumbles, his face completely closed off.

It feels like a slap in the face, but then it's also totally fair. He didn't know who I was—not really. In some ways he probably knew me better than anyone else in my life, but I doubt he would agree to that—*especially now.*

My body trembles a little and I know Wolf feels it by the way his arm tightens on me. I get mad at myself. I shouldn't give myself away so easily. The girl I was before...my father's death seems to be hiding. I can't find her.

I don't know if I'll ever find her again.

"It was nice of you to come to show your respects to my father," I respond, but I direct my words to Diesel.

Devil makes a sound, close to a snort, his face not showing humor at all. I let it go. Diesel doesn't respond. He just looks at me funny.

"We'll talk back at the clubhouse. I'm going to take Torrent to the graveside," Wolf says, giving my hand a squeeze.

Diesel responds to him, but for the life of me I couldn't tell you one word of what he said. Then Wolf puts his arm at my back and turns me away from the other men.

I try not to feel shame because Devil will see me wearing the cut that Wolf had made for me. I can't help but be self-conscious though. I didn't specifically want to wear it. In the past three weeks since all of this happened, Wolf has been so attentive. He's been worried about me and done his best to take care of me. I love him for that, but I definitely don't love him. I've told him that. He keeps insisting that for my safety he needs to claim me, so that other clubs, and his own club—my dad's own club—will see me as claimed and protected. I'm not blind to this world, so I can see his point on some levels, but I've told Wolf continuously that I'm not ready for a relationship.

Hell, I don't know if I'll ever be ready. I think there's something broken inside of me now. It's so hugely broken that I'm not sure I'll ever be whole again.

"Are you okay, Tor?" Wolf asks when we are a small distance away from Devil.

"I'm not sure I'm going to be okay this entire day, Wolf—or maybe ever again."

"You'll get through this, sweetheart. Dodger would be proud of how strong you are."

"I don't really feel strong."

"How well do you know Devil?" he asks and I knew that question was coming. Dad knew I had seen Devil, but he took great pains in not telling Wolf. He always tried to protect me... and maybe Wolf. He truly believed I'd be happy with Wolf, that Wolf would make me happy. Maybe he was right. I don't know. Having Wolf to lean on the last three weeks has helped me to at least function. I don't want to lie to Wolf now... but I can't make myself tell him the truth either.

"Not that well. Our paths crossed from time to time. Mostly in the park across from the convent or in the town when we would be volunteering. That's why he thought I was a nun."

"Oh. Yeah. That makes sense," Wolf says and he seems to let it drop. I breathe a sigh of relief.

I let thoughts of Devil, our past, and how we met again, slide from my mind as my father's grave comes into view. This is going to be hard enough without adding Devil into my thoughts. Besides… how I feel about him doesn't matter anymore. That's all behind me.

Nothing is the same anymore.

Nothing.

DEVIL

"*Y*ou okay, man?" Diesel asks. I've lost track of exactly how many times he's asked that shit. I down another drink of my beer in response. I could use something besides beer, but getting shit-faced here probably wouldn't be the wisest move. Partly because I don't entirely trust this club and I sure as hell won't be able to watch Diesel's back—*or my own*—and partly because if I get too drunk, I'll probably go over to Torrent, drag her out of here and demand to know why she lied to me... or fuck her senseless... *maybe both.*

Neither one of those are an option. So instead, I'm sitting on the top of an old picnic table, my feet on the seat, drinking a beer that's way too warm to drink, and staring over at the bonfire while Torrent talks with that fucker, Wolf and a few other men. There's other women here, and I've had a few come on to me, but seeing Torrent again has caused my dick to go into hiding. It's either seeing her again, or seeing her wear another man's cut.

It's hard for me to wrap my mind around the fact that I grieved over what I could never have with this woman... that I had to let her go because she would never belong in my world... and all the time...

"Earth to Devil," Diesel says and I let out a loud sigh as I slam my beer down on the table. Diesel's standing in front of me. The fucker is probably trying to block my view of Torrent, but it's not working. I see her—even though I wish like fuck I didn't.

"I'm fine. My damn beer is warm. How much longer we have to stay here?"

"You ready to leave?"

"Been fucking ready for hours," I answer.

I've been ready since Torrent walked away from me at the cemetery.

"Don't you want to try and talk to—"

"There's no point. Nothing to be said really." I shrug, cutting him off before he can say her name. I'm pretty fucking sure I'd be fine with never hearing her name mentioned again.

"You should talk to her. Find out what's going on, what happened," Diesel says, looking over his shoulder in Torrent's direction.

"Don't think your boy Wolf would agree with that assessment," I smirk, wishing I could punch the fucker in the face. Then again, every damn time I see him hug Torrent, or whisper to her, I get that urge. He'd look much better with my fist imprinted on his damn face—with his nose bleeding.

"Fuck him."

"That's a different tune than you were singing," I mention to Diesel—not really giving a fuck.

"Something about this whole club is rubbing me the wrong way. I'm not sure what, but it has my gut burning."

I frown. When Diesel says that, he's usually spot on about any situation. He's saved our hide more than a few times with his sixth sense about things. I can't say that I'm very fucking comfortable here either, but I thought my feelings about Torrent were clouding my judgment. Now, Diesel has me wondering.

"You think she's in danger?" I ask before I can stop myself.

"Danger? Nah, probably not. Trouble? I think that little girl might be in a whole heap of trouble though."

"Wolf seems very protective over her," I tell Diesel, my eyes going to the couple in question. I watch as he puts his hand on Torrent's shoulder, his fingers tangling into her hair on her shoulder. I tighten my hand into a fist so fucking hard my arm goes numb, all in a hope to keep myself from going over there and choking the life out of the bastard.

I've never been jealous... right now I'm not sure what I'm feeling is jealousy. There's a rage inside of me—the likes of which I've never felt before.

"He seems like he's choking her to death to me." Diesel shrugs.

"What?" I ask, my attention going to him immediately.

"He's not letting her out of his sight. She gets more than a couple steps away and he pulls her back to him—literally. That's not normal, man."

"Maybe. Or maybe we've never been—"

"He's controlling her. She couldn't even reach for her own drink. He took over when she tried to reach out to the cooler."

"Maybe he's just being thoughtful. The Torrent I know wouldn't let anyone control her."

"The Torrent you know wasn't kidnapped and beaten."

His words are like a fucking knife... *a punch of reality.*

Until this moment, I had been so fucked up over seeing Torrent again—over seeing her wearing another man's cut and finding out who she truly is to piece it all together.

Torrent was the daughter that was kidnapped. Torrent was in the clutches of a gang for weeks and lost her father.

"Beaten?" I ask Diesel, realizing that up until now I hadn't asked for details about what had happened, mostly because I didn't care.

"From what Wolf said she was fucked up bad. Besides, didn't you notice the darkened area around her mouth? Bruises and puffiness that even makeup couldn't completely hide after almost a month? Dude, that doesn't scream good news to me," Diesel says and my chest goes tight as I think over his words. Fuck, I never noticed the bruises. How is that possible? How could Diesel see it and I didn't?

"There's no way I can get her away from Wolf long enough to talk to her anyway." I shrug, even while trying to figure out a way.

"There's always a way. Wolf's drinking pretty heavily. There will be an opening soon… I mean, if you want it," Diesel says, but he's looking at me and his face dares me to call him a liar. He knows me like the back of his hand.

"You going to help me keep the fucker distracted."

"Oh yeah."

"This might not end well," I feel obliged to warn him.

"I figure it might not, but if that little girl over there is hurting as much as I think she is, ask me if I care."

"What's it to you?"

"How long we known each other, Devil?"

"Too fucking long," I joke, my gaze drifting back to Torrent against my will.

"In all that time—you have never—and I mean *never* mentioned a girl to me. You've *never* even thought of claiming and settling down with one, and you have *never—not once*—been lost in your head for months over a chick. I figure I owe it to you to find out what's going on. If she's a bitch, then find out and move the fuck on."

"And if she's not?"

"Then you decide if she's worth bringing the hammer down."

"And if she is?"

"Then we prepare for hell, because God knows getting her away from that man won't be easy."

"I think it could be pretty easy. I could kill the motherfucker," I mutter, liking the idea more and more.

"That girl is haunted, Devil. When you talk to her, look in her eyes, watch how she moves—put the anger aside and watch and listen. Whatever you do, buddy, you got to go gently where she's involved—or she might not survive."

I listen to Diesel's words and they burn through me. Part of me was hoping Diesel was right and Torrent is being controlled by Wolf, that maybe there is a chance...

But I don't want a chance with her, if I'm only getting it because she's so fucking fragile she's going to shatter on me... That's fucked up. Torrent... at least the Torrent I knew...deserves only happiness.

Fuck.

TORRENT

*T*here should be a limit to how much a person can handle. Today has definitely been mine. I watch as Wolf empties another glass. He's getting trashed. I understand it. He loved my dad. But, I have zero desire to stay around a drunk man. Actually, I don't want to be around a man in general right now.

"I'm tired, Wolf. I'm going to go lay down."

"We haven't had the bonfire yet, Tor," he responds, his words slurring just enough to tell me he really is drunk as hell. Wolf can handle his liquor—he can drink most men under the table, even my father. For him to slur means that he is drunker than I've ever seen him. Since I've known him my entire life, that's saying something.

"I don't really want to see the bonfire. That's for the club. I don't want to be here for that," I tell him and it's the God's honest truth. I have no wish to see them burn my dad's cut and say goodbye to him. I wanted to keep the cut and wrap it around me and smell him on it.

"I'll take you back to your room," he says and I bite down the urge to scream at him. I don't want him to take me to my room. I want to be strong enough to take myself back to the room. The truth is, however, that on the few occasions that I've walked alone, I keep seeing shadows and hearing laughter. I feel like someone is following me...waiting to jump out and hurt me at any second. I disgust myself with how weak I've become, but I've not been able to shake it. Of course Wolf doesn't give me much of a chance to try either and that's both a blessing and a curse. He's starting to smother me and I have a feeling that if I don't try to be independent now, I will never be again.

"I'll be fine. You need to be here to start the bonfire," I tell him, hoping I'm right and I will be fine. "Besides, no one will bother me with me wearing your cut," I remind him—since that's the very reason he said I should wear it.

"I still want to take you back to the room, Tor. I don't know some of these men from the other clubs, at least not well enough to trust them. It will take—"

"Hey Wolf, I was wondering if I could ask your advice on something? I've been admiring the way your courtyard is set up. The security is top-notch," that man from earlier—Diesel—says, suddenly appearing behind me.

I look around for Devil, but I don't see him anywhere. Maybe he left... That's for the best. For a second, Wolf's hand tightens on me and then relaxes.

"It will have to wait. I'm going to take Torrent to—"

"Red can take me," I compromise, wanting to get away. I don't want to see Devil and part of me is scared with his buddy so close that he will show up. I've had enough today... more than enough.

"Sweetheart..."

"I'm fine. Besides, Red is probably more sober than you at this point." I force myself to smile up at him, to soften the words to make it seem like I'm joking. Inside, I'm annoyed he's drunk, which is unfair, but I needed my friend today and when he's drunk, being around him just doesn't feel the same.

I'm too afraid now to risk being around someone who doesn't have control...

Wolf leans down and kisses my forehead and motions to Red. I avoid Diesel's eyes and I walk away.

I really want tonight over with.

Red and I walk back to my room in silence. That's nothing new; Red and I never talked much with each other. I try to concentrate on walking and ignoring the moving shadows or that feeling like someone is going to jump out of the darkness and hurt me. That alone is exhausting. There's a part of me wondering if I will ever feel normal again.

Somehow I doubt it.

We make it to my door and I open it with a heartfelt sigh.

"Thanks, Red."

"Lock the door behind me, Tor. It's our club, so you should be safe, but there's too many unknowns here tonight to be entirely sure."

"Got it," I tell him, but I want to laugh. If he only knew how quickly I lock doors and windows these days.

"Good enough. Night, girl," he says. I close the door on him, lock it and lean against it while I let my knees stop shaking.

A second later I feel the knob move and then hear footsteps walking away.

He checked to make sure I locked the door.

That should make me feel better. Instead, I kind of feel like a prisoner...

DEVIL

I watch as the man with Torrent walks away. It feels like my damn heart is pounding so hard in my chest it could jump out. I stare at her door, wondering if I truly want to see her. There are a million scenarios running through my head. The urge to turn around and walk out of this damn place is strong and it's warring with my need to talk to Torrent. I don't know why I'm even here. It's obvious that Torrent wasn't who I thought she was. Diesel's words come back to me.

That girl is haunted.

I reach out my hand to knock on the door with Diesel's voice still in my head.

"Who… who is it?"

"It's me," I answer, wondering if she will open her door. I don't have to wait long for the answer as I hear the lock tumbler move with a clicking noise that seems extremely slow and loud.

"You shouldn't be here, Logan," she says once the door is opened. She doesn't open all the way; instead it's barely enough to peek her head out.

"I was just saying that to myself," I admit, searching her face. My eyes zero in on the spot Diesel mentioned earlier. She definitely has a bruise, it's faint and clearly hid by makeup, or at least the majority of it is, but it's there.

Motherfucker it's there.

"Then why are you here?" she asks.

"Because I care," I tell her honestly.

Her eyes widen in shock and her lips separate at my answer— but only for the briefest of seconds and then she wipes the surprise away and it's like a mask comes over her face.

"You shouldn't."

"That's me. Always doing what I shouldn't," I respond. "Are you going to let me in there to talk, or are we doing this out here?"

I ask the question and then watch as her hand comes out and she pushes her fingers in her hair to tuck a stray strand behind her ear. Her eyes look down on the ground and that's when I see the way her hand is trembling.

"I... I don't think we should talk, Logan."

"Are you scared of me, Angel?"

She looks up at me then. Her eyes truly are haunted and seeing the pain in them is gut wrenching.

"I don't want to be," she says and her voice drops down to the point that I have to strain to hear it.

"I'd never hurt you, Torrent. Never. I give you my word on that."

"We don't really know each other."

"That's not true. You know me, Angel. I've always given you the real me."

I watch as she rubs her lips together and swallows down her nerves.

"But... people aren't always who you think they are, Logan."

"I'm starting to see that," I tell her and instantly regret it. Her face closes up. I didn't mean it as a barb directed at her for lying to me—at least not intentionally.

"It's late. You should go before—"

"Before your boyfriend finds me?" I ask, my anger getting the better of me.

"I don't have a boyfriend."

"That cut you're wearing says differently."

"Is that why you're here? To see what he had that you didn't?" she asks, and for some reason I love what she said. This shows signs—the first signs—of the Torrent I know. The Torrent who... *I still want.*

"Don't flatter yourself, Angel. You left me months ago. I'm not looking to pick back up."

"You're not?" she asks.

"Hell, no," I tell her and I'm pretty sure I'm not completely lying. My attraction to her is *not* the only reason I'm here.

"Then why?"

"Because whatever else we were, Torrent, I think we were friends."

"Friends..."

"Yeah, and I think you really look like you could use one right now."

"Don't pity me, Logan," she responds, her eyes suddenly looking haunted again.

"Why would I pity you?"

She studies my face for a bit. She looks so tired I fight the urge to take her into my arms. If ever there was a woman who needed someone to lean on it would be her.

"So you're here... *out of friendship?*"

"Is that so hard to believe, Torrent?"

"After the way I left things... Yeah, I guess it is."

"I admit, the way you kicked me to the curb wasn't ideal, but it wasn't all bad," I tell her with a grin—even though nothing about this entire situation is worth smiling about.

It takes a minute, but I see when my meaning registers with her. Her face blooms with a bright pink color. She shakes her head and some of the sadness leaves her eyes. Those subtle changes bring me hope that the Torrent I knew is not completely gone.

"I can't believe you went there! It was just a m—"

"A moment I will *never* forget."

"I was going to say a mistake," she mumbles, avoiding my gaze.

Unable to stop myself—even if I should—I put my hand along the side of her neck and pull her gaze up to mine, needing her attention.

"It didn't feel like a mistake to me, Torrent. Hell, I think about touching you… I think about you often."

"You should go, Logan," she answers, fear threaded in her voice.

"You could go with me."

"Why would I do that?"

"Because there are things we need to talk about. Things we didn't get to finish."

"Devil—"

"You call me Logan, Angel. You've always called me Logan."

"Things are different now, Dev—"

I put my fingers on her lips, stopping her from talking.

"Logan," I remind her.

"Things are different now, *Logan*."

"So we're different. Does that mean we can't talk, especially since I'm in town?"

"Is talking all you want?" she asks. Right now wouldn't be a good time to be truthful; besides, I don't honestly know what I want from Torrent anyway.

"Isn't that what friends do, Torrent? Talk?"

"I—"

"I'm staying at the Golden Pecker off of 63. I'll be there for a few more days. Do you know it?"

"You're horrible," she says and she smiles—it's weak, but it's a smile.

"It sounded like the place was made for me," I whisper, stepping in a little closer, and giving an easygoing shrug—like I don't have a care in the world.

"It's called The Golden Woodpecker," she mutters.

"Potato, Po-tat-toe," I mutter, watching her eyes and memorizing the bright flecks in her dark eyes and silently counting them.

"I shouldn't," she says, but she doesn't outright say no, so that encourages me.

For a minute, we're so close that I can smell her sweet vanilla scent and it fires the memories I've been trying to bury. A man could get drunk on that scent. She stares up at me and there's not much space between our lips. I could lean in a little farther and kiss her. The urge is there and I'm having trouble finding the reasons why I shouldn't...

Until...

"What's going on here?" Wolf says, his voice harsh.

And just like that the chance is gone and I see the light go out of Torrent's eyes.

Motherfucker!

"I'm merely saying goodbye to an old friend. No harm in that, is there? The woman is allowed to talk to old friends, isn't she?" I ask, innocently. I see the hate in his eyes; he's not trying to hide it. I can't say as I blame him. If our roles were reversed I'd probably hate me too.

"Torrent, are you okay, sweetheart?" he asks instead of answering me.

"I'm fine, Wolf. Devil was only offering me his condolences."

"That was awful nice of him," Wolf answers, his voice cold.

"That's me. Mr. Nice Guy. Torrent, you know where to find me if you ever want to talk," I tell her, walking backwards so I can keep my eyes on both of them as I walk away.

"I'll be fine. Have a safe trip back home," she answers.

I ignore the disappointment I feel at her words. Give them both a half-salute with my hand and keep walking away.

TORRENT

"*How's* my favorite girl?" Wolf asks the next morning.

I'm sitting at the kitchen table eating cereal. It's early, probably around five by now. I've been wide awake since four and it was becoming apparent I wasn't going to go back to sleep, so I got up. The nightmares aren't new, but sometimes they are more vivid than other nights. Yesterday's ceremony brought too many memories to the forefront.

"Why are you awake?" I ask him, stifling a yawn.

"I've got business in Alabama today. Me and a couple others are going to head out soon. I'd take you with me... *but...*"

"Spare me. I've never wanted in the club business. I don't really want to go to Alabama on the back of a bike either. It's like a hundred degrees outside."

"Are you sure you're a biker's daughter, Tor?" Wolf laughs and I can't stop the sucker punch of pain at his words that nearly robs me of my breath. I know it shows in my face the minute Wolf changes. "Fuck, sweetheart. I'm an idiot," he growls, squatting down in front of me. He turns my body to face him, resting a hand on each of my legs. "I'm a moron," he says, sadness thick in everything about him.

When he's like this I'm reminded of the Wolf that has always been in my life. The one who cares about me, tries to take care of me and protect me. The Wolf who I once brought to school for show and tell and he proceeded to scare all the bullies at school who were making me their favorite target—not to mention scare the principal and teacher into being more aware of the problem.

He was my hero. And now I'm very much reminded of that man… the man I care for. I reach over and use my thumb to brush out a wrinkle under his eye. His eyes are green and when he stares at me like this they warm in color.

"Stop. You shouldn't have to walk on eggshells around me. I'll be okay."

"I know you will, Tor. You're strong, stronger than any of us ever gave you credit for—even your dad."

"I don't feel very strong right now, Wolf. To be honest, I'd like to check out for a bit and sleep the world away."

"Then you do that, sweetheart. You do whatever you need to do and let your heart—" He says as he brings his hand to my chest and places it over the area where my heart is located. "—and your mind rest." He finishes his words by leaning in and kissing my forehead.

Before I can think about it, or even stop myself, I lean into him and wrap my arms around him. The tears—which always stay close to the surface—begin without warning. Wolf goes down on his ass, right there in the middle of the floor—and pulls me into his lap, rocking me.

"I'm sorry," I tell him in a sob, burying my head into his shoulder.

"Don't be sorry, sweetheart. You're having a hard time. I'm going to cancel my trip today," he says.

"You don't have to do that, Wolf."

"I know I don't have to. I want to. I can go tomorrow, it's not so urgent it can't wait a day. Today, you and I are going to get on my bike and spend the day like we used to."

"I'm a little old to go to Pizza Playland, Wolf," I laugh.

"So you say. Get dressed and let me prove you wrong."

"You can't be serious," I tell him, pulling away to look at his face.

He brings his fingers up to wipe my tears away. "Totally serious. Get dressed and I'll show you."

"But, you have things to do, Wolf. I—"

"I think you're underestimating my love of pizza while watching dancing mechanical bears."

I can't help but smile, even through my tears.

"Go get dressed, Tor. Time is wasting and I can't have my best girl standing me up and making me wait all day."

"You're sure about this?" I ask, suddenly looking forward to the day.

"Never been more sure," he says simply, but leaving no room for doubt.

"Thank you, Wolf," I tell him, leaning up to kiss his cheek.

I hold him close and breathe in his warm scent, which brings in memories of my childhood—tender, loving memories of my youth, memories that make me feel...

Safe.

DEVIL

"**Y**ou ready to head out?" Diesel asks, opening my door wider. I'm sitting on the bed, my bags packed. I really thought I was ready, but I'm not. I look up at him and I know he sees it before I say anything. "You're not leaving," he says, walking deeper into the room and closing the door behind him.

"I don't think I can yet."

"I thought you talked to her last night?"

"I did, but—"

"It's two in the afternoon, Devil. Man, if she was going to show up, she would have by now," Diesel says and I can't disagree with him, not really. But... something is nagging at me.

"Something doesn't feel right. I can't leave yet," I tell him finally.

"Your gut talking to you?"

"Something is," I respond.

My whole body is tense. I feel like I'm preparing for something and I don't have any fucking idea what it is. It's that feeling I get sometimes that there's a damn shoe over my head and that usually means it's going to drop sometime soon. I thought I had pretty much gotten over whatever fascination I had with Torrent, but my time with her last night proved me a fucking liar. I felt more alive standing next to her than I've felt in forever. I can't explain the pull between me and Torrent, but it's there and from what I saw, even with everything she's been through, she still feels it too.

I don't know if that's enough.

"So what's the plan? You going to sit around here all day and try and look pretty?"

"I'm not the one of us that spends a fortune on their hair to make it soft so all the girls want to touch it and fall to their knees to worship you."

"Fuck you. You can't talk. You tatted your fucking cock with the sign of the devil."

"Not my cock. Just close to the cock. Besides, there was a reason for that."

"What's that?"

"Well I'm called Devil for a reason. Plus, women love to play with the bad boys. I wanted to point them in the right direction."

"You're such a cocky bastard."

"Never claimed to be anything different." I shrug and he flips me off.

"So we're going to stay in this damn place for another day?" Diesel asks, and I frown, thinking about that. I scratch the side of my face through my beard and think his question over.

"No, man. You have Ryan and I know how hard it is for you to be away from him right now. You go on home, I'll be fine."

"Not going to happen, Ese."

"You've seriously been hanging around Skull too damn long," I mutter at his nickname. Diesel's not got anything Spanish about him, but he uses words here and there—most commonly Ese, because he's heard it often, because he likes it... *Who the fuck knows really?*

"Let's go find some lunch and check the town out if we're going to stay for a few days. I like to know the lay of the land."

"Torrent might—"

"Christ, we won't be gone that long. Your dick can't be so wrapped up in her already that you can't go find dinner," Diesel mutters and I frown.

"You need to get back to Ryan. Just because we foiled the last kidnapping attempt—"

"Crusher and Dani will keep him safe, but I'll head back tomorrow. You decide tonight if you're going to stay another night. If you are, I'll give one of the other men a call and have them come down here to watch your back."

"Don't you think that's going more than a little overboard?" I ask him, frowning.

"If the way Wolf was looking at that girl is any indication? Fuck, no I'm not overreacting. You're getting ready to wade into some dangerous territory, Devil."

"Wouldn't be the first time," I respond and not to be a bigger asshole, but I don't care what he says. If there's a chance that I end up with Torrent when all of this is said and done, I'll take that chance every day of the week.

Which is further proof that I really am wrapped up over this woman. The biggest problem with that is, I can't be sure what Torrent will do... *or how she feels*.

TORRENT

"*Y*ou really think you got what it takes to beat me, Tor?" Wolf asks, gripping his hammer tightly.

"Dude, you are so going down!" I boast, holding my hammer the same way.

"You willing to make a bet?"

"What are we talking?" I ask, eyeing him warily.

"A little friendly wager, Tor, unless you're... *chicken?*"

I narrow my eyes at Wolf, and fight the urge to smile.

"Fine. What is it that you want to bet?" I ask, determined to win.

"If I win, we eat at La Pena's tonight."

I cringe, because I hate Mexican food. I can handle taco salads or tacos at home, but to eat out I avoid those places.

"And if I win?"

"You tell me," he says and I think it over.

"If I win, you let me move back into Dad's house, no bitching."

His face goes hard—like I knew it would.

"Damn it, Tor. I can't do that. I need to know you're safe and right now you're safer inside the club."

"You took out Crash and anyone involved."

"The club still has other enemies, sweetheart. You know that."

"I need this, Wolf. It's not like Pop's house isn't right next to the club. I can practically stand on the porch and yell at you if you're in the back courtyard."

"Tor—"

"I don't want to be at the club, Wolf. It's not my life. And you don't need to be my nursemaid all the time. You have a life and it's one I'd rather not… witness."

"What's that mean?"

"Come on, Wolf. Those damn club girls hang all over you."

"There's one way to stop that, Tor. You got my jacket. Everyone knows how I feel about you—including you. Give in."

"Wolf—"

"You love me, Tor," he says and my heart squeezes. I ruined a lighthearted moment bringing this up. I should have left it to later, been wiser about picking my battles. It's too late to stop it now, though.

"I do love you, Wolf. You know that. But I don't love you like… I should."

"That can come in time," he says, and he sounds so confident. He was my father's pick for me. He's protected me and cared about me my entire life. He loved my father as much as I did. Things would be so simple if I could give him what he wants. He's a beautiful man, caring, loving…

He doesn't make me feel like Devil does…

That forbidden thought springs up, even though it shouldn't. I do my best to squash it down. I can't think about Devil. The temptation to go to him this morning was so strong. There's no point though. Devil's life is on the other side of the state and it doesn't include me.

"What if it doesn't, Wolf? That's not fair to either one of us."

"I'm willing to take my chances," he responds.

"I—"

"Change of plans," he says and I frown.

"What does that mean?"

"If I win, you give me two weeks where you seriously think of me as your man, and let me prove to you that we can work. Oh… and we eat at La Pena's."

"But—"

"And as an added bonus you can move back into your dad's house."

"There's no catch?"

"I'm going to have security beefed up and men outside, but no… no other conditions."

"And if *I* win?"

"Then, you move back into your dad's house, but you have to give me one week where you let me prove we could work as a couple *and* we eat at La Pena's."

"So either way, you get what you want?" I grumble.

"Either way we *both* get what we want," he corrects. I study him, still not sure if I'm doing the right thing. But, in a way I want him to prove things to me too. What if he's right and we could be good together? It's what my father wanted and I got him killed. It's one of the last things he ever told me. I need to try. I owe him that.

My hand moves down and I hit start on the machine. The little moles pop out, one on my side and one on Wolf's. He wasn't ready, but I was and I whack mine hard with the sponge hammer and I'm hitting the second before Wolf even realizes what's going on.

"Motherfucker, Torrent, you don't fight fair," he growls, slamming his hammer down so hard the material bends back as it strikes the poor plastic mole a little too hard.

I giggle despite myself.

"Man up or shut up," I laugh.

We spend the next five minutes hitting the poor defenseless moles that pop up. All around us are kids and their parents with tortured looks on their faces and it might be one of the best days I've had.

When it's all finished, I am forced to look up into Wolf's smiling face.

"I win," he says twirling the cord to the hammer on his finger.

"Crap."

"Shall I take *my* woman to La Pena's for dinner now, or do you want me to show you how good I am at Skeeball?"

"I hate La Pena's. What does that even mean, anyway?"

"It's penalties or sorrow or something. I don't know. I never worried about English much, let alone Spanish."

"Well, it sounds like Little Penis—just so you know. And since when did you get so good at all these games? I distinctly remember I used to spank your ass at Whack-A-Mole!"

"You were a little girl and I let you win. These days you're very much a grown girl and when I think of spanking your ass—as you put it—it's in a much *different* context."

My gaze shoots up to his heated one and I feel butterflies in my stomach that are not all that unpleasant. Nervousness flutters through me too.

"Wow…"

"Ready, sweetheart?" he asks, and right now he looks every inch a wolf…

And I'm pretty sure I'm his prey.

"Ready," I squeak—not sure if I am at all.

DEVIL

"**W**hy are we here again?" I ask Diesel as we park up in the lot of a Mexican restaurant.

"You're having food with me before I head out."

"Diesel—"

"Wherein, I'm going to enjoy my fajitas and beer while you promise me not to do anything stupid until Fury gets out here to watch your back."

"What the hell does La Pena's mean anyways?"

"Hell if I know, but apparently it's the only Mexican place around."

"Couldn't we go for pizza? Or fuck, what about a good old steak?" I grumble.

"You always want pizza. What is your hate against Mexican food, Ese? It's good shit."

"It tastes like shit, I'll give you that," I say with a sigh as we walk inside and I take off my shades, tucking them into the pocket of my vest. Diesel does the same with his as we wait to be seated. They take us back to a table, but both of us shake our heads no.

"We'll take that booth over there," Diesel says, finding one against the wall. The waiter looks at him strange but takes us over there with a shrug. Years of our lifestyle and being nomads until we found our own spot in this life has taught us both to keep our backs to the wall and our eyes on the crowd and the doors. "Two drafts," Diesel orders as the waiter puts down salsa and fresh baked tortilla chips.

"You going to order for me too, *Baby-cakes?*" I ask sarcastically.

"If you don't quit whining like a baby, I'll order you a hamburger off the kid's menu. Does that count?"

"At least it's American food."

"They have steak you know," Diesel laughs.

"Do you see a baked potato on the menu? Or a loaded salad that has tomatoes and onions? Shit, eggs and bacon are nice too—with those crispy croutons."

"Jesus, you really are a baby," Diesel says disgustedly.

"Only about food," I tell him, trying to defend myself. Once the waiter comes back we order our food and I go with a steak fajita and figure I'll pick and choose what I eat. "Can I skip all that rice and bean shit? Just bring me French-fries," I tell the waiter, making Diesel laugh.

"French fries?"

"At least it's a potato," I tell him and flip him off when he laughs harder.

My gaze moves around the room, automatically taking stock and monitoring it—even if I don't need to. I even peg the two exit possibilities and the door that leads to the kitchen. Hell, maybe I have been in this life too long.

"So I called this morning and Fury will be here by evening," the bastard says once he quits laughing at me.

"I don't need a goddamn nurse maid, Diesel. I'm a grown man. Been taking care of myself for a while now. Hell, I can even wipe my own ass after I shit."

"Quit being a prick. You know what's going to happen if Wolf sees you sniffing around his woman."

I go over Diesel's words in my head. I take a drink of my beer and still replay them again. Finally, I look up at him and lay it out.

"I'm not convinced that she's his."

"She's the daughter of a man who ran the club."

"So?" I challenge him.

"Fucker, she's not new to this life. She knows what wearing a cut that says you're someone's property means. She might be lost and in a world of hurt, but he's laid claim to her and you trying to get in her pants puts your dick in jeopardy."

"My dick?"

"I figure that's what he will be cutting off if he finds it anywhere near Torrent."

"Weren't you the asshole that encouraged me to talk to her last night?"

"Yep, that'd be me," he admits.

"So what the fuck is your problem now?" I ask him, more than a little irritated.

"You talked to her, she made her choice and I think you need to move on."

"We don't know that she's made her choice yet," I answer right as the waiter brings our food. Both of us remain quiet as that happens, but as soon as the waiter is out of earshot, Diesel starts again.

"Looks to me like her choice is pretty much made, buddy. Not to be a dick about it, but I think you need to realize that too."

"What do you mean?"

"She didn't meet you today—"

"Well, no. But—"

"And she's looking pretty tight over there in the corner with Wolf."

His words cause me to shut down. My gaze seeks out every fucking corner in the place.

I see her across from me in the far left. There's a darkened booth and a couple facing me. They don't see me though and I can't decide if that's a good thing or a bad thing. Wolf has his arm around Torrent. She's resting her head on his chest. And he's feeding her a piece of chicken from his fork. She's smiling and he's staring at her... with eyes only for her.

Fuck me... Diesel's right.

She looks happy. She looks like she loves him.

She sure as hell doesn't look like she ever thinks of me...not the way I do her and that shit burns hard.

The waiter comes by and leaves two more beers and I'd give anything if it was something stronger... *right now I need it.*

TORRENT

"*I can* feed myself you know," I tell Wolf, trying not to laugh as he brings another piece of grilled chicken to my mouth.

"What? The bet was I show you what it's like to be my woman. That's all I'm doing, baby."

"By feeding me?"

"I'm enjoying it," he laughs.

"I've enjoyed everything today. Thank you for this, Wolf. I hated you changed your plans for me, but I really did need it."

"I wouldn't take nothing for today, Tor. Even though you're insistent on moving into your dad's house."

"I need to—for several reasons. If you really want to give this dating thing a try, it's needed."

"What the hell for?"

"So that we're in separate spaces, of course."

"I don't know how you date, but most people these days have to be together to date."

"To date, sure, but they don't *live* together."

"I don't see anything wrong with that," Wolf argues and the disappointed look on his face makes me smile.

"That's because you're a pig."

"Hey, Tor! That's not nice. I *like* you."

I roll my eyes at him. "We should head out. I want to get started moving."

"I thought we were going to try this relationship thing. How do you plan on doing that if you're going to be moving the whole time?"

"Oh, but you see, this is how you show me what a wonderful boyfriend you are, Wolf."

"I'm not sure I'm following," he grumbles.

"You get to help me move and carry all the heavy stuff while flexing your muscles."

"You're a little crazy, Tor," he laughs. "So, I help you move. What's in it for me?"

"What do you want? And while we're on the subject, why do I feel like I'm always making deals with you?"

"No idea," he says with a smirk. "How about I get to sleep over?" He wiggles his eyebrows and that, combined with the smile on his lips, makes him look years younger.

"Oh no, not happening."

"Tor, there has to be some PDA in a relationship."

"PDA? How does sleeping over qualify as public displays of affection?"

"I was thinking of another P word... *private.*"

"I'm thinking of another P word too," I tell him, sticking my tongue out.

"Dirty girl. I could show you that too if you want," he says calmly.

"What? Oh! Oh my God! You are a pervert—which is a P word too, but I was thinking prick earlier."

"I prefer it be called dick or cock, but penis is doable..."

"Can we stop talking about your *thing*? We're only starting to date so the most we're going to share is PG-13 at best, mister."

"What does one get in a PG-13 relationship?"

"Hand holding, snuggles on the couch or a bed occasionally."

"Gee, all of that?" he says dryly.

"And *maybe* if you're nice some kissing and a little bit of touching."

"Tell me more about this touching," he urges, but I stop talking —because out of the corner of my eyes, I see the one face I wasn't expecting and he's looking right at me. "Tor?" Wolf asks, and I hear him, but I can't tear my gaze away from across the room.

Devil is over there with his buddy and he's looking right at me. His gaze is so intense that it feels like it's branding me.

"Is that the asshole who was bothering you last night?" Wolf asks, his voice hard.

"He wasn't bothering me."

"He was outside your room when he shouldn't have been," he counters.

"I told you, we're old friends. He was paying his respects and checking on me before he headed out of town," I lie. I try my best to keep my voice normal, because it's clear that Wolf is upset. It doesn't take a rocket scientist to read the signs either. He doesn't like Devil around me, but then, Wolf has never liked any man being around me. It's a side to him that always set me on edge and one of the reasons I ran away from a relationship with him.

I like men who take charge, but I don't like men who try to control every damn aspect of my life. Wolf definitely has a tendency to do that. Dad thought that was great. He wanted me to be with his friend and I know I should try because I owe it to my father. Still, this is another side of Wolf and it makes me nervous. I need to try and divert his attention here. The last thing I want is for Devil to get in Wolf's crosshairs. That would be bad, especially with Wolf's temper.

"Doesn't look like he's left town from where I'm sitting and I don't like the way he's staring at you, either," Wolf growls.

"Let's ignore it and get back to our date," I tell Wolf, trying to defuse the situation. I shouldn't have even bothered, because

Wolf's body tightens beside me. His arm around me stiffens too, his fingers biting into my shoulder to the point it's on the verge of painful. I don't even have to look to know that Devil is walking over here.

Crap.

DEVIL

"*Hey.*"

I sound lame as fuck. I should have remained in my seat and then got the fuck out of town. Proving I'm a stupid asshole who is hung up over the wrong woman, instead I walk over here. Jesus. If Beast could see me now, after all of the grief I've given him, he'd be having a field day.

"Devil..." Torrent says, shock and something else in her voice and on her face that I can't name.

"I thought you were leaving town," Wolf says before I can respond to her. He's easy to read, however. It's clear from his tone and the look on his face that he *wants* me gone.

"I was enjoying the sights and entertainment this place had to offer," I answer, looking at Torrent. She might not get it, but Wolf and I are on the same wave length. He knows there's only one *sight* I want to see here—and it's currently sitting at this table, staring at me with those damn whiskey sunny brown eyes.

"Find anything of interest?" Wolf asks, his voice cold.

"Still looking," I answer.

"I can see that," he says dryly.

"How are you doing, Torrent?" I ask the woman our conversation is about.

"I'm okay," she answers.

I study her—*really* study her.

"Now why don't I believe that, Angel?"

"A better question might be why you are so interested," Wolf responds.

"Wolf," Torrent whispers.

"I'm worried about a friend. That's not against the law, is it?" I ask him, finally bringing my gaze back to Wolf.

"It's not needed," he answers, leaning on the table as if to get closer to my space. If he wants to intimidate me he's shit out of luck. "I can take care of Torrent just fine. She doesn't need your concern."

I let my eyes flicker over briefly to Torrent and the pale look on her face and the tightness that's there.

"That's strange," I answer, forcing myself to look at Wolf again, and not reach out and caress Torrent and make her relax. It's not my place...*not right now.*

"That Torrent has someone in her life to take care of her? Or that she doesn't need you?" Wolf asks like the cocky asshole he is.

"That she needs anyone to take care of her. The Torrent I know can take care of herself."

I hear her intake of breath, but I still don't look away from Wolf. It never pays to ignore an enemy and that's definitely what this son of a bitch is.

"Are you about done here, Devil?"

"Not really. Haven't really ate yet. Our food just came."

"Then maybe you should go back to it, before it gets cold."

"I suppose," I agree, because there's really nothing else I can do here.

"Maybe you should head back to your part of the state too."

"And why's that?"

"Well, this can be a rough area if you don't know anyone. I'd hate for you to get hurt or something by accidentally going somewhere you shouldn't," the bastard says.

"Wolf!" Torrent gasps, but in this instance both of us ignore her. This is between me and him.

"Is that a threat?"

"Not a threat. Merely showing some friendly concern."

"I see. Well your concern is noted, but I'll be heading back tomorrow."

"So soon?" Wolf answers, sounding way too happy with my answer.

"I don't really have anything to keep me here. At least not that I know of... do I, Torrent?"

"I... No... at least I don't think so. I mean, I didn't know you knew anyone here," she says, her face filled with color and my question making her so nervous that she's gripping the side of the table so hard her fingers are white.

"I thought I did," I tell her and this time it's her I look at—her I'm giving all of my attention to. "I guess I was wrong."

"You were?" she asks.

"Apparently, and that makes me damn sad, Angel," I tell her.

"I think you should go now, Devil. I can send some men out to help give you safe passage out of town if you like in the morning," Wolf says, and I bet he'd like that. I have to wonder if I'd live to see the city limit sign. Somehow I don't think I would.

"I believe I can find my way. Unless something happens to change my mind," I say with a slight shrug of my shoulders.

"See that it doesn't," Wolf responds, his voice hard.

"Goodbye, Torrent. If you need me—*for anything*—you know where to find me, Angel," I tell her and ignore Wolf's growl of dislike. Torrent's gaze locks with mine, but she doesn't respond.

That's okay. I think I got my message across. I turn and walk back to my table where Diesel is waiting and I can tell from the look on his face...if I stay here, it will be with Fury watching my back...

And maybe that's not such a bad thing at this point.

TORRENT

"Thanks for the ride into town, Red. I really appreciate it."

"No worries. Give me a second to check in with Wolf and we'll go in," he replies.

"Oh, uh, there's really no place for you to go in. It's a small spa and—"

"Tor—"

"Red... that building is small. A total of three rooms," I warn him.

"So?"

"I'd rather not have you sitting in the small waiting room with a grand total of four chairs while I'm in the next room getting a bikini wax and screaming in pain."

"Wolf wants me to keep an eye on you. He told me you were being harassed by one of those men from that charter close to Sevier County."

"Red, there's not even a back door to that building. You can watch me from this SUV. I don't really want you hearing me cry over my lady parts."

"There's no back door? How is that even legal?"

"I don't know, but it's true. You want to go in and look?"

"Yeah, I guess if I make sure the building is secure, and can monitor who goes in then Wolf should be satisfied."

I stop myself from rolling my eyes. I understand why Wolf is being so cautious. The problem is he's always been overprotective and right now it's about a million times worse. Agreeing to "date" him has only made him more possessive too. I know this is what my father wanted, but those doubts I had before are nearly screaming at me now. My head is a mess; my emotions are a mess... *I'm a mess.*

I wait once we get inside the small spa—which is really a small office trailer that has been converted. Murfreesboro doesn't have a lot of choices. The receptionist knows me well and smiles when I go in, but her gaze immediately goes to Red. He probably scares her to death. He's a huge man who stands at 6'9" and is built like a linebacker. He's got long red hair that's curly and might look good if he took care of it, but he doesn't. Instead, it's a massive, huge afro. One of his arms looks like a tree trunk along the biceps.

Red goes through the small area and then starts to open the main room before the receptionist screeches at him.

"Sir! You can't do that!"

He looks at her and then opens the door—which is followed by more screeching as the woman who is getting a bikini wax doesn't appreciate his intrusion at all. I hold my head down as he checks out the bathroom and ignores the receptionist again, while checking out her area.

"Fuck. There really isn't a back door to this place. How in the hell do you guys stay in business?" Red barks to the poor innocent girl who probably wishes she had called in sick this morning.

"I...uh...well..." She trails off, because it's clear she doesn't know what to say and how could she?

"Satisfied?" I ask Red when he comes back to stand beside me.

"I'll be out in the truck and I'll be watching the entrance. If you need me, you call and I'll be here in seconds," he says in his gruff voice. I nod.

"You could go for a bit, you know? This is going to take a while."

"How long?" he growls.

"I'm an hour early for my appointment, Red. I warned you."

"So?"

"I don't think they can work me in early, can you, Sharon?" I direct my question to the receptionist. She knows me well and right now I'm praying she knows what I need from her. She studies me for a minute and I hold my breath when she starts to answer.

"I… well, Torrent, to be honest we are behind schedule today. So it may be an hour and a half before Jamile can even take you back."

"You're fucking kidding me," Red answers and his voice vibrates with so much anger poor Sharon jumps.

"Told you and then I'm getting the works while I'm in there."

"What does that mean?"

"That once I get back there it could take up to three hours to finish."

"You'll do this another day then. I got shit to do."

"Then go do it. I'm getting my spa day."

"Torrent—"

"*Red,* this place is the *only* spa in the area. I'm not traveling to Nashville to go get everything done."

"Why not?"

"Because I'm not letting strangers look at my hoo-hah."

"Christ."

"And besides that, Wolf will be home in two days."

"Torrent, you're starting to get on my damn nerves."

"The feeling is mutual. Besides, I'm pretty sure Sharon can't work me in if I cancel today."

"I'm afraid not. We stay booked up," Sharon pipes up helpfully. I smile at her, silently giving my thanks.

"Then, you'll reschedule and comeback whenever," he mutters.

"Red. I am not going to look like…. well, I don't want to have your hairstyle between my legs when Wolf gets back."

"Fuck, Torrent, I don't want to hear that shit."

"I'm just saying it's going to be your job to tell Wolfe why our romantic date ends at a handshake."

"Fine. I'll get a prospect to come and watch the door, but understand me, Torrent, you better be ready to leave when I get back."

"In five hours?" I question hopefully.

"Four, tops. You better make that work."

"I… uh… think we can work with that can't we, Sharon?" I ask, turning to her so she can see my face silently pleading for her to agree.

"I think so…" she says and I don't miss the confusion on her face, but thankfully Red does.

I watch as he stomps out without saying anything else. When the door closes, I think that's the first free breath I take today.

Slowly I turn to Sharon and wait for her questions. I don't have long to wait.

"Torrent, you don't have an appointment today and you know it doesn't take—"

"I need a way out of here, that's not in the front and I need you to try and cover for me, Sharon."

She studies me and maybe she sees the sheer panic on my face, but she gives me a grim smile of agreement.

God, I hope I'm doing the right thing.

DEVIL

"**W**as that Fury?"

"Yeah. I told him he didn't need to come up after all, that we'd be leaving in the morning," Diesel answers. "Unless you've changed your mind again?"

"I thought we agreed, I should back away?"

"Never thought you were the kind of man to give up that easily," Diesel says with a shrug.

"Man, you're giving me whiplash with your back and forth," I growl at him. It's not him I'm frustrated at—it's myself.

"The same could be said about you, Ese," Diesel smirks.

"Don't I know it," I mutter, leaning back against my pillow.

I'm propped up on the bed, leaning back against the headboard with two pillows behind me. Diesel is sitting at the table beside the bed and I'm not sure why. He has his own room, or hell, he could be gone by now. I'm trying to get the image of Torrent in another man's arms out of my head and not being that successful at it.

"We need to get you out. You're worse today than you were yesterday."

"We could head back now," I respond. "Not like I have anything holding me here," I add with a shrug.

"Now you're talking. How long will it take you to pack your shit up?"

"Gee, let me think about that. Two minutes?"

"You're such a smart ass. I'll grab my gear and meet you at the bikes," Diesel says, opening the door. He's gone before I even get the energy to get up myself.

I go over to the dresser and grab my bag—which is really a ratty, blue, Walmart piece of crap that I shove down into my saddle bags. Then I head into the bathroom to get my deodorant and shit. I barely make it to the door when the knocking starts.

"Diesel, fuck, you just left. I'll be ready to go in a minute. You haven't even given me two—"

I stop as I open the door and see Torrent standing there. She's wearing faded jeans and a black T-shirt with a leather jacket—though thankfully not that fucker Wolf's cut. Her hair is brushed down her back and she doesn't have as much makeup on today. I can definitely see a few light bruises on her face and I flex my hand behind the door, trying to keep control of the anger it makes me feel.

"Hi…"

"Torrent. I didn't really expect you to show up."

"You're leaving," she says.

"It didn't seem I had anything to hang around for. You coming in or are you going to stay out there?" I ask her, stepping back from the door.

"I'm coming in," she responds.

She walks in and behind her I see Diesel.

"I take it we're not leaving anytime soon?" he asks, but he's grinning.

I flip him off and close the door on his laughter.

I turn to face Torrent. She looks nervous and I smile because

I'm a bastard and I kind of like that she's nervous around me right now.

"Does your boyfriend know you're here?"

"He's not my boyfriend—at least not yet," she grumbles, giving me a defiant look.

"And does he know you're here?" She doesn't answer, but she looks down at the ground and that gives me enough of an answer. I give a short laugh. It's not funny, but then again the look on Wolf's face if he ever finds out Torrent sought me out would be. "I didn't think so."

"He's the reason I'm here," she mumbles, rubbing her hands down the leg of her pants, nervously. I'm sure she doesn't mean to call attention to her curves, or the way those pants cling to her body like a second skin—but she does.

"Now that, I didn't expect and I don't want to call you a liar, Angel. Got to say though, I find it hard to believe."

"He doesn't like you."

"Now *that* I believe. But, if you came all the way over here to tell me that, you kind of wasted your time. I kind of already knew that," I joke, walking over to the bed and sitting down where I was before. I fluff my pillows and then fix them again against the headboard, all before turning back around and looking at Torrent.

"Comfortable?" she asks, obviously put out with me, which makes me strangely happy.

"I'm getting there. I'd be better if you'd come over and join me though," I tease, patting the bed beside me.

"That's *not* going to happen."

"Eh, maybe not right now."

"It's *never* going to happen, Logan."

"Didn't anyone tell you that you should never say never? Besides, that's kind of a challenge for me."

"A challenge?"

"Yeah, now my goal will be to make sure I get you on the bed with me."

"Well, I hate to burst your bubble, but you shouldn't look for that to happen. Especially since you will be back home and I'll be here."

"That's semantics, besides we're both here right now."

"Yes, well. That's why I'm here. Wolf doesn't like you."

"You're starting to repeat yourself, Angel."

"You've got on his radar."

"I have no idea what that means. Did I mention there's room here on the bed for you?"

"Devil, will you try and be serious for a minute? Wolf isn't a man you should cross."

"Angel, it sounds like you're worried about me. I can't decide if I should be offended or flattered. Now, about this bed…"

"Will you stop being an idiot. This is serious. You don't know him like I do. He's very… *protective* over me."

"I think the word you're looking for, Angel, is possessive."

"Whatever. Listen, Wolf is a good guy really, but he can be…"

"Torrent, I don't really want you to defend your boyfriend to me."

"You need to leave."

"You carted your sweet little ass over here to tell me that?"

"I felt the need to warn you," she mutters. "Though now, I'm starting to wonder why."

"Because you like me, even if you don't want to."

"Maybe I do. Will you take me seriously, please?"

I let out a deep breath and turn to put my feet on the ground and face her.

"You don't need to worry about me, Torrent," I tell her seriously, leaning my hands on my legs and watching her.

"You don't know Wolf like I do, Logan, you don't understand how he can be," she says and she looks lost. I get up and walk to her. I pull out the chair that Diesel had earlier and basically force her to sit down. Then I slide down on my knees in front of her, bracing my hands on each arm of the chair. I have a lot of questions I want to ask her, but somehow when I open my mouth only one comes out.

"And that leads me to one question, Torrent."

"What's that?"

"Just how well do you know, Wolf, Angel? And did you *know* him when we met?"

I stare up into her eyes and wonder exactly why I need to know the answers.

I only know I do.

TORRENT

I try to sort through all of my thoughts. Then I frown up at the man who is causing me even more problems than I already had. I wish I knew what it is about him that appeals to me so much. It could be the sparkling deep blue eyes that shift from mischievous to sexy and then serious. Maybe it's the smile, or the wrinkle he gets in his brow when he concentrates on something. Or maybe it's his scent and the way I react to it. I read somewhere that people are attracted to each other by scent. Maybe that's it, I have no idea… I just know how he makes me feel.

"You do realize that's two questions, Logan."

"I realize you haven't answered either one," he answers. I look down at his hands on the chair. On one hand, his fingers are covered in ink and I've seen men with tats my whole life, but it's never been quite this sexy before.

"I've known Wolf my entire life. He was my dad's best friend. He helped raise me."

"I'm pretty sure he doesn't think of you as a daughter, Angel."

"You're right… he hasn't for a while. He says he's in love with me."

"And how do you feel about him?"

"I don't know. It's complicated. I love him."

Devil frowns and I know my answer doesn't make him happy.

"Maybe you should leave then, Torrent."

"I shouldn't even be here now," I respond, knowing he's right. He falls back on his legs, moving away from the chair.

"Then why are you?" he asks.

"I was worried about you. I needed to warn you."

"Bullshit."

"What?" I ask, getting he's upset but annoyed at his response.

"I said bullshit. You're not here to warn me."

"I am. I was trying to protect you, Devil."

"Will you drop that act with me? It might work on someone else, but it's not going to work on me."

"I have no idea what you're talking about," I tell him, getting up. "And I'm starting to see this was a mistake." I take one step toward the door before Devil grabs my leg and he does something to my leg that unbalances me—causing me to tip forward. I start falling and he pulls me down on him. "What the hell are you doing?"

"That's what I'm asking you, Torrent and you need to quit lying to me."

"I'm not lying to you!" I growl, pushing against his shoulders, trying to get free.

"Then maybe you're lying to yourself."

"You're crazy!"

"I probably am, but there's no way you're in my hotel to warn me your boyfriend has me in his sites."

"But I was! And he's not my boyfriend!" I huff, and for some reason I'm starting to panic. My heart is rapping heavily against my chest.

"You said you loved him," he says and this time he's growling.

"Not like that! Will you let me go!?!?" I cry out when he won't let me push away from him.

"Then why in the fuck were you wrapped all around him at the bar?"

"I wasn't wrapped around him! We were…"

"*What?*"

"We were on a date! I agreed to give him two weeks to convince me we would… we could…"

"I don't believe this shit. You gave him two weeks to convince you to spread your legs for him?"

I reach up to slap him, but he grabs my hand, making me want to scream again.

"You're an asshole!" I tell him when I can't get any satisfaction with hitting him. "And I agreed to *date* Wolf for two weeks to see if there was anything there."

"*Date?*"

"Date!"

"Christ, what is it about you that makes a man tie his balls around your little finger and jump through hoops for a pat on the damn head?"

"What are you talking about?"

"I guarantee that Wolf has never *dated* a woman in his life. He's only doing this to get to you and he's jumping through your hoops to get there. Just like you had *me* jumping through hoops to get to you when I thought you were a goddamn nun!"

"I never asked you to jump through hoops, Logan," I answer, trying to defend myself.

"No, you kept coming to me looking sweet as sugar with a body that promised nights of sin."

"I never promised you anything, Logan!"

"Then why did you keep coming back? You did it because you knew you had me on the line and—"

"I did not!"

"Then why? If that's not the reason then tell me why, Torrent. Why did you keep coming back to me if you knew you could never be mine?"

"Logan—"

"Tell me!"

"I don't know," I try and defend, but he brings his hands up and puts them on each side of my face and doesn't let me look away.

"You do. Tell me, Torrent. Tell me," he urges.

"Because I couldn't stay away," I finally answer, even though I don't want to. "There! Are you happy now, Logan? I kept coming to see you because I couldn't stay away. I wanted to see you," I answer. By the time I get to the last words I'm whispering. He pulls my face closer, and doesn't stop until I look at him.

"Then, why did you come to me that last day and push me away? Why did you disappear?"

"I didn't have a choice. Dad was worried about the mole. He didn't want me to bring attention to myself. It was dangerous. There were things... I needed to help my dad, Logan. I was going to..."

"And?"

"I was kidnapped and then Dad tried to save me and..."

"Oh God, Angel. Come here," he whispers, kissing my forehead and pulling me deeper into his arms.

I should resist him, but since I'm being honest with myself right now, I have to admit I don't want to. This is yet one more reason I've been resisting Wolf. There's only been two people who make me feel like I'm whole when they hug me.

My father and Devil.

DEVIL

$\mathcal{I}$t takes some maneuvering, but I manage to get up from the floor carrying Torrent. She's holding me and sobbing into my neck. She's so full of pain and I had no idea. I sit on the bed and resume my earlier position. Once I've reclined back on the pillows, I make sure Torrent is comfortable and I let her cry. I don't say anything; now isn't the time for words. I content myself with holding Torrent, combing my fingers through her hair, kissing the top of her head and breathing her in. God, I've missed her. I missed her even when I didn't realize it.

"It's okay, Angel let it out," I whisper.

"I shouldn't be here. I… I needed to warn you," she murmurs.

I should let it go at that, but I find I can't. I don't know where in the hell this is going. I don't even know what we are, but whatever else happens I want nothing but honesty between us.

"That's not why you're here, Angel. You knew I was leaving. That's not why you're here. Admit it."

"Okay fine. That's not why I'm here," she huffs and her bottom lip sticks out in a pout. I can't resist moving my finger along it, stroking it.

"Why are you here? I want to hear you say it, Angel."

"I missed you, Logan," she answers.

It's a simple statement and there's no huge meaning behind it, but knowing she missed me—like I miss her—slides deep inside of me and makes something shift. I wanted Torrent before. Now I don't know if I can let her go.

"I missed you too," I respond, because it feels like I should let her know she's not alone.

"I got you all wet," she mumbles, her hand petting my shirt.

"That's usually my line."

She looks up at me and rolls her eyes. Then elbows me.

"You're such an ass, and it has not escaped my notice that you tricked me, Logan Dupree."

"What do you mean I tricked you?"

"You got me on the bed while I was vulnerable and weak."

"Are you saying I took advantage of you?"

"Are you going to admit it?" she asks.

I move her so she lies on top of me and our faces are close together. Her body is pressed against mine like this and even with our clothes on it feels perfect. Maybe more perfect than anything I've ever shared with a woman.

"That wasn't my intention, but I'm not a damned bit sorry, Angel."

She pulls her head back enough so she can see me clearly. Her fingers dive into my hair and she uses the pads of her fingers to press against my scalp tenderly.

"I'm not either, but I shouldn't be here. My mind is a little messed up, Logan and my life… I have a lot to sort out right now."

"This is not so different than the first time we met—except then I thought I was going against the Big Guy upstairs. Can't tell you how fucking glad I am that you're not really a nun, Angel."

"It might be better if I was. God is probably more forgiving than Wolf."

"You realize the way you talk about Wolf doesn't fill me with confidence that you're safe around him."

"I'm fine. Wolf would never hurt me," she defends. I frown. I can tell she truly believes that and maybe he wouldn't hurt her—physically. Instinctively I know that right now is not the time to argue that with her.

"I guess that leaves us with one question, Angel."

"What's that?"

"Why are you here with me, when you're *dating* Wolf?"

"We seem to be going around in circles," she sighs. "Maybe I'm here because I'm a horrible person," she mutters, trying to avoid my eyes again. I lean up to kiss her forehead.

"I don't believe that for a second," I tell her and it's the truth. I think Torrent is mixed up and been through a fucking lot.

"Maybe I'm warring with what I want and what I should do," she says, looking up at me under her lashes, her lips pressed together and a shudder moving through her body. She's got so much emotion and fear churning through her body it's a wonder she can keep going. I've seen women on the edge before and that's definitely Torrent right now—even if she's trying to hide it.

"Why *should* you do anything, Torrent? Life happens. You're a free person. Why *should* you do anything?"

I watch her throat work as she swallows and my gaze is glued to the way her lips purse as she considers my words.

"Logan... my entire life I've kind of done what I wanted. When my dad was in trouble...he asked me two things... to keep my head down and to stay where he put me, so he could make sure I was safe while he got to the bottom of things. Instead of doing that... I went out to meet this man with blue eyes that made my knees weak—even knowing I shouldn't."

"Torrent—"

"And when he asked me to stay there and be safe, I tried to leave and... and..."

"Damn it, Angel—"

"I got my father killed, Logan. If I had done what he asked of me, he never would have walked in there and laid his life down like he did. It's all my fault," she whispers and I hate that the tears begin to fill her eyes, sliding out along her face as her body shakes from the need to sob. "It's all my fault," she says again. "I killed my father, Logan."

"Torrent—"

"I killed him," she whispers so brokenly it hurts to hear her. In some ways it would be so much better if she would cry again, let the grief overtake her body. She doesn't. Instead she looks up at me with tears there, but refusing to do anything about them. They slowly fall while her face is filled with misery. "I killed him," she repeats and I'm left wondering if I can ever help Torrent heal... or worse...

If she will let me help her.

TORRENT

*H*e doesn't understand. Devil means well, but he wasn't there. He doesn't have the nightmares or the memories of my father's last words. He doesn't comprehend how cold I feel inside. I'm trying to live my life hiding that from everyone. Mostly I'm afraid if I don't...if everyone can see how frozen I feel inside, it will be like giving the cold life and it will take me over. I feel like I'm bleeding on the inside and it's a race against the clock until that moment when I drown.

The temptation to tell Devil that is there. *It's strong.*

I don't give in. Telling him will change nothing. There's nothing I can do to fix any of it. I let myself be weak, ignoring the pain in my chest, and not giving in to the need to fully cry. Instead, I hold onto him until the urge to give him everything passes. I listen to his heart beat against my ear as I lay on his chest. I feel his hand hold me, his fingers combing my hair and I let myself be weak, if only for a little bit.

"You okay, Angel?" he asks softly a bit later.

"Yeah," I lie. "I need to tell you something," I whisper, afraid to tell him—afraid not to.

"What's that?"

"My dad wanted me to let Wolf take care of me, he wanted… he wanted Wolf… for me, and I… I need to try to see if I can give him that, Logan."

Devil's hand tightens in my hair and I feel the muscles in his body tighten underneath me too. I close my eyes.

"What do you want, Torrent?"

"I don't know if that matters anymore."

"What if it did? Tell me, Angel. If you could choose for you, what would it be?"

"I don't know…" I whisper and I know my answer disappoints him. I feel his legs shift under me. Before he can move us, I decide to tell him what I want—at least for right now.

"We should get up. You need—"

"But I do know if I were free right now, I'd really like for you to kiss me," I tell him, feeling guilty and more than a little foolish.

Devil is completely still, not saying anything for a minute or two. I begin to feel uncomfortable and when I try to move off of him, his fingers tighten into my hips—not letting me. I strain against him, feeling foolish.

"Look at me, Angel," he urges and I close my eyes before giving in. I stare at him and he doesn't say anything for a bit.

The look on his face is so intense, I feel flushed just from that alone. He brings his hand to the side of my neck, holding me there so gently it makes me ache. His thumb sweeps across the corner of my mouth and I prepare myself for his goodbye.

"Logan—"

He stops my words by bringing his mouth to mine and swallowing them. I close my eyes, savoring this moment—this stolen moment, that I shouldn't have. This intense moment that I want more than I want my next breath. My tongue comes out shyly to move across the seam of his, craving nothing more than a simple taste of him.

Immediately his mouth opens, letting me inside. A vibration of noise moves through him and I can feel it rock through me. He has cinnamon on his breath, the taste is heated, the flavor strong, spicy and only adds to the pleasure. His tongue is slick, wet, and smooth and he uses it like an instrument designed to own me. Never have I had a kiss like this, nor did I know they existed. It's not consuming, or even hurried. I feel like he is taking his time tasting me, exploring, and it makes me feel special. I savor it, because I want to commit everything to memory.

Too soon it's over and I keep my eyes closed while I breathe deeply, my heart pounding.

"Give me two weeks, Angel."

My brain is cloudy. I have so many thoughts, so much emotion running through me that I don't understand at first.

"What?"

"You gave Wolf two weeks because you feel you owe it to your father. Give me two weeks."

"Logan—"

"Don't you owe it to yourself to see, Torrent? I get Wolf is who your father chose for you, but he never saw us together. He never got to see the pull between us, or if I can make you happy. I can't pretend to know what you've been through, but I'm telling you whatever is between us is special and worth investigating—"

"Logan, I don't…"

"And whatever you think you know, if your father truly loved you, he would want you to be happy. Give me two weeks to prove to you that I'm the only one who can do that."

His words wreck me. They burrow deep inside of me.

They give me hope.

But I can't hold on to that hope.

"Logan… Wolf, there's no way he'd… I mean, I moved out of the club. I live at my dad's house now, but still. There's no way he's going to be good with you coming around. I don't think—"

"No way he can handle the competition?" he jokes. I want to smile with him but I know there's nothing funny about this situation.

"Logan, honestly I…"

"Torrent, you haven't seen me in my world. I need you to trust that I can take care of myself. I'm not worried."

"You might not be, but I am. I don't want to risk getting into another bad situation. I don't think I can handle someone else I care about getting hurt, Logan," I respond, knowing that it's the truth. Devil seems to study me for a minute and then shrugs.

"So we'll do it like we did at the convent—only better. Let me handle it. I need to hear you say that you will give me two weeks to prove to you that this thing between us is worth holding on to."

"I shouldn't…"

"But you're going to, aren't you, Angel?"

I ignore the panic I feel inside, and the fast beating of my heart. I ignore my common sense that tells me this is a *bad* idea. I ignore everything but the light in his eyes and the smile on his face.

I give in to the need inside of me.

"I'm going to…" I whisper and I'm rewarded with another kiss.

I bury all my doubts in that kiss, which probably isn't the wisest thing to do, but it feels good.

DEVIL

*J*t is unbelievably easy to sneak into this damn compound. The clubhouse itself might have more security, but Torrent's home is a piece of cake to get to and break into. Hell, I only saw three cameras and none of them are around the window on the back porch. The windows are also way too damn old. A small flick of the point of my knife in the right place and the lock gives way. I don't know what kind of club president her father was, but apparently he didn't feel the need to protect himself or his family like he should have. Plus, he wanted his daughter with that asshole Wolf. All that combined doesn't leave her old man smelling like daisies—more like a pile of cow shit.

I make it through the window to what looks like a spare bedroom. I frown thinking how fucking easy it was. There's not much I can do to help, but I'll be figuring something out before I leave her here. I listen for a few minutes before I leave the room. I don't want to walk out and have someone besides Torrent out there.

The house is silent.

Shit. She might be gone. I open the door carefully and then walk into a wide hallway. There's a bathroom across from me and another bedroom, but they're both empty too. The living room is empty, and looking through the rest of the house—dining room, kitchen, and utility room—it's all quiet too. On the other end of the house, there's a double set of doors. I open one of them carefully; the clicking of the lock seems abnormally loud. This room is obviously a master bedroom. The bed is made and the room is empty but there's another set of doors to my right and although they are closed, I can hear music coming from them. I open them slowly, not sure of what I'll find.

I don't get time to look around the minute the door opens a scream lights up the room.

I jump and then when my eyes focus on Torrent, who is in a bathtub full of bubbles, her arms clutched to her chest, her hair wet and her toes peeking out over the side of the tub—I relax.

"Now that's a view worth breaking in for."

"Logan! What are you doing here?"

"I came to see you," I explain, although it should be pretty evident. I walk farther into the room and Torrent dives deeper under the water—*and the disappearing bubbles.*

"Get out!" she squeals.

"Is that anyway to greet your date, Angel?"

"My *date?*"

"You told me today you would give me two weeks."

"Well yeah, but I mean, we just saw each other today, Logan."

"Yep. I was going to show up a little earlier, but I decided showing up later was a better move."

"And *why* was that?"

"So your guards would be drunk—which, by the way, they mostly are."

"Oh... I thought... I mean..." she stutters.

"You thought what, Torrent?"

"I thought you showed up late so you could catch me..."

"Wet and naked?"

"You're horrible," she grumbles, blushing.

"I can't lie, Angel. I wanted you wet and naked... but I wanted to be the one to get you that way."

"You really are insane," she laughs. "Are you going to step out so I can get out of the tub?"

"I'm leaning towards... *No.*"

"Asshole," she mutters, but she's still smiling. "At least grab me a towel over there."

I walk to the cabinet she motioned to and there's bath towels, wash cloths and hand towels.

It's not like she was specific.

"Here ya' go," I answer, sounding sweet and innocent—even if I do say so myself. Then I hold up a small blue hand towel.

"I hardly think that will dry my whole body, now do you?"

"I think it'd be fun trying. I'll even donate my services."

"I bet you would. Hand me a real towel, *please.*"

"I really thought you were more adventurous," I mutter, teasingly. I replace the towel with a large bath one, reaching it to her. She stares at it for a minute with a frown. "What's wrong now?" I ask, curious as to what is running through her head.

"I um... Can you hold it out for me?" she asks, blushing a bright red again. Torrent is such a mixture of shyness and sarcasm that she intrigues me every minute I'm with her. She leaves me wanting to see what happens next.

I stretch the towel out, holding it in both of my hands. I look at her over the top of it, leering with my face showing nothing but challenge.

"Like this, Angel?"

"I'm trusting you not to peek," she warns.

"Scouts honor," I grin.

"Turn your head."

She waits until I do it, and then stands. The sound of water sloshing makes my mind go wild. I know the visions I'm picturing could only pale next to the real thing...

"You're looking!" she gasps, pulling the towel around her

quickly. She did it before I barely got a glance, but what I did see was fucking amazing.

"Darlin', I'm called Devil for a reason. There's not a straight man alive who could pass up that chance. Hell, some gay ones too."

"Whatever. You were never a scout, were you?"

"In the most technical sense... *no*," I laugh.

"Can I get you to go back out into the hall while I get dressed?"

"If I say no?"

"Then I think our date will be over pretty quickly," she says stubbornly.

I think she's bluffing, but I'm not willing to test that out. I lean over and kiss her quickly, and walk away.

"Don't keep me waiting too long, Angel. You never know when I might be forced to come back in—*to check on you, of course.*"

"You never know when I might be forced to clobber you over the head with that baseball bat by my bed—*in shock, of course.*"

And there's the old Torrent, mimicking me and giving as good as she gets. I laugh as I leave the room, because I could see her doing it, and I'm as fucked up as everyone has always accused me of being—because I like it.

TORRENT

I smile as he closes the door. I really wasn't expecting him tonight. I actually wasn't sure how this would work. I'm surprised he's here and I keep looking around, certain that some of my dad's men will find him—or know he's here.

I throw on a pair of pajamas. I should probably dress up since Devil is here. This isn't exactly a normal date, though, and I want to relax tonight. I look at my jeans and T-shirts hanging in the closet and second guess myself, but finally say fuck it and close the door. I towel dry my hair and stare longingly at my blow dryer. My hair will be an untamable mess by morning, but I don't want to delay being with Logan. I can admit that I'm happy he's here—even excited. It's probably not fair and makes me all kinds of horrible—but I'm glad that Wolf is out of town.

"What are you doing now?" I ask Devil when I finally track him down in the kitchen.

"I'm hungry," he says with a grin. "You're looking good, Torrent," He takes a bite of a banana. The same could definitely be said about him. Eating a banana shouldn't be sexy, but somehow on Devil it is.

"I'm pretty sure there's something more filling in this kitchen than bananas," I laugh, sliding into a stool at the breakfast bar. He pulls off a piece of his banana and brings it to my lips. I'm almost hypnotized by the look on his face and without thought find myself opening for him. He slips the sweet bite between my lips and I suck it from his fingers. I don't think it's my imagination that his eyes darken in color. My heart feels like it's kicked into overdrive in my chest and I forget to breathe.

"I know," he says. "There's peanut butter."

I blink, wondering if I misheard him.

"Peanut butter?"

"Angel, you haven't lived until you've had a fried banana and peanut butter sandwich."

"I... if you tell me you're really the King of Rock n' Roll, I'm going to go running now."

"No Elvis here, but if you're a good girl I'll show you how well I can move my hips later."

"I bet you would. You really are a freak, aren't you, Logan?"

He winks at me and I find myself laughing. I haven't felt like laughing in a while, but around Devil I tend to do it all the time.

"What's all this? I thought you just put the peanut butter and banana together?" I ask, trying to pay attention to what he's doing as he gathers ingredients.

"Sacrilege! The secret to making a sandwich fit for the King is the honey."

"Honey? Do I even have that?"

"Found it in the cabinet. See peanut butter alone is more than filling. It's enough to make you lick your lips and moan from pleasure, but if you add a little sweet honey so it sticks to the peanut butter making it slide down your throat while the flavor explodes on your tongue. And *then* there's the cinnamon."

"Cinnamon?" I'm whispering because his words conjure up images that have nothing to do with a sandwich or cooking.

"Anything thick, sweet and moan-worthy needs a little spice added so you always remember it."

"Does it?"

"Definitely. A little something extra so you always remember it and come back for more."

"Why do I get the feeling you're comparing your sandwich to your dick?"

"Actually it's sex. All good cooking should remind you of sex."

"Seriously?"

"Definitely, Angel."

"What about fruitcake?"

I giggle when he screws his face up in distaste.

"I said *good* cooking, woman."

"Well, hand me some bread and I'll spread the peanut butter stuff on it. I'm suddenly hungry."

"Now we're talking," he jokes, while handing me the bread. "You do that and I'll add the bananas to the other side."

I get one done and he takes his slice with the bananas and smashes them together—*being really messy*.

"Uh—"

"Sometimes the best things in life are messy, but when it all comes together it can be perfect," he says and he leans over to kiss me.

It's not a long kiss, it's short and sweet, but it makes me feel happy. It makes me feel like I matter to him and I'm starting to believe I really do. Why else would a man go through as much as he has and still be in my kitchen tonight making me sandwiches... and mostly making me smile?

All signs are pointing to the fact that Devil likes me.

Like I do him...

"You have peanut butter on you," I tell him when he pulls away.

"I do? Where?"

"Right here," I tell him, grinning. I take my finger and smear some of the peanut butter I got on it from handling the sandwich and rub it on his nose.

He doesn't do anything for a minute and then his eyes light in mischief and he grins really big.

"You know this means war, right, Angel?" he says and I start to get a little nervous and then he grabs me by the arms and pulls my face to his and rubs his nose against mine, making me laugh so hard I snort.

Yeah... I really like him.

DEVIL

"I've had a really good time tonight, Logan," Torrent whispers and I hug her closer.

We're lying on her bed. Unfortunately, we're both completely clothed. She has her head on my shoulder and one of her legs draped over mine. I'm holding my other hand out and she's put hers against it. Her fingers, to my fingers, her thumb to mine and needless to say mine is much larger, definitely darkened from the sun more, and covered in ink. Still, there's something hypnotic about the way they look together.

"I did too, Angel. Probably the best night I've had in a long damn time."

"I'm not only talking about tonight, though to be honest I now have a new favorite food in peanut butter and banana sandwiches."

"I told you, it's all about the honey," I grin, sliding my fingers between hers and bringing our joined hands to my lips to kiss hers.

"I liked the cinnamon sugar you topped it with more, I think," she giggles. "But seriously, this whole day has been great. It was good to ride on the back of your bike again too," she says quietly.

I think back to when I left the hotel with her. She tried to talk me out of it, but there was no way I was going to let her go all the way back in town without me. Instead, I put her on the back of my bike and took back streets until we were a block from the spa. Then I walked her around back and helped her inside. I honestly don't think it's dawned on her how much she's trying to keep from upsetting Wolf. She might not *think* she's afraid of the man, but clearly there's something going on.

"You belong on my bike, Torrent," I tell her, steering away from my thoughts of Wolf. I will deal with that son of a bitch soon.

Very soon.

"Things are complicated, Logan."

"We'll un-complicate them," I promise her and I will. Torrent doesn't know it yet, but I'm not about to give her up this time.

"You make it sound so simple, Logan."

Torrent sighs, turning over on her back and disengaging from me. I turn to my side so I can see her.

"Most things are simple, Angel. It's people who fuck everything up."

"I've fucked up a lot where you're concerned," she confesses.

I let my finger trace an imaginary line along the side of her face, staring at her and taking in everything about her. My finger slides to the corner of her mouth, and I can't resist stroking in the corner where there's a tiny dimple showing.

"I'm still here, Angel. I'm not leaving."

"Why?" she asks.

"Because I have faith that we're meant to be, even if you don't."

"What makes you so sure?" she asks.

"What's more meant to be than an angel and a devil?" I ask her and she grins, deepening her dimple and making it impossible not to kiss her.

I taste her lips, kissing her softly, eating from her mouth with a sweet slowness, meant to show her only one thing—how special she is to me. She kisses me back, almost shyly. Her fingers slide under my shirt, teasing my stomach. It takes control I didn't know I had not to force my hand, but I don't. I need to handle Torrent with an easy touch, until she can see what's going on. I wasn't around when her father died. I wasn't here to save her, but it doesn't take a genius to see it's messed with her mind. It's even easier to realize that Wolf is playing on that. I have a lot to overcome when it comes to winning Torrent, but I'm damn well going to do it.

"I love the way you kiss, Logan."

"Feel free to take advantage of my skills anytime," I invite.

"I might take you up on that," she replies.

I try not to moan as her fingernails make an upward motion and graze my nipple.

"I—" She stops when her doorbell rings and I bite down the stream of curse words that come to mind. "Oh no," she whispers, her face going completely white. "Logan—"

I reach up and hold her face, when she'd move away completely. I force her to look directly at me.

"Breathe, Torrent."

"That could be Wolf. Logan, if he catches you here... Oh God..."

"Torrent, baby, it's going to be okay. Just breathe," I tell her again.

"But—"

"I'll hide and you get rid of them, tell them you were sleeping and not feeling well."

"You can't be here! If he sees you... If *anyone* sees you, Logan..."

"I'm not leaving until I'm sure you're okay for the night."

"I don't think—"

She practically squeals when instead of the doorbell ringing again there's a pounding on the front door that you can hear even here in her bedroom.

Someone is getting anxious.

I kiss her before she can scream when the man yells so loud you could swear he's in the room with us and not through a locked door two rooms over.

"Torrent! Open the door!"

When we break apart, her eyes are wide. She brings her fingers up to her lips.

"That's Red, not Wolf."

"Put your robe on. I'll be close by, so I'm promising you that you will be safe."

"I—"

"Stop arguing and let's get this done so that fucker will leave."

"Okay," she whispers and then she surprises me by kissing me this time and it's a quick kiss, but the fact she takes the time to wrap her tongue around mine and growls into my mouth is nothing but encouraging. "Don't leave," she says and this time I'm the one that's surprised. "Promise you won't leave, Logan."

"Wild horses couldn't drag me out of here right now, Angel," I swear to her.

"Then let's get rid of that *fucker*," she says with a grin and for some reason she looks completely at ease right now. I don't know what brought on the change, but it's good to see and I definitely want to stick around to see what my girl has on her mind.

TORRENT

*J*feel like skipping on the way to the door. I'm dreading
dealing with Red and whatever his damage is, but in
my head there's this voice sing-songing.

"Devil cares for me. He really cares for me."

I've never really had a man that I've liked this much—never
had someone in my life that was necessary except for my father.
Devil has been different from the beginning. My reactions to him
and the way he makes me feel are unlike anything I've ever experienced. The simple truth here is that I care for him. I care...
deeply for him, even if I shouldn't.

"Try to leave my door hanging please," I growl as I cinch the
belt of my robe at my waist. I look over my shoulder nervously
one last time to look for Devil. I don't see him, and I guess right
now that's a good thing. Before I turn my deadbolt I take a deep
breath and then force myself to look completely natural—*and
sleepy.*

"About fucking time," Red yells the second the door is open. I
quickly jump in front of him when he'd come pushing his way
inside.

"I was sleeping," I lie. "Which, by the way, is what most sane people do at this hour. What do you want, Red?"

"Wolf called and said you weren't answering your phone."

I blink. I really hadn't thought about my phone. I heard it ringing once, but I ignored it because I was enjoying spending time with Devil. I should feel guilty for worrying Wolf, I guess, but I don't. I'm actually a little relieved I didn't answer.

"My battery was down, so I turned it off and let it charge."

"He wanted to talk to you," he says stubbornly.

"Well, I'm sorry. There's nothing I can do it about it now. I could call him?"

"He can't talk now because he's doing some business for the club tonight. He said to tell you he'll call in the morning, but he's going to have to be out of town for a couple of more days."

"Oh. I hope everything is okay," I murmur. I hope I sound upset, but inside I'm happy. That means I'll have more time with Devil without the real world coming between us. I really am going to have to make some tough decisions—*and soon*—but for now I have this small reprieve and I'm glad.

"It's fine. Wolf has everything under control. Your old man left things in a mess and Wolf has a lot of roads to repair," he says and I immediately get pissed at his insinuation. "It's club business," he goes on. "Not your concern. Wolf has a big fucking headache to fix, but he will do it. Dodger burned a lot of fucking bridges, Tor."

"I think maybe you better go," I mutter, unable to even pretend to keep a cap on my anger.

"You make sure you keep your doors and windows locked," he orders, watching me closely.

"I will, though no one bothers me unless you count men who bang on my door and wake me up—"

"I—" Red interrupts, but I speak over him because I want to get my point across.

"Waking me up," I repeat, my tone annoyed. "Just so he can insult my father."

"Make sure you lock your damn doors. I swear you're a pain in the ass. I don't know why Wolf fools with you," Red mutters, turning and walking away. I slam the door loudly on him, wishing I could slam his face instead.

"Logan?" I ask when he doesn't immediately come out of hiding. I retrace my steps going through the kitchen and hall. When I get to my bedroom he's over by the window holding my broom—or *what's left of it*. "What did my broom ever do to you?" I ask, wondering why he's broken the wooden handle. I grimace when I think of the strength it must have taken to break it. That couldn't have been easy.

"Hey, Angel. Get rid of the idiot that quickly?" he asks and I frown as I watch him put the largest pieces of my broom handle under the bed and wedge it so he can use that to help break off another piece.

"Yeah, I guess. What *are* you doing?"

"Securing your windows," he says like that's a perfectly natural reply. I watch as he wedges the piece of broom he broke into the top part of my window. Once he's satisfied with the way he's secured it, I watch as he tries to open the window. The handle of the broom makes that impossible and I have to say I'm kind of impressed at his ingenuity.

"That's a really good idea," I remark as he does the second window the same way.

"I'd rather they were safer, but this was the best I could do under the circumstances. We'll try and do each window and then when I leave you can secure the window I use and—"

"I was… I mean…"

"Spit it out, Angel," he urges and I struggle with my embarrassment. Still, I take a deep breath and try.

"I was hoping you'd stay the night. No sex or anything," I say hurriedly, before Devil can get the wrong idea. "But, I'd really like to fall asleep in your arms tonight."

He looks at me and for a minute I'm scared he's going to turn me down. Then he grins a full smile, and that's when I lose myself a little more to Devil.

"Then let's get these windows secured. I want to hold my woman tonight."

I really should correct him, but I don't.

I want to belong to Devil.

So, like a fool, I help him secure windows and remain in my dream world where Devil is my man and we have a future.

I need to find a way to make that a reality.

DEVIL

"What are you doing, Angel?" I ask, my voice thick with sleep and... *hunger.*

Torrent is lying on top of me, nibbling on the side of my neck. Her warm breath heats my skin and every time her teeth gently nip at my skin chills of awareness shoot across my body. I have my hands on the cheeks of her ass and I'm holding her against my hardened cock. I was hard last night and it seems this morning won't be any different. It feels like the hard fabric of my jeans has rubbed my dick raw. My balls ache. It's a miracle I didn't attack Torrent last night while she slept. I've tried to hold myself in check with her, but she sure isn't making things easy for me right now.

"You smell so good, Logan," she whispers. Her voice is deeper than normal, huskier and it only makes me ache more.

"Angel you need to stop. I'm only human," I groan as those sharp little teeth bite into my earlobe and pull. I close my eyes, my fingers clinching into those luscious, thick mounds of her ass. I wish she hadn't worn pajamas to bed. My body shakes with the need to have her naked.

"I don't want to stop," she says as her tongue plays with my ear.

"I'm having a hard time…"

My words break off in a moan when she shifts and her hand cups my cock through my pants—squeezing.

"I noticed," she moans. "You feel really big, Logan. Are you?" she whispers in my ear. "Are you big and wide? So thick that you leave me aching when you're gone?" she asks. Her voice is wicked, full of mischief, but still…*hungry.*

"Motherfucker, you're killing me, Angel. It's not nice to tease," I groan, my voice sounding like thunder in my own ears.

"Maybe I'm not teasing," she says right before she slides down my body. She sits on my knees, straddling me. Her hair is mussed from sleeping and her face is flushed with desire and maybe a touch of nervousness. She looks like a temptress and it's all I can do not to reach out and grab her.

"What *are* you doing?" I ask, watching how each breath she takes vibrates in her body like she's run a long race.

"Something occurred to me last night while you were sleeping," she says.

"What's that?"

"You were sound asleep, but you were holding me close, using your body to almost shield me. I woke up once from a nightmare and even though you were sleeping, your hand brushed through my hair, you kissed me on the temple and hugged me tighter."

I let her talk. I don't tell her that she had nightmares all night long—some more powerful than others, and some that didn't wake her—even though I wish they had. I hate that she was trapped in her own personal hell and there was nothing I could do to help her.

"Torrent," I begin, but I don't finish when she shakes her head no. She has something she wants to say and hell, I'm just glad to be here at this point, so I let her go with it.

"I don't know where this is going to go, Logan. My life is kind of a mess, and I have some things to work through with Wolf—"

I can't stop the growl that bursts through at the mention of the man's name.

"He's been good to me, Logan. He always has. I care for him and my dad loved him like a brother," she says, her voice going sad. I bite my tongue. There's nothing to be gained by telling her what I think about the asshole. Torrent has been manipulated by Wolf and maybe even by her father. I hope I can eventually make her see that. "It will be okay, eventually. I need to handle things carefully with Wolf—and I will. But..." She stops talking, biting her lip and those beautiful dark eyes with amber flecks pin me to the bed.

"But?" I prompt, almost afraid to push it.

"I don't want to lose you, Logan. Last night in your arms, well even before that, I knew."

"Knew what, Angel? It's early in the morning and you got my dick screaming hard too. You're going to have to spell it out for me."

"Well, I mean I think I knew... or *know*... maybe... but I know at least how I feel and—"

"Angel, breathe. I keep having to remind you of that. I don't think you've grasped it yet, but you are completely safe with me. I'm not going to hurt you. I'm not going to judge you or even push you in a direction you don't want to go. I'm here *with* you because I want to be and because—"

"You care about me," she blurts out and the shock on her face is enough to make me grin. It's clear that she didn't mean to say that. I rush to make her feel at ease.

"I do care for you Torrent—*very much.*"

"I mean, I thought so. I was pretty sure last night and stuff," she says with a shrug and I laugh and reach out to touch her face. Her gaze comes back to mine and she smiles with a deep blush on her face. "It's still really nice to hear you say it," she murmurs.

"I could show you too, if you're not convinced," I offer— praying like fucking hell she takes me up on the offer.

"Well, actually that's what *I* was trying to do."

"What's that?"

"Show you how much... I care... *about you*," she confesses.

I've been called many things in my life. Some of them true, some false; some were well-deserved and others not, but one thing I've never been is stupid.

"Then show me, Angel. I'm all yours," I invite and hope like hell she doesn't back out.

TORRENT

I sound so crazy. I hate it, and I'm probably giving Devil whiplash with the way I war with myself and switch my brain around on him. I'm having trouble being the Torrent I was before all of this. The Torrent who saw what she wanted, took it and to hell with anyone else. I miss her because there are times now she's replaced by someone shy and timid and that has never been me. I'm afraid to take the wrong step. Still, I know I need to tread carefully. I can't go through anything like I did with my father, not again. I may hate it, but I am... *delicate* right now. I'm so unsure of everything. The one thing I'm positive of right now is... Devil.

I'm safe with him.

Everything in me feels that and I'm going to trust in it—even if I have to fight myself to do it.

I take a breath and then bunch my fingers in the hem of his shirt. He laid on my bed fully clothed last night. He slept all night in his jeans and shirt. It couldn't have been comfortable, but he didn't press for more either.

"Lean up," I ask quietly as I pull his T-shirt from his body. He helps me navigate it over his head and I ignore the way my heart keeps slamming against my chest. Once I'm done I throw the shirt down on the floor. "I've been wanting to do that all night," I tell him. He grins up at me lazily.

"No one was stopping you, Angel," he says, but he's wrong. I was stopping myself. I second guess myself constantly now, but I've vowed to stop doing that with Devil. He says I'm safe with him, and in my heart I believe him.

I drag my gaze back down to his now bare chest. He's not one of these pretty boys who has waxes and man-scaping done. I always suspected that, but looking at the hair on his chest, it's confirmed. I actually like that he has hair there. It's not overly hairy, but enough that I want to press my chest against his and rake my breasts through it, *feel it...*

"How did you get this?" I ask, my finger moving over an old scar, which is obviously a knife wound. It's so close to his heart that I inwardly cringe.

"Someone tried to kidnap Diesel's kid. I made the mistake of going easy on them because it was a woman..." He shrugs. My fingers stall over the scar and I look at Devil.

"Women can be as deadly as a man," I tell him, knowing that to be true. How many times in my past was I overlooked because of my sex? I always used it to my advantage... at least until I found myself a prisoner with no chance of escape.

"Learned that the hard way, Angel," he says.

I lean down to kiss the scar, feeling the hard raised ridge against my lips.

"You can trust me, Logan," I tell him, needing him to understand that. "I know I haven't made it easy, but I've had a lot going on. I never would have lied if—"

He brings his fingers up to my lips to stop me from talking.

"It's the past, Torrent. All in the past. The only thing that matters is what's between us and in front of us right now. The only thing I regret about the past is that I didn't try harder to find you after that damn nun told me you left."

"You tried to find me?" I whisper, feeling happy at his words.

"Not hard enough and for that I'm sorry," he tells me, his words solemn and forthright.

"It's all in the past. Nothing matters but what's between us right now," I respond giving his words back to him.

I let my fingers travel down his body, drawing an imaginary line that only I can see. I pass a few other scars and one looks like it was caused from a bullet. I don't ask about it; I'm not sure I really want to know right now. Even with the scars marring his skin, he's utter perfection. Men usually don't like to be called beautiful, but there's no other word for Devil. I don't share that with him, however. My hands go to his jeans and I unlatch the button and carefully slide the zipper down over the large bulge pressing against the denim.

My hands shake a little. It's been a while since I've been with a man, but it's been a long time since I've wanted to be with one too.

I trace the tattoo that hangs low on his groin. It's a 666 that starts black and slowly fades into different hues of red until the tips of the 6's all are bright, fiery red.

"I can't believe you have this tattoo," I smile, then slide further down his legs so I can bend down and trace the numbers with my tongue.

"Don't worry, baby. I promise my dick's not cursed and it's only evil if you don't touch it," he jokes. His fingers slide through my hair as I'm kissing him, massaging my scalp and tenderly caressing me. It's nice.

It's more than nice.

"I guess I'll have to touch it, then," I murmur.

It takes some work, because my legs are shaking at best, but I slide off of Devil and stand on the floor. I'm a mess of desire, hunger, and nerves. Devil helps me take his pants off and we do the work in silence, the air too thick for words. The only sound you can hear is the mixture of our breathing.

His cock springs out almost immediately—no boxers or briefs for him. I wasn't wrong about him either. He's big, so big that I grow wetter from looking at how impressive he is. Every feminine part in my body tightens in response. He's a vast range of colors, from darkened flushed colors around the head to lighter and brighter colors down the shaft. There's a bulging vein that runs along the center of his cock that I'm dying to press my tongue to. I can't really tell how long he is. I've never really thought about it much with a man; as long as they had enough to get the job done it has never really mattered, but the truth of it is that Devil is generously endowed and I find myself being more than thankful. He's also so wide there's a part of me wondering how he will fit inside of me.

"Shit..." I groan without meaning to, as I see a large pearl drop of pre-cum drip down off the large, dark head of his cock. It's beautiful and though every man might have this certain appendage, I'm sure there's not one that looks as good as this one.

"Like what—oh fuck, Angel," Devil growls his fingers tightening almost painfully on my head when I bend down to lick the head of his cock, stealing his pre-cum.

I hum in approval as I taste him. I expected something almost bitter in flavor, but instead it's sweet and tangy and I want more. I stretch my hand around him. He's so broad that it's hard to do, but I use it to stroke him tightly, squeezing his cock and milking him without thought—only knowing I want more.

More pre-cum slides out onto his head this time, this one larger, and it fans out sliding over the edge and running down so that it lands on my finger. I lean down to lick it off of my own hand and take my time letting my tongue trace the path back up his cock until I suck the entire head in my mouth.

"Mmm..." I moan around him, because never has anything felt so good. Then again, I've never had feelings for someone the way I do Devil and that makes all the difference.

"You need to slow down or I'm going to come much too fucking soon," Devil nearly snarls, his body vibrating beneath me.

I look up at him from under my lashes, refusing to unseal my lips around him. I want to keep him in my mouth until I've managed to take everything I can. That's something else Devil makes me that I've never been before... *Greedy.*

I try to hold his gaze as I swallow his cock down, trying to take all of him—even knowing it's impossible. He stretches my mouth impossibly and all too soon he's at the back of my throat and I'm forced to stop. I slide back up, moistening his shaft with a mixture of my mouth and his own cum. His cock shines as I let his head free from my mouth, for just a second, right before gliding back down.

Devil gathers my hair in one of his hands and I look to see him staring at me, taking in everything I'm doing. The pleasure on his face is enough to make me want more, try harder to make him lose control.

"Fuck, Angel. You're beautiful," he groans.

He doesn't put pressure on my head, which I kind of expected with his hold on me. Instead, he lets me keep control as I run my tongue over his shaft and bring him closer to the edge. I use my free hand to massage his balls. They're warm, almost hot to the touch, and I'm surrounded by the musky scent of Devil and it feels like heaven.

I'm so wet I can feel my juices dripping and sliding—painting the insides of my thighs. I don't think I've ever been this turned on before and Devil's not even touched me... at least not sexually. I continue sucking him, squeezing his cock tight with both my mouth and my hand. Devil pulls a little tighter on my hair and I cry out from pleasure.

"I'm going to come, Angel."

"Yes..." I moan around his thick shaft, because that's what I want. I want his cum shooting out of his cock, sliding down my throat and out of my mouth. I want to know that I made him lose control, took him to the edge and made him explode. Just the thought of it makes me feel like the most powerful woman ever born.

"Take your top off. I want to see my cum running down your neck and over your breasts. I want you painted in my cum," he cries, his voice hoarse.

I'm already clawing at my own shirt, because his words are exactly what I want. It's almost as if he looked inside of me and could see what I wanted. I have to let go of his cock to finish getting the shirt off of me. I whimper in disappointment as he literally rips the top off of me, throwing it crazily across the bed.

"Please," I whimper when he makes it impossible to slide my lips back down on his cock again right away.

Instead, he aims his cock at the valley between my breasts, painting his juices on my chest so his pre-cum makes me slick and wet.

"I'm going to titty-fuck you soon, Angel. Your tits are too fucking perfect not to do it," he warns, or hell, maybe that's a promise.

All I know is that I'm done waiting. I grab his cock and move to take control again. I take him back into my mouth and I've barely made the complete stroke until I hear his groan, signaling his climax is coming. His body stiffens and I squeeze his cock as I stroke him again with my mouth. His cum releases and slides down my throat. I can't keep all of it in, can't swallow it fast enough, but I try.

I feel Devil's hand tighten into my hair again as he comes. I hear his groan of pleasure that is almost anguished and then I hear words that make me feel…too many things to decipher.

"Torrent," he cries, my name never sounding sweeter. "God, baby… don't stop. Hold on to me… never stop holding on to me."

Maybe he's talking about right now, but it feels like more and I find myself hoping he really means more…

DEVIL

"**W**hy are you pouting?" Torrent asks and I frown at her. I'm not pouting, but I don't especially like the fact she didn't let me reciprocate earlier. I hate the fact that I'm getting ready to leave her too.

"I'm not pouting. I just don't want to leave you. Besides, I don't see why I couldn't make you feel good too," I mutter and fuck it, maybe I am pouting.

"Because you said yourself you need to get out of here and go check on Diesel and let him know you'll be staying in town. You have things to do. I'll be fine. Honestly, I know I'm cautious around Wolf, but that's for *your* sake, not mine. I'm perfectly safe here. I'm going to clean house and relax a bit. I might get one of the boys to ride me into town to get some groceries."

I frown. I don't understand why she can't see what is clear to me. The fact that she feels the need to have one of Wolf's men run her into town is bad enough. The fact that she doesn't think she's being extra cautious around Wolf at all times is so much worse. I'm beyond knowing how to make her realize what she's doing. But the fact she wanted me in her bed, that she gave me her mouth so sweetly this morning… I'm hoping that means that she will break away from him in time. There's a chance her confidence in Wolf isn't misplaced, but I have a feeling it is. It doesn't matter; I'll deal with the motherfucker on my own… I have to make sure that none of it touches Torrent.

"Am I your man or not, Torrent?" I ask, gently. I'm pushing, I know it, but I can't stop myself.

She blinks up at me. Her face loses a little of its color, indicating that my question jarred her, despite me trying to go easy.

"Am I your woman?"

"Absolutely. You're fucking right you are, Angel."

She studies me for a minute and closes her eyes.

"Then yes, you are—"

"Then we walk out of here together. You get on the back of my bike and I'll take you to the store," I tell her. I want to tell her I'll take her back home with me, but I'm not sure she's ready to hear that right now.

"I want that, Logan, I do, but—"

"Then we do it. It's not going to get any easier, Torrent. It's best we come out now and face it head on. This hiding shit is not who I am."

She looks more than a little panicked, but she doesn't back away from me. She brings her hand up and gently curves it around my neck while another hand rests against my heart, feeling it beat. She goes up on her tip toes and I tilt my head down so I'm closer to her.

"We only have to hide until Wolf comes back. I'll tell him, Logan. I promise. But I owe it to him that he hears this from me, not one of his men," she says.

I bite down my argument. It wouldn't do any good, and I made a decision early on to handle Torrent carefully. That hasn't been the wrong call. I'll let her have this. That son of a bitch will be back soon, and when he is, all bets are off. I'll let her tell him, but she'll tell him with me there. Torrent might have faith in him, but I sure as fuck do not.

"I'll be back at dark," I grumble.

"You don't have to sound so happy about it."

"I don't think you understand how much I really *dislike* the fact that you're not leaving this place with me, Torrent."

"I'm picking up on that, Logan," she says, laughing. She steps into my arms and pulls me to her, linking her arms around my back. "It's going to be okay, you know. You'll see. I have to make Wolf understand how much I lov—care about you. He only wants what's best for me."

"That's me, Torrent. Don't you start doubting that and second guessing your decision," I tell her and maybe that's my biggest fear. I don't have the best track record with women. I've steered away from relationships with everything in me. Torrent is the first woman that's made me want a relationship and I'm claiming her. There won't be another woman after her. She's all I want.

I need to make her mine.

"I won't. I promise, Logan," she says, pulling away enough so she can look at me. "Thank you for not giving up on me."

"I don't think that's possible, Angel. Give me your mouth. If you're going to send your man away without the taste of you on his tongue, the least you can do is kiss me."

"You're horrible," she whispers, leaning up to kiss me.

I take her mouth slow, memorizing everything about it like it will be my last time ever touching her. I don't know why I feel so desperate when it comes to Torrent, but right now that's the over-riding emotion.

"Tonight," I promise her and she nods her head in agreement.

I turn away to the window I used the night before, when something sticks in my head so I ask.

"Are you on the pill?"

"What?" she asks, coloring but I can see she's trying not to laugh.

"Are you on the pill?" I ask again.

"And if I wasn't?"

"Then I'm going to need to bring some rubbers with me tonight, but for the first time in my life I really don't want to use them. So tell me, Angel. Are you on the pill?"

"You don't want to use a rubber?" she asks, clearly shocked.

"Fuck no. I plan on yours being the last pussy I sink inside of and the last thing I want around my cock separating us is latex."

"I… I don't think I know what to say to that. You plan on me being… You…"

"Torrent, in case you haven't figured it out yet, I've always been in this thing with you for the long haul. If you think after getting a taste of you that I'm going to let you go now, you need to think again."

"I'm in it for the long haul too, Logan."

"Good to know. So, can you answer me please? Do you take the pill?"

"Well no, but I mean, I have birth control. I could never remember the pill, so I took umm… other measures," she shrugs.

"Good enough, unless it's dangerous. We might want kids one day and you don't want to do anything that might hurt those chances. We can talk about it later."

"I… uh… Okay," she says, clearly confused.

"My number is programmed into your phone. You call me if you need me. I'll be here so quick you will think I never left," I promise her.

"When did you program your number into my phone?"

"While you were sleeping," I grin. "So don't hesitate to call."

"I won't."

"Good girl," I tell her and then hike my damn body up and through the window. I thought about using the back door but I think they have every entrance monitored—the assholes aren't smart enough to worry about a random window on the side of the house. "Hey, Torrent?"

"Yeah?" she asks, looking through the window.

"My number's stored under Torrent's Sex Slave." I grin with a wink, and then I sprint toward the tree line before Wolf's men can see me. I hear Torrent laughing in the background and it makes me smile. I love that I make her happy. It's something I want to do the rest of my life.

DEVIL

"*Y*ou have the look of a man that's been knee-deep in pussy all night," Diesel says when I shut off my bike. We're in the parking lot of the hotel and it's clear Diesel is anxious to leave. I feel bad that he didn't yesterday. I know that he hates being away from Ryan for this long.

"Wish I could say the same about you," I tell him, and wish I could. Since Violet fucked him over, Diesel has had it with women. He keeps saying he's going to get laid, but he never does. I don't want to say he runs from pussy, but he sure as hell turns his back on it.

"Where's Torrent at now, then?" he asks and that tension I've been feeling since I left her creeps back in.

"It's complicated," I tell him, rubbing the back of my neck.

"What the fuck does that mean?"

"It means she wants to have a heart-to-heart talk with Wolf before we go public."

"Jesus. Are you sure you're Devil and didn't switch places with Skull or someone? Seems like you're letting your woman call too many fucking shots," Diesel growls.

"Yeah, I know. She's...fuck, man, she's been through a lot. I haven't got the story out of her yet, but I've seen her nightmares and they're nothing to laugh at."

"Just don't get caught with your dick in your hands on this, Devil. I get the feeling Wolf has secrets," Diesel warns and I get the same vibe, so it doesn't make me real happy to have it confirmed.

"I take it you're not going back today," Diesel says.

"I can't, man. I'm going to do my best to convince Torrent to head out our way—with me."

"What if she doesn't? Women can be funny. This is where she's lived her whole life. What are you going to do if she doesn't, Ese?"

I think that question over. I honestly don't know the answer. I'm happy in the Savage crew. I don't want to live here. I love Torrent and I don't want to give her up. I love my club too. It's a choice I'm hoping I never have to make.

"I'll cross that bridge when and *if* I have to," I tell him. I think when Torrent finds out how fucked up Wolf is, she will leave. I have this feeling that he's going to show his true colors sooner rather than later.

"Fair enough. Fury should be here soon. I called him when your girl showed up yesterday. I'll head out when he gets here."

"I don't need a damn babysitter, Diesel. I can watch my own back. You take Fury home with you."

"You need someone to—"

"Listen, man. Of the two of us, you have more enemies after you than I do. You can't deny that," I tell Diesel. I'm also being serious. I know he hates it, but Diesel needs someone watching over him and his son 24/7.

"That's why I've come to a decision," he says and I get a horrible feeling in the pit of my stomach. I know what's coming. It's written all over his face. I want to tell him to fucking forget it, I want to yell at him, but I know it won't do any good.

"You're leaving the club," I respond, knowing the truth, hating it, but not running away from it.

"I need to go away with Ryan. At least for a while, until I figure out why Vicky is trying so damn hard to get my kid."

"I don't know if that's smart. It hasn't been that long ago that they took Ryan and left you for dead beside the road. I still remember the call I got when I was with Beast and Hayden. It was pure luck the state police pulled that sorry bitch over and recognized Ryan from the Amber Alert."

"Yeah, I know and don't think I'm not still having nightmares about it. I can't help but think this is club related. Not to mention the fact that because I'm tied to the club they know exactly where to find me. If I disappear with Ryan, so does any chance Vicky and whoever is helping her has of finding us."

"Someone needs to kill that fucking bitch," I growl, rubbing the back of my neck.

"That's a fucking fact and one I keep praying for, but I don't think God really listens to my prayers."

"Well, you're praying for someone's death. I don't know all the rules in the Bible and shit, but pretty sure that's against them," I tell him with a smile I don't really feel.

"Whatever," he sighs, looking damn tired.

"When are you leaving?"

"Today—"

"I don't mean here—I mean the club. When are you disappearing with Ryan?"

"As soon as I get back. I've already told Crusher. He's not real happy, but he understands."

"Fuck. You'll be gone when I get back."

"Yeah."

"Will we be able to get in touch with you? How in the fuck are we supposed to know you're okay?"

"I don't want to tell anyone. I trust you guys, but the more that know, the better chance for a leak. Crusher will know; he can find me if I'm needed," he says and his answer pisses me off. Crusher is a good man, and as Diesel's VP I understand why he might be the one to know. But fuck, the rest of us men were around when Crusher was a member of the Kentucky Chapter of the Savage Brothers. I don't tell him that shit. I've never had a kid; I couldn't know how I'd react in Diesel's shoes.

I'm not happy though.

Nothing about any of this shit with Diesel, or the fact that Torrent wouldn't leave with me today, makes me happy.

Nothing about it at all.

TORRENT

"*I* was beginning to wonder if you were going to show up," I grin, running into Devil's arms. He catches me and pulls me up into his body, kissing me until I can't catch my breath.

"Sorry, Angel. It's been a bad day," he says and when we break apart I notice the tension on his face.

"What's going on?" I ask him, almost afraid to know.

Devil rubs the back of his neck, a move I've noticed happens often when he is frustrated. I take his hand and lead him into the den. I don't use this room often, mostly because my father always used it as kind of an office. I much prefer the living room because of the open feel and the many windows. But, windows are not good with Devil in the house and too many prying eyes close by. I have blinds drawn, but I don't want to take a chance. Once we get to the den, I lead him over to the sofa. He sits and I slide in behind him, immediately massaging his shoulders and neck. He hasn't answered my question yet, but I don't push him. I want him to tell me when he's ready.

"That feels like heaven," he groans, letting his head drop forward.

"You're so tense," I tell him and it's completely true. I can feel the way his muscles are knotted up under my fingers and I work to try and get them to relax.

"Diesel left today," he says, but I can't figure out why that has him so upset. My fingers fumble a little as a thought occurs to me.

"Did you... I mean do you wish you had gone back too?" I ask, and he looks over his shoulder at me.

"Why do you ask that, Angel?"

"Well, you're clearly upset and..."

"I'm worried about him, Torrent. He's going through some stuff. He's worried about his boy."

"He's the one whose ex was trying to get the boy back, right?"

"Yeah. There's something going on there. Diesel thinks an old enemy is behind it."

"And not his ex?"

"Someone is bankrolling that bitch. If not she wouldn't keep at it."

"Oh... What's he going to do?"

"He's leaving the club, Angel."

"Leaving?"

"He's stepping down as president and taking his child and going dark."

"But... I mean, is that safe? Wouldn't it be better to have his club behind him?"

"Fuck, baby. I don't know. That didn't work out great for your dad, did it?"

I try to keep my reaction from him, but I can't stop the pain his question causes. My heart hurts.

"Christ. I'm an asshole," Devil growls, turning around.

"No. It's fine. You're right," I respond, trying to reassure him. I'm feeling self-conscious, and like a big baby.

"I'm a stupid asshole," he says again, and he gathers me up in his arms and pulls me into his lap.

"It's fine, Logan. I promise."

"It was insensitive. I'm worried about my brother, but that's no reason to hurt you."

He squeezes me tightly and kisses my temple. I make my body relax. I know he didn't mean anything. Devil would never hurt me.

"You're just worried about your friend. It's my fault, isn't it?"

"Of course not. Why would you say that?"

"If it wasn't for me, Logan, you would have traveled back with him. He's traveling home alone and that's dangerous."

"He's got someone watching his back—at least from a distance."

"What's that mean?"

"Diesel had another member come up to watch my back while I was here so he could go home. I talked with him and we both agreed Diesel needed more protection than I did. So he's following him back and once Diesel gets settled, he'll come back—if I'm still here."

"You're thinking of leaving?" I ask, trying not to be too needy, but I can literally feel myself panic at the thought of Devil not being here.

"I have a life back home, Torrent. You know that. It's a life that I like. I have a family there."

"Oh…"

"That said, I'm hoping you will think of coming home with me."

"You want me to…"

"I told you I'm in this for the long haul. You had to know I wanted you to come home with me, Torrent."

"I guess I never thought about it…"

"Then maybe you should," he says and my heart kicks into overdrive. "Would you be willing to come back home with me?"

"I… I guess I never realized how complicated a relationship between us would be."

"Torrent—"

"I'm not saying no, Logan. I'm not. I'm just thinking maybe we pick our battles one at a time."

"Wolf," he says and I nod.

"I think that's the biggest thing, don't you?"

"Have you heard from him any more?"

"He's planning on being back in town in two days," I tell him and saying that out loud makes me nervous.

"Good. I want him back here and things out in the open. I got to tell you, Angel, I'd do anything for you, but I'm getting damn tired of sneaking around to see you. It's a pattern we've done way too much of."

I can't argue with him. At the same time, I can't help being nervous about the future.

Can I move away from everything to be with Devil? Everything I ever shared with my father is here...

Can I leave my past behind to have a future with this man?

DEVIL

"Now you're the one that's quiet, Angel," I whisper into the dark room. I'm lying in bed with Torrent and it's been a good night, but definitely subdued. I'm worried about Diesel and I know Torrent has a lot on her mind—most of which is my fault. There's a chance I pushed her too hard tonight, but it had to be done. She can't hide from the truth forever, and I think that's what she is doing.

She curls back into me, kissing the side of my neck and I guess I should be glad that she hasn't pulled away from me. I'm not sure how I would have handled that. I'm trying to handle Torrent gently, but I'm not this man—the man who sneaks around to see his woman. I'm too fucking old for this shit.

"I'm... not looking forward to what needs to be done."

"Torrent—"

"No. I mean it's okay. I may not like it, Logan, but I know I need to take control back. I know it has to happen. I'm dreading it and that's allowed, right?"

"Yeah, Angel. That's allowed," I tell her, sighing because I hate that I can't make all of this right for her. Torrent has been through so much and I think before this is over, she'll have to face the truth that Wolf is not the man she thinks. She'll have to have her eyes opened to see that he's playing on her sorrow and emotions to control her. Torrent is a smart woman, part of her already knows, but knowing it and recognizing the pattern you are in are two completely different things.

"What I feel for you, Logan… It's real. I promise," she whispers sweetly.

That's when I've decided we have had enough seriousness for the night. I've let my worry over Diesel and the pressures of being here with Torrent, when I should have my boy's back, bleed through when I shouldn't have. There are times that I forget everything Torrent has been through. I don't even know all of it, I've not asked her to talk with me about it and she's clearly not dealing with it and pushing it into the back of her mind. Eventually she will have to work through it, but for now I need to remember she's got a lot to deal with—a lot more than the fact she has two men in love with her.

I haven't told her I love her, but the emotion is there. She had me from the very beginning. I don't know Wolf's game, but I know mine. I'm in this for Torrent. I want her back home with me. I want her by my side. I want her on the back of my bike and in my bed.

Fuck… I want babies with her.

"How real are we talking?" I ask her, pushing my heavy thoughts away. I pull her body over mine, her legs sliding to my sides as she straddles me. She looks down into my face, her hair falling around her. Even in the darkness her beauty shines through.

"What are you talking about now?" she asks and I can literally hear the smile on her lips. This is what I want for Torrent…

Happiness.

"You said what you feel for me is real, I'm kind of wondering how real."

"I have no idea what that means," she laughs.

I let my fingers hook the end of her T-shirt and tug on it.

"When a woman cares for a man very much, it causes her clothes to come off," I instruct her.

"I thought that was tequila?"

"Well, that too. But when a woman has fallen under a man's spell, there are certain signs to watch out for."

"Like what?" she giggles.

"Well, first she has an uncontrollable urge to kiss her man. She'd rather have his kiss than air in her lungs."

My voice is stern, filled with a seriousness as I joke with her. I slowly let the pads of my fingers splay out against the warm skin of her stomach.

"Oh no," she gasps.

"What's wrong, my Angel?"

"I think I may have symptom one, because I really want your lips on mine much more than I want to breathe," she whispers. I don't know if she realizes it or not but she's grinding slowly against my body, her hips moving in a slow, seductive dance that is designed to take me to heaven.

"Maybe you're mistaken. We should kiss to see if you're really that desperate," I tell her, already leaning up into her. She bends down and gives me a kiss, one that's wet, playful, full of desire for more. Her tongue traces my bottom lip and then slides inside. That's as much as I can allow and then I take over the kiss. I push into her mouth, needing her so much my body is vibrating with it. I plunder her mouth, memorizing it, praising it… *worshipping it.*

When we break apart, we're both winded and Torrent's breathing is so ragged the sound echoes in the room.

"Definitely have symptom one," she whispers, her voice trembling. "What's symptom two?"

"That's where the hunger is so bad, your clothes have to come off."

"I think you already have this illness, Logan. You're naked," she whispers, making me grin.

"I've had it since I first saw you, Angel. I've just been waiting for you to catch up."

She leans back and takes off her T-shirt, flinging it to the floor.

Christ.

There are few things in life that can steal a man's breath. The sight of Torrent sitting astride of me, her breasts free, a smile on her lips and her hair falling around her face softly is definitely one of those things.

"I think I'm starting to catch up to you," she whispers, her fingers moving over my chest, rubbing the hair she finds there, and teasing me.

"Not quite yet," I tell her and my fingers grab the silky material of her panties.

"No?" she asks.

I stretch the fabric tight until it gives. I rip it in two places and then pull it away from her body. I groan because once she settles back against me, my cock slides between the lips of her wet pussy, welcoming it against her heated center. I need inside her, but this teasing is almost too good to stop.

"That's better. Much better. I'd say we're almost ready to see if you have the third symptom now," I groan as her fingers grab one of my nipples and pulls. I bring my hands up her stomach to palm her breasts, squeezing them, kneading gently. Her hips move back and forth, as she begins to grind against the ridge of my cock, coating me in her sweet cream.

"I thought clothes were supposed to fall off... not be ripped off." She moans the words as her nails dig into my skin and she grinds harder on me. If I don't take control soon, she's going to come and I don't want that, not like this. When she comes, it's going to be with my cock buried deep inside of her so I can feel every fucking delicious second of it.

"I'm definitely farther advanced than you, baby. I couldn't wait any longer."

"What's the last symptom?" she whimpers, her head falling back, her hips moving faster and harder.

I grab Torrent, stopping her from moving and causing her to let out a soft, long wail of need and disappointment that makes my cock jerk against her.

I lose sight of our game, hunger and need fueling through me with the force of a rocket.

"On your knees, Torrent. Get up on your damn knees," I order her. She groans, but does as I ask.

Fuck, she's as eager as I am.

I circle my hand around the base of my dick. I'm drenched in the juices of Torrent's pussy. Christ, it's going to feel like fucking paradise to be inside of her. I help guide her down on my cock, my eyes closing as the head squeezes into her tight entrance.

"Oh, damn. You feel so good, Logan," she whispers, sliding further down on me. She takes me slowly. I can feel inch by inch as her greedy little cunt swallows my cock. The inside walls of her pussy quiver around my shaft and once she takes me completely, she sits there, not moving.

It's a delicious torture.

"You okay, Angel?"

Torrent opens her eyes, and even in the darkness there's light coming from the hall and I see her face clearly. This is one of those times a man will never forget. If I live to be a hundred, or live a million other lives, this will be a memory I carry with me every second possible.

"I've been waiting for this for a long time, Logan. I've been waiting for you," she whispers. "I love you."

I wasn't expecting the words. They shake me to my core. They are the spark thrown on a keg of gun powder. There's no holding back now. I lean up to take her mouth. Before I do, I growl against them.

"Ride me, Torrent. Ride me."

I take her mouth roughly then, grinding her breasts against my chest as hard—if not harder—than she's grinding that pussy. She's taking us both to heaven and it's never been better in my life. This right here is why I put up with all the bullshit. This is why I kept coming back.

Torrent.

She's the reason. She's my world.

This woman is everything.

That's my last sane thought as I reach down and massage her clit, making her go off like the Fourth of July and emptying myself deep inside of her.

She's everything.

TORRENT

*T*wo days of pure bliss. That's exactly what I've had with Devil. He's not left. I love that I go to sleep with him and I wake up with him. I know the peaceful happy times are coming to an end shortly. They can't help but stop, because Wolf is coming back tomorrow. Devil is pushing for me to tell him. He hates hiding. He's ready to be done with it all. He also wants me to come back with him. That makes me nervous, but there's really not much here for me now. The clubhouse and my father's buddies are not my family. With the exception of Wolf, it's not like I've been close to any of them. I blame them for my father's death. If they had been quicker, if they had stopped him from trying to do it all himself, my father might still be alive. Someone inside, someone they chose to be part of their group, betrayed my father. What if Crash had an accomplice? What if there are more traitors? I have so many questions and I really don't have answers. Most of all…

Except for Wolf, I don't trust any of them.

"What are you thinking about over there, Angel?"

I'm sitting on top of the breakfast bar, Devil is sitting on a stool in front of me and we're sharing an overfilled plate of sausage, scrambled eggs and pancakes. For some reason, Devil wants to hand feed me. I could feed myself, but I like him constantly touching me, so I'm not about to argue.

"I'm thinking that things are going to change soon," I tell him. I have to wonder if he can hear the fear in my voice. What if once we get back on the other side of the state, what if when we settle in Jelico, where Devil says he has a house—everything changes? What if Devil grows bored with me? What if it doesn't work out? I told him that I love him last night. I hadn't planned on it, but I did. He didn't say it back. What if he doesn't feel as strongly for me?

"That's good though, Angel. Things can't stay the same. We have a life to start living and as much fun as I've had with you the last few days, I'm really not one to live hidden from the world."

"I guess that means I can't kidnap you and keep you in the basement."

"You have a basement?" he asks, surprised.

"A storm cellar really. It's connected to the club. We don't get tornadoes often, but they do happen."

"Good to know. I'll make sure I don't let you lure me down dark stairs," he says with a wink.

"Well, the trap door is in the den, under my father's desk, but I promise it's very well lit, and... there's a king size bed in my part of the shelter..."

"Now we're talking," he laughs. "You're going to have to stop getting that sad look in your eyes, Angel. My heart can't stand it." He reaches up to smooth his thumb along my jawline. I look down at him and do my best to give him a full smile.

"I'm fine. Just having a few memories of my dad. You didn't get to meet him, but I think he would have liked you, Logan."

"Not sure about that, but I could have given him one promise that he might have liked," he answers.

"What's that?"

"I would have told him that I'd bust my ass every damn day I'm alive to make sure his daughter smiles and is happy."

"You definitely make me happy," I assure him.

"What are we doing today?" he asks. "Is there something you want to do before we talk to Wolf tomorrow? Are you packed and ready to leave?"

"I haven't packed yet. Will we really need to leave right away?"

"I'm afraid so, darlin'. I got a call from Fury and Diesel had a part on his bike go out. He'll be back home tomorrow, though, and the men are staging an intervention."

"An intervention?" I ask, confused.

"To show him that he needs the club, that we are stronger together than apart," he says and I think over his words and close my eyes at the bittersweet feeling that envelopes me. "Hey now, what's that look for?"

"What?" I ask, opening my eyes to look at him. "It's nothing really. It's... Well, if Dad had men like that around him, maybe he would still be alive."

"I thought you said he had Wolf? That they were really close."

"Well yeah, but there was a leak in the club, so Dad felt mostly alone. If he had the support that your friend Diesel has..." I stop talking and end with a shrug.

"Things would have been different," he finishes. And I nod in agreement.

"Things would have been different," I whisper and Devil leans up and kisses me.

"Have I told you how much you mean to me?" Devil asks and my heart skips a beat in my chest. Will he tell me he loves me? If I knew that some of my nervousness about leaving here would ease. I know the word love is just that... *a word*, but still... It'd be nice to hear it, to have it returned since I've already told him that I love him.

"No... but I really would—"

I stop when there's a knock at the door. My gaze locks with Devil's and now my heart speeds up for a different reason.

"Tor! Baby, you in there?" I hear Wolf yell.

"Shit," I hiss and Devil frowns. "Wait a second!" I scream out, wincing at the panic I hear in my own voice.

"Okay, hurry. I'm dying to see you. You owe me a date!" Wolf yells back.

Crap. Crap. *Crap!*

"Looks like it's time to tell Wolf," Devil says, standing up.

"No!" I hiss and that panic is definitely full-fledged terror right now.

"No? What the fuck, Torrent? We've talked about this," Devil growls. I have visions of him ignoring what I want and stomping to the door. That's followed closely by visions of Devil dying because Wolf kills him.

Shit!

"I know! I know! But we can't tell him like this! You're barely dressed! I owe it to Wolf to be more… *delicate.*"

"The fuck you do," he growls and I know the situation is about to get out of control.

"Please? Hide this one last time. Let me get rid of Wolf and set up a time later to talk with him. I promise I will, I have to work up to it."

"Motherfucker, Torrent. It's never going to be the perfect time," he barks. "I've had enough of this shit!"

I wince, because Devil is laid back—easygoing. He's never been hateful around me, especially not directed at me. I know he's close to the edge and I don't want to lose him. I've got to have a little more time to prepare. *I know Wolf.* If I blindside him like this, things will be so much worse than they need to be.

"Please?" I beg again. "This will be the last time I ask you to hide, but please, *please* do this for me, Devil."

Something goes over Devil's face then. I don't know what it is, but it's not good. He doesn't even respond to me. He stomps off and I take a deep breath, watching him go. I hope I can smooth this over once I get rid of Wolf. Somehow I think that's going to be a really big job.

I might need a miracle.

DEVIL

*M*otherfucker!
What if I've read this all wrong?

It didn't escape my attention earlier that when Torrent was begging me for more time, that she slipped and called me Devil.

She didn't call me Logan. She didn't touch me, or talk to me like I was her man. She begged me, like a man she was afraid of and she called me...*Devil.*

I stomp down the hall, like a fucking idiot. I ought to go out there and have it out with that son of a bitch. When did I become this man? A man who lets his woman put his balls in a jar and call the fucking shots?

"Damn baby! I thought you were going to leave me out there all day. Come give me a hug."

I listen to Wolf and I clench my hand in a fist to keep from killing the son of a bitch.

"Wolf! You're home early," Torrent says and I have to wonder if Wolf can hear the panic in her voice as well as I can. I take pleasure in knowing she doesn't call the bastard by his name—only his road name. Then I remember that she called me Devil and the good feeling I was enjoying is gone.

212

"Couldn't stay away from my girl any longer. Did you miss me, baby?" he asks.

Not for a minute, motherfucker. She was too busy begging for my dick.

"Of course I did. I was...well, I've been thinking about things and I was hoping we could talk."

"I hope it has been good thoughts," Wolf jokes.

Keep joking, you son of a bitch. I'll make sure I give you all the details to really laugh it up.

"Well, I think it is. I've been thinking things over and I think I know what will make me happy."

There's a minute of silence and I have to wonder if the asshole is starting to get a clue. Maybe the fact Torrent is wearing my T-shirt has caught his eye by now. I doubt it has dawned on Torrent. She had her pajama shorts on under it, but you can clearly see she's wearing a black T-shirt and it's clearly a man's too. In fact, it's the same one I was wearing at Dodger's wake. Will he notice? I hope to fuck the bastard does.

"I've only ever wanted your happiness, Torrent. You know that," Wolf responds.

"I know, Wolf. I've always known that. Do you think we can have dinner together? I'd like to talk to you about some decisions I've made," Torrent says and I grin.

I grin really fucking big.

"I have some shit to catch up on. But we could have dinner tonight if you want, or maybe tomorrow would be better?" Wolf responds, and yeah the asshole knows what time it is. He's gone from anxious to have time with Torrent to putting her off.

"Tomorrow would be awesome!" Torrent is so relieved at having one more day before she has to tell Wolf, I doubt she even realizes the change in him. I do and I can almost feel his anger brewing.

I listen as Wolf talks with my woman and thankfully for him, he doesn't try to kiss her. Just the same, I don't breathe easy until the asshole leaves. I walk back into the kitchen and adjoining living room. Torrent is leaning against the closed front door, staring at me and looking really nervous.

I plant my feet apart and I have my arms crossed at my chest. Torrent and I are going to have this shit out right here and now.

It's time Torrent sees the man I really am and she's never calling me Devil, damn it. To Torrent I am Logan.

Spent the majority of my life being called Devil and right now I hate that fucking name and all because Torrent used it. Damn woman is driving me crazy.

TORRENT

"**You**re mad," I whisper, and that's probably the understatement of the century. Devil is fuming. You can literally feel his anger in the room and it's so thick you can cut it with a knife.

"And here I was worried you didn't have a brain in that pretty little head of yours," he responds.

I blink at his harsh words. Devil has never talked to me like that. As much as I understand that he's upset—maybe even has a right to be that way, I still don't appreciate it.

"That's not nice."

"My woman pushed me out of the room and let another man touch her. I'm not feeling real *nice* right now, Torrent."

"Oh stop! It was just a hug!"

"From a man who wants between your legs!" he yells back, and I blanch as the force of his anger is hurled in them.

"Please stop. You're being ridiculous—"

"You need to shut up right now, Torrent. So help me God, if you try to tell me I'm being ridiculous right now, I won't be responsible for what I do to you."

I feel fear skittering down my back, but I do my best to ignore it. This is Devil; he wouldn't hurt me.

Unless it's with words.

"But it is. You know it's you I love Devil."

"That right there!" he explodes, and I jump because his voice is so loud and raw.

"What?" I cry. I'm trying to keep it together, but the way Devil is acting, his yelling and the *hate* coming off of him, combined with Wolf being back, has me so nervous that I can't catch my breath. I haven't been this panicked since I was chained and treated like a dog. I've done everything I could to bury those memories and the helplessness they make me feel. Devil is bringing them all back right now and I'm having trouble holding onto my sanity.

"When in the hell did I become Devil?"

"What? I don't understand. That's your name and—"

"Not to you! Not to you, Torrent. With you I've always been Logan—*always*, Torrent. Then this son of a bitch gets back in town and you're begging me to keep quiet about our relationship and calling me Devil."

"But that doesn't *mean* anything."

"Really, Torrent? Because from where I'm standing it means a fuck of a lot. In fact, right now I'm starting to wonder if I mean anything to you!"

"I love you," I whisper. I'm losing it. Flashbacks of the men holding me hostage are trying to surface. Their faces are overlapping Devil's and I can't catch my breath.

"You've got a funny way of showing it. I don't know if you realize the kind of man you've hooked, but I don't hide for no-fucking-body. I've let you have your way because you've been through a lot, but it's becoming clearer and clearer that was the wrong way to handle things with you."

"*Logan*, I think we both need to calm down and talk about this like two mature adults."

"You want me to calm down, Torrent?"

"Well, yes. It's not like we should be upset with each other. I *am* telling Wolf. I have to make sure I do it the right way."

"And you think dinner with him is the *right* way to go about it?" he mocks, clearly not happy about that at all.

"Well, yeah. It will give us a chance to be calm and relaxed so I can explain that this thing…"

"I'm not a thing, Torrent. I'm supposed to be your man."

"Quit twisting my words. That's not what I meant. Please Dev—Logan, I love you, I'm giving up everything to be with you…"

"I didn't realize you viewed being with me as giving everything up," he says, and now he's not yelling. Now his words are quiet and cold as steel. Somehow that scares me even more.

"Maybe we should take a break and let our tempers ease before we talk more," I suggest.

"Am I invited to this dinner with you and Wolf?" he asks.

"I… Well…"

"You're not planning on me going at all, are you Torrent?"

"I thought it would go over better if I go alone," I whisper, knowing even as I say it that it's the wrong thing to say to him.

"So you want me to sit on my hands while that fucker takes you to dinner and convinces you that he's the better option?"

"What? No. De—Logan, he can't do that."

"Why not? After all, he has Daddy's seal of approval right?"

"Please stop," I whisper.

"I thought I was involved with a woman, but you're a child playing at being an adult."

"Are you done?" I ask, not sure I can take anymore—not from him.

"You should be careful, Torrent. While you're trying to control everything you might find that your precious Wolf isn't as clean and harmless as you think."

"What does that mean?"

"Just what I said."

"You're being mean now. Does it make you feel good to hurt me, Logan?"

"I guess I should appreciate the fact you remembered my real name this time. Somehow I don't. I'm not being mean, as you put it. Real men, Angel, they don't let you lead them around by the short hairs, no matter how fucking good your pussy is. I've let you have your way too damn long. I'm done chasing you, Torrent. If you want me, then you're going to have to chase me."

"You're leaving?" I ask, absorbing his words that are so harshly spoken, they feel like a physical blow.

"Fuck yeah, I'm leaving. If you want me, you know where to find me."

"Logan—"

"And if you think I'm going out the fucking window this time, you need to think again," he growls. "You can keep my shirt as a souvenir."

I stand while he walks away from me. I hear him rummaging around in my bedroom, probably getting his cut, shoes and his gun. It's not too long before I hear the back door slam so loud I have to wonder if it falls off the hinges.

I stay that way until I can't stand any longer, and then I slide to the floor and let myself cry.

DEVIL

$\mathcal{I}$ stomp out of Torrent's house ready to kill. I probably was too fucking harsh with her, but damn, even a saint has his limits and I've never been a saint. Sometimes when I look at Torrent now she doesn't even remind me of the girl I met in the store giving me sass. She's a shell of that person. Then, other times, when it's just me and her, she's back. I can't figure it out and all I know is I've had it. She's got some decisions to make and I'm done jumping through motherfucking hoops.

The thing about anger—especially when you're lost inside your head with it—is that it makes you stupid. That's the only excuse I have for not seeing the motherfucker who knocked me along the side of my head with a fucking baseball bat. One minute I'm headed into the tree line where I've hidden my bike and the next I'm falling to the ground seeing stars.

I fall hard on the ground. The world is monochromatic—a grayish white all around me. I have a whistling in my ears so loud it's like a roar. I lay there trying to figure out where I'm at and what's happening. I feel wetness running down along the side of my head. It takes the longest time for me to realize that it's probably blood I'm feeling. Slowly the sound dies down and I can hear voices. I look around to try and see faces, but my vision is blurry as hell.

"Stupid ass motherfucker you think you can come onto my land, try to get my girl and live?" I close my eyes as I finally hear the asshole.

Wolf.

Maybe it would have been a good idea to listen to Torrent and use the motherfucking window again. Especially since I was stupid enough not to pay attention to what was going on around me.

"I hope you enjoyed your time with her, because there's going to be nothing left of you when I'm done," he sneers.

I want to respond; I try but all that comes out is a grunt. My tongue feels like it weighs a hundred pounds.

"We got him now, Boss! We got him good!" another man laughs, sounding like a sniveling little kid who needs an ass kicking. "Ow! What did you do that for?"

I really wish I could see. I heard the sound of a fist making contact and I can only assume Wolf beat the asshole. From the muffled sound of his *"Ow!"* I'd say he punched him in the nose.

"Fuck-head. It was your job to make sure Torrent was safe and no one got to her! I left you in charge for a fucking week and I come back to this shit!"

"We've watched the place like a hawk, Boss! I swear! I don't know how he slipped by us," the other guy answers and shit... If I could, I'd laugh out loud. If this is what Wolf has for security, then I need to survive long enough to get my wits about me and then break free. That sounds easy enough, if I could see.

"Shut up, while you're still breathing. If I wasn't worried Torrent would hear the shot I'd finish you along with this asshole right now," Wolf responds. Then I hear some muffled sounds that could be another punch being thrown, I can't be sure. "Red!" Wolf yells.

"Yeah, man?"

"Drag this prick into the cellar. We'll deal with him tonight after I do some recon. Did Gator find out where this son of a bitch has been staying?"

"You mean besides with your woman?" the man he called Red replies.

I blink and I can see the swing of the bat enough to watch "Red" take one to the gut.

"He...has... the...info," Red moans out, one word at a time and gasps in between each.

"Drag him down there. Tie him up from the ceiling. I want to play with him before I send him back to Diesel in pieces."

"Got it."

Just when I think I might be getting less addled, and might try to break free, I feel a blinding pain along the side of my face again. I hear Wolf laughing. I vomit from the pain and claw at the ground, but the blackness is chasing me.

I can do nothing before it overtakes me.

TORRENT

J pull up to the red light and while I wait for it to change to green I check my cellphone for the hundredth time. There's no call, no voicemail and no text from Devil. I know he was mad. I thought he'd go silent for a while, but I didn't think I'd never hear from him again.

I look in my rearview mirror, half expecting Wolf to be behind me. There's no one there, though. When I told him I was driving myself into town, I expected him to argue. He didn't. He didn't even demand I take one of the men with me. I don't understand the change in him, but I'm glad for it right now.

I've been thinking about the fight with Devil and he was right to be upset. I can't be mad at him. I'm all messed up in my mind right now. I didn't realize how much, until Devil forced me to take a hard look at the way I was acting. I've been trying to keep everyone around me calm and happy. The minute they start to show signs of anger... *I panic.* That's when Devil became Devil and *not* Logan. Realistically I need therapy, not for Devil, not for anyone other than me. I need to put my past behind me... and live...

With Devil—*if I can find him.*

I dial Devil's number. The light changes and I press the gas.

"You know what to do."

I listen to Devil's recorded message and I want to cry. I've listened to it way too many times. I called it over and over last night—not because I thought he would answer, because I'm beginning to give up hope he'll ever talk to me again. I listened to it because I really had to hear his voice.

"Logan, it's Torrent. I... I really miss you. I'm sorry. You were right. Please call me."

It's a different version of the same message. One I've left over and over. Devil is either not checking his messages, or ignoring me—maybe both of them.

I throw my phone into the passenger seat and try to pay attention to the traffic. Thankfully the roads aren't crowded today. I take my exit and all too soon I'm sitting in the parking lot of the Golden Woodpecker.

I grip the steering wheel so tight my fingers go pale white. I hate that I'm scared of what comes next, but I am. Still, I make myself get out of the car and walk to the room where Devil is staying.

I knock on the door, but silence is all I get in return.

"Logan please, open up," I call out, knocking again.

"There's no one in there, lady."

I jerk when a guy comes out of the room beside Devil's.

"Oh. I'll wait until he gets back then. Thank you," I answer, feeling embarrassed.

"I don't think he's coming back. He had his bags and said he was headed home."

"He did?" I ask. Before, I felt horrible. Now that feeling is a million times worse.

"Yeah."

"Oh... Okay. Thank you," I whisper, my voice almost silent. I couldn't speak any louder if I wanted to right now.

I can't believe that he'd leave without at least giving me the chance to say goodbye.

I refuse to believe it.

I'm like a robot and go through the motions of going to the front desk. It takes some convincing but I somehow get the manager to let me in Devil's room. I know it's too late, but I just have to see it for myself.

He lets me through the door and I look around at the empty room and I want to cry, but I don't... *not yet.*

"Could I have a second, please?" I ask the guy. He looks at me strangely. He shrugs and walks out, closing the door behind him.

I go and lay on the bed, pulling the pillow into my face and breathe deep. There's not a trace of Devil's scent. I don't smell him at all. Not on the pillow, not on the bed...*Not in this room.*

He's gone.

I'm alone.

He left me...and he's not coming back.

He's given up on me.

DIESEL

"Y ou want to explain to me why in the fuck you are here
and not back in Murfreesboro with Devil?" I growl
at Fury.

"Devil and I decided you were the one who needed to have
your back watched the most. Devil was worried about where your
head was at."

"Jesus Christ! Last time I looked I was still wearing the patch
that said I was president of this fucking crew."

Silence around the table meets me and that's when I know that
Devil has opened his big mouth.

"When were you going to tell us?" Crusher asks, leaning up on
the table to lock gazes with me.

"I hadn't decided yet," I mutter, pushing my hand into my hair
and getting it off of my face.

"Bullshit. If you're going to leave and back out like a punk then
at least have the balls to tell us the truth," Crusher responds.

Anyone else, I'd nail to the wall—with my fist.

Not Crusher. For one, Crusher doesn't take shit. I made him
my VP for a reason. We'd be a pretty even match, but my heart

wouldn't be in hitting the asshole. But, even that's not the reason I don't slap him down.

The reason is guilt.

I'm the reason that Crusher is here. I convinced him to leave Dragon's crew and start over here. He and his old lady both needed it, and I needed someone I could trust to help me build a club that could wear the Savage name proudly. Until we put roots down here in Tennessee and Crusher came, my crew was mostly nomads searching for a home. Crusher was the first piece of the puzzle that made us… a family.

"I'm tired. I've been fighting this unseen enemy for too fucking long. I can't keep it up."

"Leaving isn't going to fix that," Fury answers.

"It might," I respond with a shrug. "The club is the reason I have enemies. It's definitely my enemies that are bankrolling Vicki's madness. She's not smart enough to do this shit on her own. Christ, I know you all mean well, but you don't know what it's like. You see it… but you don't live it every fucking night. I'm tired. I'm bone tired." I lay it out for them, because I'm damn tired of fighting.

"You're not thinking this through," Gunner says. He's a former member of Dragon's crew too. He joined up a few months back. He and Freak couldn't work together anymore. They were brothers in the crew, but they were also brothers in real life. There's a story there and I didn't ask the particulars, I only know that Gunner needed a place to land. With Dragon's blessing I opened my doors. I need men I can trust and Gunner is definitely one of those.

"I am," I argue, but he's not wrong. I'm tired of thinking. I just want some peace.

"If the enemy finds you or Ryan and we're a part of your life, we can help. You leave the club, and the club protection, how in the fuck are we supposed to help you if you get into trouble? We won't know a damn thing about it. Think this through, Diesel, man. Every man in this club would die to protect you and Ryan," Crusher adds.

"I don't want you to. I don't want a single one of my men dying because of my choices."

"Christ, you don't even know if it's your choices that's to blame for this shit."

"Maybe not, but Vicki is my mistake and she's tangled up in this crap. That's definitely on me. It's my mess and it's not the club's place to clean it up," I argue with them all.

I know they all mean well. Crusher, Gunner, Fury... all of them, they care about me. We are a family, so I get they're upset. But this is my life. This is the life of my child. I'm tired of staying here and being a sitting duck—not knowing what to expect. It's time I take control and change up the battlefield.

It might be the wrong move, but fuck, at least it's a move.

"So that's it?"

"That's it," I answer Crusher. He's not happy, it's written all over his face, but he's not going to argue with me any further and I guess I should be thankful for that.

"When do you leave?" Gunner asks.

"Not until we get Devil home safe. He's in some hot water up that way with a girl."

"Jesus, when is that man going to learn to keep it in his pants?"

"This is different. I'll explain later," I tell Gunner, cutting him off. "For now we need to talk to him and I want Fury and at least three of the prospects to head out to help him."

"He didn't let on like there was anything serious," Fury argues. "You sure about this, Diesel?"

"I'm more than sure," I answer, pulling out my cellphone. I frown when the call connects but goes straight to Devil's voice mail.

"Gunner, get Scorpion to do a trace and locate on Devil's phone. It's ringing into voicemail."

"Fuck," Fury growls, probably because he knows Devil is addicted to that damn phone. He would never leave it unwatched.

"Let's forget about me and concentrate on Devil. My gut is telling me he's in trouble, and my gut is rarely wrong."

"Looks like I'm headed back to Murfreesboro," Fury responds.

"We'll be lucky if we all aren't," I tell him once I try Devil's phone and he still doesn't answer.

Something is going on and it's not good. I feel it.

Why can't anything be simple anymore damn it!?!?!?

DEVIL

I know I need to wake up, but the temptation to remain sleeping is strong. I need to stay alert, but I think that may be more than I have in me right now. I can't be sure how long I've been here. A rough guess says not long. I keep drifting in and out, but I don't think it could be over two days.

I know if my club discovers I'm gone they'll stop at nothing to come and save me. The problem is I'll most likely be dead before they know. The only one who might miss me right away is Torrent and after the way we left things, she'll not think anything of me disappearing. I played right into Wolf's hands like some wet-behind-the-ears pup, walking into a slaughter. If I had the energy, I'd be pissed at myself.

The pain in my upper arms, shoulders and even my elbow is indescribable right now. They've roped my wrists and then strung me up on a hook, leaving me about three feet off the floor. That doesn't sound like a lot, but it's left my arms taking all my weight —and right now that's dead weight.

If there's a bright side, I think the bleeding has stopped from my head. It feels dried and tight against my skin now, and my vision is back, though still a little blurry. I have so much pain in other places, it's hard to tell but I think my headache has lessened too.

They've done little more than ignore me since they strung me up, but I know that too is coming to an end soon. There's been talking behind me. I can't hear what they're saying, but I can make out words here and there. There's two distinct voices, so I doubt it's party time just yet. Wolf's not here. He'll want to be the one to finish me off. I know because I'd be the same with him.

I'm not going to get that chance now. It's not that I'm giving up, it's that I'm a realist. My men are hours away and most likely don't even know I'm in trouble. After the way I left things with Torrent, I doubt she does either.

I fucked up there. I always knew my life could get me killed. I didn't take it for granted and I've lived a good fucking life. If I have any regrets at all, it's Torrent. We needed to have it out, but I should have kept my head a little more. I shouldn't have been so damn harsh. I hate that her last memory of me will be…

"Well, boys, it looks like our little doggie has finally woke up."

I blink and slowly bring my gaze to the right. Wolf is standing there leaning on a bat. There's nails sticking out of the sides, and barbed wire too. No wonder I went down like a baby before. That fucker has been watching too much television. Still, I have to say that will be effective. Too bad I can't mention it to Diesel.

"Did you have a nice little nap?" Wolf asks.

"Not really. The accommodations here suck," I answer.

I try to keep my voice cocky if for no other reason than to not give the bastard any satisfaction, but son of a bitch, it comes out weak.

"You hear that, boys? Our little puppy's not comfortable. We'll have to see what we can do to make that better," Wolf says and I close my eyes.

I'm not stupid. I know what's coming. With any luck it will kill me, but I have a feeling whatever Wolf does, it will be slow. He'll want to draw this out.

"Fuck you," I groan as his bat connects with my knees and tears into my flesh.

"Shut up, puppy. I don't have time to talk. I have to hurry. I have a date with my woman in a bit. You remember Torrent, right? While you're hanging here, bleeding to death, I'll be sliding in her bed. I'll make sure to show her exactly how a real man treats a woman," he yells and this time the bat hits me in the stomach. The hit is harder, the nails claw into the skin and the barbed wire holds onto the flesh so that when he pulls the bat away, pieces of my skin are torn away too. The pain is so intense I can't respond to Wolf. I can only scream and prepare for the next hit.

And pray I pass out again soon...

WOLF

"*Y*ou look beautiful tonight, Torrent," I whisper, putting my hand over her smaller one and bringing it to my lips.

She's quiet tonight. I can see she's upset and I know it's over Devil. She'll get over it eventually. She'll have to. Her little boyfriend will soon be dead—if he's not already. There's more pieces of him on my bat than there was left on parts of his body. I got a little carried away. I saw bone on pieces of his leg and it's amazing how great my tool works on the face. The barbed wire cut through beard and all. Pretty boy is not so pretty anymore. *Not that it matters.* He'll never see the outside world again. I'll leave him in pieces and bury those where only the vultures can find his remains.

What I'm not so sure of is Torrent. I've wasted a lot of years on her, only to have her ignore my advances. Then, when she should have turned to me for comfort, she goes to another man. I was intrigued by her and fuck, I've wanted her for a lot of years. It's not the same now.

Before she was a spitfire that made my balls ache and was

begging to be dominated and tamed. Now, she's a shell of the woman she used to be. Part of that is my fault.

Well, not really.

This can all be laid at Crash's feet. That fucker messed so much shit up, I can't even begin to wrap my head around the screw-ups he made. That's why I had to kill him. Well, that and I couldn't be sure he wouldn't let it slip that I was the one behind the plot to kill Dodger. Crash was a loose end; he had to die. Still, the fact he hurt Torrent the way he did... That wasn't supposed to happen.

Torrent was a tool to get to her old man, but she wasn't to be harmed. I wanted her healthy and intact. I didn't want her damaged. I wanted her fire. I wanted to be the one to quench it. Crash fucked all that up for me too. This Torrent holds no fucking appeal, or maybe that's the stink of Devil on her, hiding it. I might give her a go just to see.

Regardless, Torrent is a piece of the puzzle that I need. A lot of Dodger's men, the loyal ones, are suspicious of me. They're not keen about sitting under me as their leader. I don't really give a fuck, but a club can't stand without muscle and it's going to take a while to find men I trust to watch my back in the meantime. If Torrent was my old lady, they'd fall in line. Then, once I had men in place, if they piss me off I'll get rid of them. This club is mine and finally I'm going to see to it that it will be run the way I want it to be. Dodger's fuck-ups with the trafficking cost us some serious money and made enemies we did not need to have. I've smoothed that over, but who the fuck knows with the Koreans? They weren't exactly filled with happiness when I told them Crash and Jin were dead.

I didn't try to save them. They could have pointed the finger at me, but with Crash gone it has definitely been harder finding my footing with them. Chul—the leader—has an American step-brother called King. I've been trying to get him on my side, but he's staying distracted over trying to get his boy from its mother or some shit.

I want kids. Torrent would probably breed some good ones, but I can't help but think they'd be weak now. She has more of her father's blood than I gave her credit for. I was hoping she'd be like her mom. Layla was hot as fire. No man could tame her.

Dodger sure didn't have it in him. That's why she came looking to me. Sweetest fuck I ever had and wild as a damn mink. We were perfectly matched, until she thought she should come clean to Dodger. She wanted to be my old lady. Started to get jealous as fuck and ignored Torrent and Luke completely.

I had to silence her. I gave her a good time before I did it. I let her ride my cock and when she was about to climax, I choked the life out of her. To this day it was the hardest I've ever come in my life.

If only Torrent had a little of her mother's fire...

"Wolf? Are you listening?" Torrent asks, and I jerk myself out of my memories. I've got to concentrate on the here and now. I still have moves I need to make.

"Sorry, baby. It's been a rough day. Running this club was never what I wanted. Some days are harder than others. I sure miss your daddy," I lie.

Torrent's face goes pale, and I contain my smile as she trembles. Her hand reaches out to mine and she holds it tight.

"God. I do too. It's so empty without him here—isn't it, Wolf?"

"It is. I still expect the bastard to come storming in ready to tell me some damn story and make me laugh."

"I keep having nightmares of him. He's trying to tell me something, but I can never understand."

"It's the trauma, Tor. You saw too much. I'm sorry I couldn't save you sooner."

"I owe you so much. More than what I've given you, that's for sure. I need to talk to you about something, Wolf, but I'm... *scared.*"

Fuck... that right there... weakness. The Torrent I wanted

would never admit to being scared. I manage to keep the distaste off my face, but it's not easy. I can't play my hand yet.

Not yet.

"You never have to be scared with me, Torrent. You're always safe with me. You know that. Your father knew that. I will always protect you."

"I know. My father loved you so much, Wolf. You were the only one he truly trusted."

That's because he was a stupid son of a bitch.

"It will be okay, Torrent. You'll heal and I'll be here to help you. Don't keep things inside. I want to be your friend too, you know. I want to be here in any way you will let me. You can tell me anything."

"You might not after I tell you what I…have to tell you," she says and I stop myself from rolling my eyes.

Get it over with, bitch.

"Tell me, baby," I urge.

"I've been seeing… Devil."

I pull back, trying to act like what she's telling me is a shock. I should win a damn Oscar.

"When did this happen, Torrent?"

"While you were away. I went to him to ask him to leave. I was afraid him being here would upset you more and I… I didn't want that."

Maybe she's smarter than I gave her credit for.

"It kind of just…happened, Wolf. I didn't plan it—I swear."

"I thought you promised to give us a real shot, Tor. I love you," I tell her, my voice so full of disappointment and sadness, it's hard not to cackle at the shame that swamps her face.

"I'm sorry," she whispers, her voice so full of guilt, I can't help but find some satisfaction in it.

"So, your decision is made," I answer and then breathe heavily, as if I have any intention of losing gracefully.

"Well, yes. I'm sorry. Of course it's not like it matters anymore. Devil hates me."

"No one could hate you, Tor."

Except for me. I'm getting there faster and faster.

"He does. He left. He went back to his club," she whispers and fuck if the waterworks don't start. I hope I can make it through this fucking dinner without choking her like I did her mother.

TORRENT

I shouldn't be talking to Wolf, I guess. I know that it would upset Devil even more, but he left and I'm alone. I don't have friends. I had my father and his men. Other girls stayed away from me because of my family and those that didn't... they used me to try and get closer to the men. I learned the hard way friendships weren't worth it.

"He left you?" Wolf asks. I can hear the shock in his voice. Maybe he finds it hard to believe, but then he doesn't know everything I've put Devil through. Devil deserved better. I'm surprised he stayed around as long as he did.

"He was upset because I wouldn't let him talk to you. He wanted to tell you about our relationship. I wasn't going to hide it from you, Wolf, I promise. I felt I needed to be the one to tell you. I didn't want to spring it on you. I felt I owed you more than that."

"Well, you were right."

"I was?" I don't know if I'm shocked or confused by Wolf's answer. I didn't expect a man to see my side.

"Of course you were, Tor. We have a special relationship and a lot of years between us. It hurts knowing that you found someone else to make you happy. You know how much I love and care for you. I've made no secret of the dreams I had for the two of us."

"Wolf—"

"It's okay, baby. I just meant, as much as it hurts now, it would have hurt a lot more if you hadn't been the one to tell me."

"That's what I thought. I wanted to make Devil understand, but I couldn't. It's… you're my family, Wolf. You're all I have left. I don't want to lose you."

"You won't lose me, Torrent," he murmurs and then he pulls me in to kiss me gently. There's nothing romantic or sexual about it. It's meant to reassure me and I try to hold on to it. I need Wolf right now. I don't have my father and now… I don't have Devil. Eventually I will get stronger and I won't need anyone again. *Someday…*

"Thank you for being so understanding—especially under the circumstances, Wolf."

He pulls back, and smiles at me, though I think he's still sad.

"Maybe it's because I'm older than this Devil and mature, but it could be because I love you so deeply. All I really want is for you to be happy."

"Devil makes me happy," I assure him. "I have to find him."

"I can't believe he left you, Tor. That's not right. Maybe he doesn't care for you—like you do him."

"He cares. I mean, he's never really said he loves me, but he definitely cares," I murmur, trying not to let the doubts fill me.

"I don't know this Devil enough to tell you either way, Tor. But I do know one thing."

"What's that?"

"Real men don't leave. If it had been me, they would have had to kill me to get me to leave you," he says.

His words make me feel weird… It feels disloyal to Devil. I mean, it's good to hear—I wish Devil was the one telling me that —but, at the same time, Wolf doesn't know what our relationship has been like. He doesn't know the hoops Devil has jumped through for me.

"I—"

"A real man never leaves the woman he loves. It doesn't matter what the argument is about, Torrent."

I think over his words. He's really taken this better than I thought he would. I might be able to keep my friend out of all of this and that makes me feel better. Wolf is the only family I have left and I need him—especially if Devil won't forgive me.

"I need to talk to Devil."

"Torrent, are you sure that's a good idea? It's clear he doesn't want to talk to you. I don't want to see you chasing after someone who doesn't deserve your time."

"I have to, Wolf. I have to know if we can work it out... or if it's over."

"Very well."

"What?" I ask, surprised.

"If you want to see him, I'll take you to his hotel. We can go right after dinner."

"That won't help. Devil checked out of his hotel. I uh... I checked yesterday while I was in town."

"Oh—"

"I should have told you. I'm sorry, Wolf," I rush to tell him.

"It's dangerous, Tor. I'm not sure what went on with Dodger. I've been trying to figure it out and tracking down leads, but until I can explain why the Koreans involved you at all, I don't feel comfortable with you going someplace I don't know."

"I'm a grown woman. I can take care of myself, Wolf."

"But you can't. You didn't listen before and you were kidnapped. Because of that your father lost his life. You need to be more careful, Torrent," he chastises and his words kill me.

They're true, but having them spoken out loud by someone who loves me, destroys me.

"I need to go see him, Wolf."

"See Devil?"

"Yes. I need to face him and at least try to explain everything."

"Torrent, I can't let you go that far on your own."

"Then you can take me. Please? If Devil could hear from you that I've explained everything, it might help. If he could see us together, maybe he would understand."

"Torrent, your father left a mess behind. I can't pick up and leave right now. I only just got back."

"But—"

"Besides, you don't even know if he's there. Devil could be anywhere. You don't know anything about him. He might even have another woman, baby. You need to face the facts. He left you, and a man that could do that without an explanation can't be trusted."

I listen to Wolf and think about what he says. Devil... with another woman...

It feels like I can't breathe. I don't think he would do that. He cares about me. No. There's no way.

I feel certain of that for about a minute. Then I remember how we first met... Devil at a store with a buggy full of condoms, planning to party.

Shit.

WOLF

I plant the seeds where I need to, but I'm growing intensely bored with this damn game. When I get back to the club I'm going to need a bottle of whiskey and definitely play time with some of the girls. Had Devil not stuck his dick where it didn't belong I might have been playing with Torrent tonight. At least I could have stuffed my cock in her mouth to keep from hearing her drone on and on.

A new plan is starting to hatch in my head. If I could make the club believe that Torrent and I were getting married and then kill her and leave her to be found the day of the wedding... I'd gain all the members' sympathy and cooperation and be done with Torrent at the same time.

I sift through the particulars in my mind and almost don't catch what she says next.

"I'm sure he went back to his club. His president was in trouble."

"What kind of trouble?" I ask, thinking it could be useful information. Diesel had the balls to show up at my club and help his brother see a bitch I claimed as my property. Maybe I can add to his *trouble.*

Retribution, motherfuckers... That's the name of the game.

"I'm not sure. Devil mentioned that Diesel had a little boy and the mother kept trying to kidnap him and take him away. They think she has help, maybe. Diesel was thinking an old enemy was trying to get his child to use against him..."

"That can definitely be a weakness exploited. Look at what happened with Dodger and you," I respond, enjoying the look of pain that comes across her face. Now that I think about it, I'm probably the one taking her fire away. I'm controlling her without trying much. It's really... *so easy.*

"Yeah," she whispers. "Devil's gone back home. I know it. They said the last time Vicki tried to get her son, she left Diesel for dead. Devil would have gone to be with his brothers."

"Vicki?" I ask, starting to get more and more interested. It's a long shot, but that name sounds familiar and so does the situation. *Surely it couldn't be that simple.* Then again, the gods might be shining down on me.

"Diesel's ex. Devil told me her name during some of our lunches together during my time at the convent."

"I see... I tell you what, Torrent. Give me a few days to see what I can find out about Devil and if he is back with this crew, I'll get in touch with him for you."

"You will? Even though... Well, I mean..."

"I will," I tell her, squeezing her hand. "I keep telling you, Torrent. It doesn't matter to me how needy you are right now. I care about you. I want to help you."

"I... Thank you, Wolf. That means a lot. You're always here for me," she says, and I pull her into my arms and hug her.

"And I always will be here for you, Torrent. I won't stop until you get everything you deserve," I whisper, my hand brushing her hair. *"Always."*

In my head I'm making plans to have Red get all the information he can on Diesel and his kid. I have a hunch and if I'm right... that solid ground I want with the Koreans just fell into my lap.

TORRENT

I've given Wolf two days now to try and find Devil. Whenever I've asked him about it, he says he's working on it. I'm trying to be patient but the more time that goes by, the more I worry. Something feels... *wrong.*

Yesterday I finally got up the nerve to talk to a therapist. It's going to be a long road, but I think a therapist is a step in the right direction with finding myself again. I haven't told Wolf. I don't know if he realizes how some of his remarks affect me, but they definitely do. I've had one meeting with the therapist, but it went well and she encouraged me to take control of my life again.

I'm going to try and the first step of doing that is to find Devil. If Wolf hasn't gotten anywhere, I'm heading down there today.

I have to.

"What have you found out about Diesel and that kid? Is that the one King is looking for?"

I stop outside of the office when I hear Wolf. At first, I don't understand but he mentioned Diesel's name. I don't know who King is, but Wolf's tone is different than I've ever heard. Something is telling me to listen...

"Yeah, fuck dude, I don't know how you got so damn lucky.

King has a hard-on for this man Diesel. He wants his head on a fucking pike," Red responds.

My heart starts beating double time as I listen. This can't be true...

"That's why he wants the kid? I thought King was looking for—"

"That's it though, man. The kid is King's. Diesel has been raising him as his own for years," Red laughs.

He laughs.

"Shit. I'll give the asshole this, he must have balls of steel. I wouldn't want to piss King off—not with the firepower that motherfucker has behind him."

"Near as I can tell, I don't think Diesel even knows, Boss."

"You're shitting me?" Wolf answers and you can tell he finds everything about this funny.

I don't think I ever knew Wolf. I definitely don't know who this person is.

"Nope. He thinks *he's* the father of that kid. It's kind of hilarious if you think about it. Dumbass has almost died repeatedly defending a kid that's not even his."

"Damn, that fucking Savage crew is stupider than I thought. Let's send King a little happiness," Wolf says and my heart lodges in my chest.

I knew that Wolf didn't like Devil or his crew, but this is so far from the man I know—or thought I knew—that I can't breathe. I lean against the wall, needing it to hold me up, but wanting to do everything I can to keep from being found. The urge to run now is strong. If I can make it to Devil and his club, I might be able to warn Diesel. I don't do that, though. I'm hoping if I keep listening I'll hear what they have planned. That will help Devil and his club more.

"What are you thinking? Kidnap the brat and deliver him to King?" Red asks and he says it so calmly that I get sick to my stomach while listening to him.

"Nah. I don't need that kind of headache—at least not yet. How about we get rid of Diesel for him?" Wolf laughs and I clap my hand over my mouth.

I'm going to be sick.

"Now we're talking. We can head out now."

"Sounds good. Take Grunt and Foley with you. We can trust them to keep their fucking mouths shut. I'd go with you, but today is the day I finish that piece of slab in the storm shelter."

"Thank Christ for that. You've done so much to him I think he's starting to rot. Fucker sure does stink. It's so bad you'd think he was already dead."

"Not yet, but that's definitely coming. I'll finish the job soon as I get back from this meeting with King and his associates."

"You still want a man following Torrent?"

"It's not really needed around here, but if she tries to leave you have them detain her. Feed her some bullshit about the Koreans having a price on her head."

"She'll buy that?"

"She's so damn gullible right now, she'd buy oceanfront property in the fucking desert off of me."

"You got it, Boss. I'll get Lester to do it."

"Sounds good. Let's get rolling. We both need to get this shit done," Wolf says and I fight down panic as I quickly move out of the hall. I duck into a small half bath my father always claimed as his because it was close to his office. I turn the lock on the door and I don't take a breath until I hear footsteps pass on the outside. Then I wait another fifteen minutes before I peek my head outside.

"Hey! Torrent! What are you doing over here?" I look up to see one of my father's men—Daniel or something like that. I don't know him that well. He was always more of a loner. He had an accident, and is now in a wheelchair. He can't ride his bike anymore and the men stopped using his road name because of that. That always seemed horrible to me, but...

Not my monkey and definitely not my circus.

Right now, I have to fight the urge to take off running. I need to act normal, calm and completely in control.

"Hey, Dan... I uh... I was looking for Wolf. I was hoping we'd be able to eat lunch together. His office is empty though."

"Oh yeah. He had a meeting today. Don't know much about it. The men don't exactly tell me shit these days. If you're looking for a lunch partner though, I'm available," he volunteers.

Crap.

"Well... I think I might run into town now. I've been wanting to get my hair done. I'll take a raincheck though?"

"Sounds good. You can let me know," he says, but he's already wheeling away.

I make my steps go slow and measured and I plaster a smile on my face as I make my way out of the club and around back to my dad's house. I need to go check out the cellar. I don't want to... but I've got a bad feeling about what I will find there.

I really hope I'm wrong.

TORRENT

*W*hen I close the door to the house, I lock it. That doesn't feel safe, because I figure Wolf has a key. Suddenly everything I've believed for my entire life is in question. I always thought I was so smart; turns out it is quite possible that I'm an idiot.

No wonder Devil was so upset with me!

I try to think of what I might need, in case I can help whoever is in the cellar. I'm praying it's not Devil, but in my heart I feel like it is. It never made sense to me why Devil would leave without a word and not answer my call. Even in our fight, he said I knew how to find him. It didn't make sense that he would completely ignore me, especially after I apologized and promised I'd do things differently.

I force my mind away from those thoughts. I need to keep it together. I need to check out the cellar, hopefully find out Devil is *not* there, and then I need to get the fuck out of here—and I need to do all of that before Wolf comes back.

Devil called his club from my house phone. I could find that number and call them—but what if I'm wrong? What if it's not Devil down there?

I run to my bathroom and grab a first aid kit, then I go into the den and find the secret compartment under my dad's desk. There's only two people who know about that compartment.

My dad and me.

Once I lift the false bottom I take out the keys I find there. I frown because there's also a letter in there. I fold it and slip it into my pants pocket for later. I need to get to the cellar before I lose my nerve. I make my way to my bedroom and grab the small dagger my dad gave me for my sixteenth birthday and my pistol—both of which I keep under my bed in a safe. I load the gun and store each securely at the back of my jeans. Then, I put on a long-sleeved shirt, to help hide it and to serve as a jacket. The cellar can be cold.

I retrace my steps and move Dad's desk enough so I can open the trap door. I don't know if Wolf knows about the cellar door here. I figure he probably does, but I doubt he thinks I'd ever use it without a reason.

My hands are shaking so much it takes me three tries to get the key to fit into the lock on the door to the cellar. I curl my nose at the musty smell that immediately greets me, but I ignore it and go down the steps.

I use my phone and the flashlight feature to light the way. I wasn't kidding to Devil. My father hated the dark so he had state of the art LED lighting installed down here and they're operated by solar power from panels on the roof. I'm afraid to use them right now. I don't want anything to tip someone off that I'm down here.

There's no sign of anyone down here, and with that knowledge I start to breathe easier. Still, I do my best to remain quiet. There's a bedroom area off to my right that was meant to be my father's and mine in times of emergency. I ignore that and keep traveling the hall, knowing it will take me to the club's section and there's where I need to be the most careful. As I near the club's section there's another door. This one is locked too and it has an additional keypad. I send up a small prayer that Wolf hasn't changed anything and I type in my birthdate. The light on the knob goes from red to green. Next I find the right key, insert and turn it. The tumbler clicks and the door unlocks.

It's a small victory—but still a victory.

I pull the door closed, but don't lock it back. I need it to look normal in case someone comes by. Next, I head toward the area my dad never wanted me to go. I figure if there's a place set up for torture it will be there. When he first told me to stay away from that side of the shelter, I thought this was where the club girls all stayed and thought it was crazy my dad was being so protective, because I had seen the men with all the girls before.

Shit. I really am stupid.

This cellar is a fallout shelter really. I don't want to say my dad believed in the zombie apocalypse, but I think he believed nuclear war would break out and he wanted a city underground. It cost the club a cool million I think to build. It's the size of two decent houses put together. I always thought it was neat... *Now?* Not so much.

I can see the light up ahead and hear someone talking. The door is closed, but cracked open. I guess they don't think they need to worry about hiding anything. I lean against the wall, hiding myself from the room, wanting to catch my breath.

"Now how did I know I'd find you here?"

I start to scream, but Daniel strains, pulling his body up enough that he can clamp his hand over my mouth.

"Since we're neither one supposed to be here right now, I don't think you really want to do that, do you?" he asks. My eyes go wide. I can't talk because of his hand, so I nod my head in agreement. "Now I'm going to take my hand away, but when I do, no screaming. You don't need to be doing anything that will get either of us killed. Got me?" he asks and again I nod.

Once his hand is taken away, I back up a step or two, my hand automatically going to the back of my pants where I have my gun hid.

"Cool it, moonbeam. I'm on your side."

"My side?" I whisper.

"I may not be able to use my legs anymore, but I'm not stupid. I know Wolf and his minions have been up to shit. When I saw you today, I figured you knew it too. Red's been making a lot of trips out of this old cellar the last few days. Doesn't take a rocket scientist to figure out whatever had you looking so spooked earlier would lead me here."

"How did you get down here?"

"Your old man installed an elevator after my accident. He did his best to make me feel part of the club if he could. He was a good guy. I'm sorry you lost him."

"Is that why you're here? Because you feel you owe it to my dad?"

"Maybe. I think the others know more about his death than they should—which means I let my friend down. I figure the least I can do is help his daughter now."

"Where's the elevator?" I ask, trying to wrap my mind around everything.

"It connects to the club. You ready to find out what Wolf's hiding down here?"

"I think it's more like a who…" I murmur, hoping I can trust Daniel. He and Dad were pretty close before Daniel's accident, but I don't remember him all that well. Considering what I'm learning about Wolf—maybe that's not a bad thing.

"All the better. I'll go first. They won't think much about a man in wheelchair being here—especially since I'm a member of the club. For some reason these ass-fucks think being in a wheelchair means you're stupid too. I've got a gun, but I'd rather not use it. One shot and it doesn't matter we're underground, they'll hear it in the control room at the club."

I nod, because I know he's right. There's a giant control room at the back of the club that contains cameras and surveillance equipment as well as the latest computers on the market. The halls are wired with cameras, but I know the rooms are too. I've been worrying about it.

"The cameras—" I start and Daniel grins.

"Took care of that. I figure we got about fifteen minutes before they discover the problem with the cameras. Which means we need to get moving. You ready?"

I nod my head and follow behind Dan, praying I'm not wrong to trust him.

DEVIL

"**D**amn, what's going on here?" I open my eyes to see an old man rolling in his wheelchair. My guard looks surprised to see him, but I can't be sure and to be honest, I don't give a fuck. I'm barely hanging on to consciousness. I'm too fucking weak to care and I've been told all day that tonight my suffering ends. I hate to say I'm looking forward to it, but I sure as hell am. Wolf has been taking out his revenge on me hour after hour and I'm in so much pain that I only want it to end. I tell myself that's not being a coward—it's being a realist.

I've lived my life with no regrets. If I have any, it would be Torrent. I should have done so much with her different and I should have carried her kicking and screaming out of this hell-hole. I should have made sure that fucker Wolf couldn't ever touch her again. Hopefully Diesel, Crusher and the rest of my crew get here soon enough and will save her. I doubt the man upstairs listens to me, but I hope he gives her a good life. She needs that. I wanted to be the one to give it to her, but if wishes were horses we'd all be fucking cowboys.

"What are you doing down here, Daniel?" the guard asks—I don't know his name, haven't cared enough to listen.

"Figured I'd see why you pussies keep coming down here all hours of the night," the man says and if I could still feel my face I'd laugh. Here's one asshole I'd probably like.

"I'd watch my mouth if I was you. You're only alive because Dodger liked you."

"I'm only alive because your new President hasn't found a way to kill me, like he did Dodger."

"You're on dangerous territory, Daniel."

"You going to deny it?"

"No, but it's none of your business. You want to keep breathing you'll roll your fat ass out of this room and not look back."

"I'd rather roll my chair over your shriveled balls."

"You—"

I hear a gasp and make myself open an eye to look at the two men. My guard is on the ground, groping his neck, which has a knife sticking out of it.

"I ever tell you, asshole, that I used to be able to throw a knife at fifty paces and kill a fly?"

I figure the bastard is lying, and I wish like fuck that was Wolf, slowly bleeding out around the blade in his throat, but this beats nothing.

"Get moving, moonbeam," the man says and that's when my world shifts. Torrent is standing there, crying her eyes out. She's too blurry to see her eyes, but I can hear her sobs.

"If...dreamin', Angel... Don't wake... m... me."

The words are a chore to get out. I can't be sure they were even spoken, but I had to try. I figure she heard something because she starts moving. She looks around the room and then pulls a five-gallon bucket over to me. I thought she was going to put it under my feet. I hate to tell her at this point that wouldn't help. I can't even feel my damn legs—at least I don't think I can. All I can feel is pain. She doesn't though. She stands up on the bucket so our faces are close together.

"Hang on for me, Logan. Hang on for me," she says.

I don't know if it's possible. I'm pretty damn close to death—hell, I already smell like a rotted corpse. But I'll try. For Torrent, I'd try anything.

I start moving and recognize immediately she's cutting the ropes. I want to tell her to stop, to leave and get as far from Wolf as she can—to go to my club so they can help her get free. I don't say any of that, because in the next instant the ropes give and I fall to the floor. The pain explodes through my body and I can't fight it anymore.

I give in to the blackness and let it swallow me.

TORRENT

I can't quit crying. Devil is so bad. God, he's so bad. I wouldn't even know it was him, from just looking at him. The only thing recognizable is some of his face and his hair… though his hair is matted with blood and is so much darker than normal. His once vibrant deep blue eyes are pale and lifeless —at least one of them is. The other is swollen to the point I don't even know if there's an eye in there, but I'm scared there's not. He's been stripped and there's not a part of his body that hasn't been cut, torn, and made to bleed. He's bruised and swollen everywhere, his arms are broken so bad there's a bone sticking through one and his legs are at odd angles too.

How one man could survive a beating this severe is unimaginable. If I hadn't heard his broken whispers, I wouldn't have believed it myself.

"I don't think you did him any favors, girl," Dan says and he's right. I shouldn't have let Devil fall like that, but I had to get him down. I'm trying to be quick and I can only do what I can do.

"I know!" I cry. It's then I realize that I'm crying so hard my body is shaking. I have no clue on how I'm supposed to get Devil out of here. I don't know what I'm going to do when I *do* get him

255

out of here. I'm scared. No... I'm *terrified* that I'm too late. If Devil dies because I was too stupid to look for him sooner, I'll never forgive myself.

"Fucking hell! I knew I was too rusty! Duck!" Daniel yells and I jerk around to see one of Wolf's men, I can't even remember his name because he came not long before my dad's death, is pointing a gun at us.

It's so weird. You would think a man with a bowie knife sticking out of his neck couldn't find the strength to hold a gun but there he is. I can even watch as it cocks and I'm not sure where it's aimed, but it looks like it is at me.

"I said duck!" Daniel growls and the next thing I know he's moving in front of me, his chair tips and he's lunging at the man holding the gun. I hear the gun go off, but it's muffled. I scream. I take my knife and hold it tightly in my hand and then I stab it into the side of the man's neck. The rest of his body is covered by Daniel—who is groaning. The man underneath is slack, and I pull Daniel away as gently as I can. He looks at me, his eyes dull.

"Oh God. We can—" I start but he shakes his head a little.

"Thanks for one last ride, moonbeam," he says and then his body goes limp, his eyes open but lifeless.

I really want to fall apart now, but I don't let myself. I pull the wheelchair the rest of the way out from under Daniel, unceremoniously dumping him on the ground. I wince.

"Sorry," I whisper, which is crazy, because Daniel can't hear me.

I wheel the chair closer to Devil, setting the brake. I pull and tug and pray I'm not doing more damage and I somehow manage to get an unconscious Devil into the chair. He's slumped and at an odd angle, but he's in there. I move his feet, carefully so he fits better against the leg rests, and then I get behind the chair and take off, pushing Devil down the hall and back the way I came. There's no way I'm going to be able to get him up the stairs in my house, so I head toward the club. I have my gun and at this point

I'll shoot first and worry later. I have to get Devil to the elevator and out to my car.

It seems to take forever, but in reality it's only a few minutes, I'm sure. When the elevator dings and the doors open I scream when there's a gun pointed directly at me, before I even get a chance to draw. Then, through my tears I focus enough to see that it's Fury standing in front of me—the guy who was always with Devil during the early days at the convent.

"Help!" I scream. "You have to help him!"

"Motherfucking hell. Crusher! Over here!" Fury screams. That's when I look around and see the chaos all around me. Devil's men have attacked the club and from the looks of who is standing and who is not... they've won. I hope they managed to kill Wolf. If not, I really hope I get the chance.

DEVIL

I open my eyes slowly. Fuck, everything in me still hurts, but somehow it's duller than it was before. I look around and know immediately I'm in the hospital.

"Sunshine..."

"Hey, Twinkle-toes," Beast cracks.

"Did I die?"

"Close, but no cigar. You'll be here to bust my ass for years to come, long as you take care of yourself."

"Then why are you here? Where's Hayden?"

"She's at Torrent's. The babies are a little too wild for the hospital. She sends her love."

I look down to see Torrent sleeping, her head is lying on the bed, her hand reaching out and cupped over my arm, right above my IV. She's pale, and she's lost weight, but she's never looked better.

"What did I miss?"

"Torrent saving your sorry sack of bones. The boys dismantling Wolf and his goons and setting fire to their clubhouse and Torrent meeting Jenn."

"Christ," I wince.

"That went surprisingly well, by the way. I don't think Torrent's ready to meet DD right now."

"I get the feeling you're enjoying my misery, asshole," I say and I try to laugh, but it's too damn painful.

"Not even a little. You almost died, man. It was way too fucking close."

"I'm actually surprised I'm still here."

"It was a close call. If I ventured a guess, I'd say the man upstairs was answering prayers," Beast says.

"I doubt the man upstairs listens to anything about me these days, Sunshine."

"He listens to her. I'd lay odds on it," he says, pointing to Torrent.

Emotion swamps me as I look down at Torrent.

"He might at that," I tell him, my chest feeling tight.

"Got to tell you something, asshole," Beast says and a laugh bubbles out before I can stop it. I moan in reaction. Beast walks over and puts his hand gently on my shoulder.

"It's good to find someone who's uglier than I am now."

"Bastard, I'll never look that bad." I cough and son of a bitch if that doesn't hurt worse than the laugh.

"Better not look in the mirror," he says.

"Logan?" Torrent whispers, looking up. I look down at her and her face is drawn and she's worried, damn worried—*sick and pale with it*. I try to think of something to reassure her, but truth is I'm starting to feel tired already.

"Love you, Angel," I tell her and that causes her face to change, a light shining so bright in those whiskey eyes that I have to worry I have died. Surely nothing on earth could be this beautiful.

"You're a lucky son of a bitch," I hear Beast say, repeating words I once told him and I have to agree with him.

"We both are," I tell him, but I don't know if he hears me, because I slowly fade into sleep.

TORRENT

TWO WEEKS LATER

"Damn man, I thought you'd be looking better by now," Fury says, as about four of Devil's brothers come walking into his hospital room.

Fury is joking, I know, but he's not far from wrong. Devil does still look like hell. He's going to be in the hospital for much longer, though there is talk after his skin grafts heal, that they will move him to a rehab facility. Devil's not crazy about that, but he needs it. Both of his legs were so badly broken that he will have to learn to walk all over again. He's got one arm that had such a huge break that he'll have to work to regain full use of it. His ribs are wrapped tight, a lung had to be re-inflated and that's only the highlights of everything he's undergone. He's worried about the skin grafts and all of the jagged scarring he will have. I'm praying they don't become infected. He spiked a fever a few nights and it scared me to death. The biggest loss has been his eye. He completely lost his right eye and I know that's bothering him more than anything. His face is bandaged up right now, and eventually they will put a patch over the wound. They've talked to him about reconstructive surgery, but I don't know what he's thinking. I don't care.

He's alive... and he's with me. I'm thankful and that's enough.

"Fuck off, I still look better than you," Devil mumbles.

Fury, Crusher, Gunner and Beast have become familiar faces to me. They're good men. The kind of men that I wish my father could have surrounded himself with.

"How's he doing, Torrent?" Beast asks. Beast apparently isn't a member of Devil's crew, but he and Devil are really close. He and his wife Hayden are staying at my house until we can get Devil shipped back home and I go down there. I haven't been home much, and not sure I want to be—not after everything that has happened. The clubhouse is completely gone now. Crusher and his men burned it to the ground. I don't know what happened to the members of Dad's club; I've decided to apply the old military standard... *Don't ask, don't tell.*

"He ate real food today," I tell him, still proud of that accomplishment.

"I don't think you can call that crap they brought me real food, Angel."

I roll my eyes, and bend down to kiss him.

"I love you, Logan," I tell him, ignoring everyone else in the room. I almost lost him and now that I've got him back, I'm going to make sure to tell him how much I love him, each and every day —as often as I can.

He brings his good hand up to my face. He touches a finger to my cheek while staring at me intently. There's sadness in his face, but there's love too.

"I love you, Angel," he says and I kiss him again.

"You're a lucky man, Twinkle-Toes," Beast says and Devil looks at him and grins.

"Don't I know it, Sunshine. Don't I know it," Devil responds.

It's a familiar exchange between the two and I don't understand the significance of it, but I know it makes Devil happy.

"Have you found Wolf yet?" I ask, and from the looks of the solemn faces around the room that answer is a no. *Shit.*

"Sorry, Torrent. We've torn the place apart, but there's no sign of him."

"And you're sure Diesel and Ryan are safe?" Devil asks and the men look around at Devil—none of them happy.

"Diesel went dark as soon as he sent us after you. He left me a note, and told me he'd be in touch, but damn it, man, I haven't heard anything from him," Crusher says and my heart squeezes in panic.

I hope and pray nothing happens to them. I feel responsible, even though they've all tried to convince me I'm not. To their way of thinking, Diesel and Ryan have had evil after both of them for a while and at least I've helped them get a direction to look. That doesn't make me feel any better. I may not want to know what happened to my father's men, but Wolf... I'd like to see Wolf die a very violent and bloody death.

"Maybe it's good he's dark and doesn't know what's going on," Gunner says and everyone turns around to stare at him. "What?" he asks us all defensively. "It will kill him to find out that Ryan is not his."

I couldn't even imagine the pain that would cause. By all accounts, Diesel adores Ryan and has tried to give him the world from day one.

"That it will," Fury agrees. But Beast growls under his breath.

"He's that boy's father," Crusher says vehemently. I smile. Devil has told me about Crusher and Dani and how they couldn't have kids. So far they've adopted five and have another in the works.

"Damn straight," Beast says. "I dare anyone to say anything different."

I feel a little shudder of fear. I'm not really afraid, but the cold tone in Beast's voice would make me feel sorry for anyone that pissed him off, for sure.

"So what's our next move?" Fury asks.

"We keep hunting for Wolf and we keep trying to monitor this damn King. That's all the moves we have right now," Crusher answers, his voice filled with anger.

"And in the meantime we hope like hell we hear from Diesel," Gunner adds and everyone in the room silently agrees.

EPILOGUE

TORRENT

Five Months Later

I LOOK out the kitchen door and see Devil standing on the deck, looking out over the lake and my heart flips in my chest. It's been a long, hard five months, Devil's been home officially two months today, but it sure hasn't been easy. He's better—so much better than he was when he first came home, but he has his good days and his bad days. Today was a mixture of both. We had a good breakfast together, but most of the day he's been in bed with a debilitating migraine. Those are something he never got before, but they happen with sad regularity since Wolf's torture. I still pray every damn day that they find that asshole and he dies a very bloody death. So far it hasn't happened.

"You okay, Logan?" I ask, opening the kitchen door. He turns to look at me and maybe it's because we spend so much time together lately, but I can sense his mood from looking at him. "Stop it, Logan Dupree. Stop it right now," I warn him.

"Stop what, Angel?" he asks, a half smile on his face, but it's not one he really means. Since waking up he has bouts of depression. He fights them, but his body has been through a huge trauma and more than the physical body has to heal. There are days I can't find a trace of the man I met buying condoms, but always—*always* —I see the man I love.

"Stop thinking I'd be better without you," I warn him and he frowns at me.

"You haven't exactly hitched yourself to a prize catch, Torrent," he warns and I walk out to him, go up on my tiptoes and link my hands behind his neck.

"I have the man I love," I tell him, letting my lips rub against his bearded chin. It's not really a kiss, but it makes me happy. His beard is finally soft and full again. For a long time, he couldn't have one because of all the healing his face had to have. I love his beard. I rub my face against it and then I kiss his lips briefly. I have to have that contact—*I crave it.*

"You deserve better, Angel. Not a broken down piece of a man with one eye and a permanent limp."

"Will you stop? It's because of me this all happened to begin with. I was so lost in my memories that I couldn't see what was right in front of my face and look what it cost you!"

"Is that why you're with me? Pity?"

"Are you kidding me right now, Logan?"

"Angel, look at me. Not to mention, I couldn't even make love to you this morning. It was your birthday and all I could do was roll around in bed… hurting."

"I'll have you know I've had the best birthday I've ever had today. And do I have to remind you that you made love to me last night?"

"It's not the same and I don't see what's so great about it. You even had to go with Fury into town because I wasn't able."

I sigh. If there's one dark spot in our lives, it's the fact that

Wolf is still on the loose and until he's caught, Devil and I live with someone watching over us. Today Fury went with me and one of the club's prospects hung around here to watch Devil's back while he was sleeping. I know that hurts Devil's ego too. No man likes to feel like they can't take care of themselves and the ones they love.

"So you'll make love to me tonight. I feel like celebrating," I tell him.

"There's not much to celebrate," he growls and tries to pull away from me. I don't let him.

"I think there is. Logan—"

"What are you going to do if I go blind in the one eye I have left? What if my back gets worse and I lose the ability to walk? What if—"

I press my lips to him, to stop his tirade.

"What if you become the best father in the world?" I ask him when I pull away.

"I don't—" I wait for what I've said to sink in. It doesn't take long. "Torrent?" he asks.

"You're going to be a father, Logan."

"I... Shit..."

"Please tell me you're happy."

"I... I am...Shit baby, I've got a lot to heal from still."

"So you'll do it. You'll do it for me, for us and you'll do it for our child."

"You have a lot of faith in me..." he whispers.

"That's because you've never let me down, Logan. Not once. You always held on to me and I'm never letting go of you."

"I love you, Angel."

"I love you, Logan. We were made for each other you know," I tell him.

"We were?" he asks and I grin.

"An Angel and a Devil? Of course we were," I tell him with a grin. "Hey! Where are we going?" I ask when he pulls on my hand and starts walking back toward the house.

"Going to take my Angel back to our bedroom and celebrate her birthday right," he says with a big smile, the sadness he had earlier gone for now. His grin makes me laugh and I follow him... because really... I'd follow Logan anywhere...*forever.*

EPILOGUE

DEVIL

Six weeks after finding out Torrent was pregnant

"What are you doing, Logan?"

"Kissing my pregnant wife's belly?" he grins, looking up at me.

"There sure is enough of it to kiss. Logan Junior is making his mommy as big as the side of a house."

"Bullshit. You look beautiful. I can't believe how lucky I am," I argue and fuck if that isn't the truth. I always knew what I felt for Torrent was special, but every day it gets better and better.

"Easy for you to say. I'm barely four months and I already look like I'm carrying twins."

"Maybe the sonogram was wrong," I joke and the quick look of panic on Torrent's face makes me laugh.

"No way, mister! I can only handle one Devil boy at a time."

"At a time, so you are saying there will be more?" I ask her, kissing her belly again.

"Hopefully, though I would like a little girl in there somewhere," she says, her voice soft.

"I can work with that," I tell her.

I let my scarred hand slide over the soft swell of her stomach with amazement. A feeling of complete contentment fills me. I'm happy. That's something that has never been in question since the moment that Torrent told me she was pregnant. I still have a lot of healing to do, and I won't exactly ever be pleasant to look at to some people, but Torrent doesn't mind. She loves me and every day she proves that more and more. She's all that matters. The rest of the world can kiss my ass. I'll keep fighting and I will heal and I'll do it because I have the world and when a man gets that kind of gift, he doesn't let it go.

I let my hand drift up Torrent's stomach to squeeze her breast. Her tits are so much fuller now. It feels like every day there are new changes to her body. Changes I love, memorize and inspect every chance I get.

I love Torrent being pregnant.

"Logan," she whimpers, her hips pushing upward.

That's another change. Torrent is horny as hell… *all the time.*

"My Angel need some lovin'?" I ask her, letting my thumb brush against her nipple.

"Please," she whimpers.

I move so I can settle beside her. My lips seek out the side of her neck, kissing her pulse point and sucking the tender skin between my teeth. She tilts her head to give me better access and my hand drifts under the covers to seek that sweet heat between her legs.

"You're so wet for me, Torrent," I groan as my fingers slide between her lips, finding her ready and hungry for me. The wetness of her depths and the heat rolling off of her makes me groan. What man could worry about the future when their woman is always so damn receptive? Most days she makes me feel like I could conquer the world.

"Touch me, Logan. God please, touch me," she begs, so hungry her voice makes my cock ache.

I slide two fingers inside her and they move easily through the drenched valley. Her muscles clench against them, making me imagine how great my cock is going to feel soon. I move my thumb to seek out her clit and right as I'm about to torture it... the phone rings.

"Fuck," I growl. "We'll ignore it," I tell her over top of her pained whimper.

"You can't. It's the private phone," she whimpers.

Fuck, she's right. A month ago, Crusher had all the ranking members of the club to get burner phones. He thought it would be added protection. We only use it to discuss Diesel. In almost nine months, there's been no word from Diesel and no sign of him, Ryan or that damn Wolf. King has gone into hiding too and with the Koreans backing him, we might never find him.

"I'll be quick," I promise Torrent. I flop over on my back and reach for the phone off the nightstand.

"This better be good," I growl into the phone.

"It's all bad, Devil," Crusher responds.

Fuck.

I sit up in bed, instantly alert.

"What's going on?"

"Got a call tonight from a woman named Rori McDaniel."

"So?"

"She claims that her boyfriend asked her to call me. Seems he was a victim of a mugging last week and has been in a coma. He came out of it and wanted her to contact me."

"I'm not understanding, brother."

"Her boyfriend's name is Westin Cross."

"Son of a bitch."

"It's Diesel, brother. He's in the hospital in stable condition in ICU."

"What about Ryan?"

"There's no sign of him," Crusher says, his voice thick with emotion.

"Motherfucker. Where's he at?"

"You won't believe this shit. He's in Whitefish, Montana."

"Montana?"

"Yeah, calling you tonight because I'm heading out in the morning with some others to find out what's going on. I'm going to need you to take over here."

"Bullshit. I'm coming with you," I argue.

"Brother, you're needed here. You're my second in charge and I need someone I can trust here. Hell, Devil, there's a chance Wolf will rear his ugly fucking head. Plus... man, you don't want to be on the road with your woman carrying a baby."

I rub the back of my neck, wanting to argue with him, but Torrent comes up beside me, holding me... *comforting me*. She doesn't know what's going on, she can't because she's getting bits and pieces of the conversation, but she's reading my mood and she's here for me...like she always is.

God I love this woman.

"I want updates the minute they're learned."

"You know you'll have them. I'll leave Gunner with you and Fury will head out with me. Dragon is sending Dance and Freak with me too and I'll take along a few prospects."

"Keep an eye on your backs," I tell him, needlessly.

"Always, Devil. Talk to you soon," Crusher says, hanging up before I can respond.

I close the phone and stare at it.

"Devil?"

"We've found Diesel."

"Thank God! I—"

"It's not good, Angel. He's in the hospital in ICU and Ryan..."

"Oh no," she whispers, knowing what I'm going to say before I say it.

"Ryan's missing," I tell her and she falls into my arms, crying. I've told her and told her that she shouldn't blame herself, but she still does. Torrent feels things deeply, and even more so since she's been pregnant.

I run my fingers through her hair, brushing it gently.

"It's okay, Angel. We'll find him. We'll find Ryan and bring Diesel home. I promise you. We'll find him," I tell her and I mean every word.

No one fucks with the Savage clan. That's a lesson Wolf and this King son of a bitch are about to learn the hard way.

The End
Preorder Diesel Now!

READ MORE JORDAN

WITH THESE TITLES:

Doing Bad Things Series
Going Down Hard (Free On All Markets)
In Too Deep
Taking It Slow

Savage Brothers MC
Breaking Dragon
Saving Dancer
Loving Nicole
Claiming Crusher
Trusting Bull
Needing Carrie

Savage Brothers MC—TN Chapter
Devil
Diesel

Devil's Blaze MC

Captured
Burned
Craved
Released
Shafted
Beast
Beauty

Lucas Brothers Series
Perfect Stroke
Raging Heart On
Happy Trail

Pen Name Baylee Rose & Re-released
Filthy Florida Alphas Series
Unlawful Seizure
Unjustified Demands
Unwritten Rules

LINKS:

You can connect with Jordan through:
   Newsletter
   Facebook
   Twitter
   Book Bub
   Instagram

All links are accessible through her webpage at
www.jordanmarieromance.com

Text Alerts (US Subscribers Only—Standard Text Messaging
Rates May Apply):
Text *JORDAN* to **797979** to be the first to know when Jordan has a
sale or released a new book.

Made in the USA
Middletown, DE
16 September 2018